The
Secret Heart
of
Maeve MacGowan

Stephanie Ascough

The Secret Heart of Maeve MacGowan
September 2024.
Copyright © 2024 Stephanie Ascough
Paperback ISBN: 978-1-7349812-6-1
Ebook ISBN: 978-1-7349812-7-8

Published by Stephanie Ascough.
Cover Art created by Dawn Davidson.

TABLE OF CONTENTS

For everyone who wonders if crossing the orchard wall is worth it.
And for Damaris, for climbing the wall with me.

Author's Note

The Secret Heart of Maeve MacGowan started as a map. I wanted to explore the Irish landscape in my imagination, if not in real life. At the same time a story was percolating in the back of my mind: a young person tasked with a mission from the village leader who discovers that the world outside is vastly different from what they'd been told. Over time this young person became Maeve.

After publishing *A Land of Light and Shadow* I had recognized, mostly in hindsight, just how much of my own life I was processing through the pages of Arden's story. I decided to more fully embrace that process with Maeve.

I am not a historian. This book is loosely inspired by late 17th century Ireland: the legacy of Cromwell, the Plantation of Ulster. Many of you will recognize elements of Maeve's world. They are just as alive and well now as they were hundreds of years ago. I hope any egregious errors that may be present do not impact your enjoyment of Maeve's story.

I. Maeve

When the breeze sends tree limbs dancing overhead, the orchard feels like another place to me. Soft currents of air caress my skin, tugging at my skirts and red hair like some invisible mischief-maker persuading me to join its playful dance. I wonder, not for the first time, where this breeze began in its long journey across the downs. If it comes from that place of rolling hills, where the wild men and their treacherous magic live, then why does it spark such wonder in me? Why does it feel like something good?

Snatches of strange things dance across my mind's eye: An endless sky of stars. Another orchard, standing without a stone fence for a guard. A faraway place where things happened, things I have no name for and yet somehow, they name me. I press a hand to the rough skin of the nearest tree and grip my basket with the other and close my eyes, trying to shut out the melody in the breeze and the images in my mind.

I dare not tell Finna about these fancies, for she would remind me that girls do not see visions. Only those with magic do, and the only one in Quin who has magic is its leader and protector, the Patrician himself. I am no leader. This orchard, which I love like the blood family I do not have, is not mine; I am only its caretaker. If I fail to be worthy of this post, I will lose it forever. So Finna has always said.

The images fade, but closing my eyes does not shut out the melody. It is more than the wind playing over rock and soil and leaves. Today I can hear the notes of something wild. I fix my gaze on a gnarled trunk nearby. The trees are like old friends, never scolding or ignoring me. Breeze or no breeze, strange fancies or no strange fancies, the orchard is my favorite place, my safety, and among these trees nothing can trouble me for long.

Girls do not see visions. But when hunger or harshness press against me too sharply, I go to the orchard. If I cannot reach the orchard, I let my mind take me there instead. The branches hold me until I can bear the present again, or until it calls me back. I always carry my—I will say it, just this once—my trees, my refuge, within me.

It is the one thing Finna can never take away.

2. Stranger

Maeve had a job to do. Finna would count the contents of her basket to make sure she had enough for a favorite recipe. As Maeve returned to her task, the breeze settled and left autumn's first chill to curl through the air and fill her lungs. She pulled another apple from the nearest bough and brought it to her nose to inhale its bright, deep scent, just as hunger bubbled in her stomach. *If only fresh apples were as good as they smelled,* she thought. She had only ever tasted them in Finna's cakes and pies, butters and jellies. Those were good, her favorites. But what did a plain, uncooked apple taste like?

"You're looking at that apple like it's caught you in a trance."

A young man sat atop the wall with his back to the downs. He was young, a boy scarcely older than she, perhaps seventeen years of age. This was no uninvited vision, no invented image. Maeve stared at him, too startled at first to speak.

A tangle of brown hair hung almost to his shoulders, and he wore a bag slung across his back. His voice carried the same lilt as those in Quin, and his hair shone with a familiar reddish tint, but he was a complete stranger. Did he come all the way from Ferre in the east, or was he from Dumar in the north? Either way, he had come a long distance, and no one ever entered Quin by the orchard.

She dropped the apple into the basket and straightened. "How did you get here?" she said at last.

Instead of answering, he jerked his head toward the wild southern hills and slouched forward, resting his elbows on his knees as he perched careless as a bird on a branch. "I understand there's something dangerous out there. What do you think it is?"

He could not have asked a more troubling question. "We don't concern ourselves with it," she answered. "No one who lives in Quin pays attention to the music."

"The music?" The boy raised an eyebrow as interest flickered across his face. "So you've heard it, too. What does it sound like?"

He jumped down and landed in front of Maeve. They were nearly the same height, and she found herself looking straight into intelligent brown eyes. She was close enough to see a thin scar that curved like a white thread down his left cheek and ended amidst the suggestion of a beard. There was an energy in his posture and eyes that Maeve had never seen before, as if he were alert to things no one else could sense. His eyes widened and sudden intake of breath mirrored hers.

She had seen wool clothing stick together many times, remembered the familiar yet unpleasant shock of separating them. This was far from unpleasant, however. She felt like a piece of wool clothing now, drawn to this stranger with a sudden and unfamiliar intensity that flooded her body and brought a strange warmth to her cheeks. Startled, Maeve took a step back at the same time he did.

The distance cleared her head a little. No matter where he came from, no one entered the village this way, and no one displayed such curiosity regarding what lay beyond. She had heard the stories all her life: wild beasts roamed and ravaged, and wild men stirred up strange powers in the dark of night, causing evil and unnatural things to happen. The breeze carried more than imaginary music: on some nights, lilting, wild tunes wove their way across the sky, and villagers shut their windows to keep the noises out.

Quin had nothing to do with such machinations.

He repeated his question in a softer, husky voice. "Have you heard it?"

Maeve collected herself. "Most of us have heard the music at one time or another, but we're wise enough to ignore it." *Wise enough . . . Am I?* "Please, this isn't safe," she said, gesturing over the wall. "Don't you know that? The gate is that way. Everyone who has business in Quin has to go through the gate."

"But you're here," the boy said. "You must not be afraid, even if it isn't safe. I only thought you might know more." He stopped abruptly and pressed his lips together, searching her face.

Maeve gulped. "You should go." She lifted her basket as proof of her innocence and took another step back, away from the broken wall, away from the stranger who was both handsome and perplexing. "My foster mother owns this orchard. I'm only here to pick apples."

"Only apples." He sounded as though her words did not convince him, but he nodded once as if reaching a decision. "I'd better leave, then." Then he stood upright, and with the same sudden agility as his descent, the stranger heaved himself back up the wall. He sat there and gave her a final searching look. "I've heard it, too," he said, and there was a disappointment in his face that Maeve did not understand. "What's so wrong with that?"

With these words, he flashed a grin and slipped over the wall, leaving behind only the fading patter of his footsteps on soft earth.

Maeve did not watch him leave, though the wall was low enough in places to see over. The wall might guard the orchard, but the orchard, blessed with magical abilities by their god, protected all of Quin. Her role was to help Finna in looking after these sacred trees. She hurried to finish her task. Tomorrow the Patrician was coming to inspect the orchard as he did every year, and Maeve's best friend Katherine was getting married. Maeve and Finna would cook, boil, and bake apples until this year's harvest was done. An ordinary autumn in the Patrician's village. Plenty to keep her occupied and make her forget everything except what was expected of her.

Successful at last, Maeve hefted her basket to the crook of her elbow and left. The last twisted tree she passed received a farewell pat and a word of silent thanks.

From the stone archway of the orchard entrance, the hill sloped down to a wide stream crossed by a wooden bridge. From there, a short path led up a broad, low hill, where Quin lay sprawled like clusters of earth-colored sheep. The crumbled remains and partial structures of a few stone cottages dotted the earth below the orchard. Before the stream had flooded and the bridge was built, families had lived in those cottages. The separation between village and orchard hadn't been so marked, at least not in a physical sense. But even with the increased distance between Quin and Finna's place, people still trusted the trees to protect them from unknown dangers beyond their realm.

Maeve, like all Quin's children, had learned the orchard's story from birth. Sir Arthur Bromley had established Quin and her orchard generations ago. When the wild men had attacked the settlement unprovoked, Sir Arthur had prayed for protection, and in the miracle that followed, the trees drove the attackers back into the downs. God also granted Sir Arthur some magical ability, which passed down with the orchard to his grandson, the current Patrician. So long as the orchard was tended with reverence, Quin would have nothing to fear in this strange and untamed land.

That must be why we don't eat the apples raw. Only a few can bear the gift of magic.

Somehow the answer didn't satisfy her, but it was the only one she had.

Finna's cottage abutted the orchard wall and faced the village. Her foster mother stood in the doorway, her thin arms folded and her piercing gaze set toward the village activity. Finna did not frown, exactly; she rarely did. It was the firmness in her narrow chin and the way she stood, as straight as the apple trees were twisted, that told Maeve when she would have an extra chore or a little less food for dinner to pay for her tardiness. Sometimes she wished Finna would simply scold her like other mothers did. One good shouting, and have it done with. But it was Finna's lack of passion that burned the most, like the frost that would soon blanket the earth. It burned icy hot on Maeve's tender heart.

She took the worn little path looping off the main route and slowed when Finna turned to her.

"What kept you?" Her voice was low, measured, emotionless.

Maeve swallowed and clutched the basket. Should she tell Finna of the stranger, the young man? Of course she should. She must keep nothing from Finna; it was foolish and deceitful to keep anything from the woman who had fed and cared for her when no one else would.

Four or five years ago, the first time she'd really heard the music and felt it tugging at her, Maeve had danced in the orchard and came back with guilt pulling her face. Finna's silent welcome spoke volumes. When Maeve went straight to her room without dinner, she found the contents of her wooden box rearranged. Neatly, but still displaced enough to let her know they'd been sorted through. Finna may not have known what her foster daughter did, but she knew Maeve had done something wrong even before her return, and Maeve spent that night with both a stomach and a conscience that ate themselves hollow. Finna always found out. She would know about the stranger. And if Maeve stepped out of line again, Finna would search her out as thoroughly as she had searched her meager belongings.

And yet, as she looked at the woman's hard gray eyes, she thought of brown ones, warm and living, their intensity and uncertainty. She did not know his name. What good would it do, telling Finna of this brief and purposeless interaction? She had the apples, there was work to be done, and Finna needed her help. With a resolve that both troubled and thrilled her, she answered.

"Not many apples are ripe yet," she said, truthfully enough. "But I found just the right amount, like you told me to."

Finna's flint gaze softened. She gestured for Maeve to follow her into the kitchen, where together they brought out the apples and placed them one by one on the scrubbed wooden table.

"These are good, Maeve," said Finna as they began paring. "You have an eye for choosing the best fruit."

Maeve relaxed at these words. Finna's world began and ended with the orchard. Entrusted to her family for generations, she knew how to utilize every part of every harvest and hated waste of any kind. She kept the best slices of pie and the sweetest apple butter and bestowed them on Maeve when she was pleased. Where words failed, apples spoke, and even if the language was inconsistent, it never failed to prompt Maeve's attempts to earn a more tender expression of affection.

They measured flour, butter, and honey, and soon the sweet fragrance of clove, cinnamon, and baked apples filled the house. The skillet with the heavy lid sat directly over the fire in the fireplace. This cake was the first they made every season, for the Patrician's visit. Maeve was always proud of the food they made. She knew Finna was too, though she never said so. Her foster mother spoke of how well the orchard was doing and Maeve relaxed a little more. She doubted she'd find the contents of her box rearranged, after all.

"I wish I could be there, for the inspection," Maeve ventured as they began cleaning up.

"Soon, you will be." I stoked the fire and went back to drying the dishes. "You'll be old enough in another year or two."

It wasn't so much that she needed to see the inspection to know the trees were thriving. It was, according to Finna, a brief affair with few witnesses, reserved for those specifically tasked with the orchard's care. But Maeve longed to have her work acknowledged. Everyone praised Finna's cakes and pies and jellies and butters, but she wanted to hear someone tell her that her part in all this mattered, and that it was noticed.

As Maeve washed the dishes, her thoughts wandered to Quin and to her friend. "Don't we need more candles? The Campbells owe us some. I could go get them when I'm done."

Finna put away the spoon she'd dried and frowned in thought. "I suppose," she said. "Yes, we'll need them soon enough. You may go. But don't stay for long, as we've got to clean the sitting room later."

Maeve nodded. A twist of sadness pierced her, and she wished she could spend more time with Katherine before marriage took her away, even if it only took her to a different house in another corner of Quin.

"No need to be sad," Finna admonished, as if reading her thoughts. "Tears can't change the inevitable."

Why did you never marry, if marriage is inevitable? Maeve wondered, not for the first time, but she knew better than to ask. She pressed down her sadness and finished washing the last bowl, then took her apron off and put it on its peg.

"And Maeve," Finna said, "don't run."

"Yes, Finna." At the warning, something heavy pressed against her heart in the void left by sadness. Finna might not know about her strange fancies, but she and every other villager knew the link between the strange music and the wild men. It was a link she, Maeve, couldn't risk forgetting.

Gathering her shawl again, Maeve took great care to leave the house in a calm and proper manner.

3. QUIN

The walk to Quin was short, beautiful, and fraught with temptation to run and skip. Maeve resisted with a restraint that would have made someone proud, but there was no one there to see it.

She passed under the narrow stone arch, one of Quin's secondary entrances, and nodded to the guard who stood watch there. The sounds of people about their business, always a background hum in the orchard, engulfed her. The rattle of carts and horse hooves on cobblestone; children, not yet restricted in their movements, laughing and calling as they left the school a few streets away; the clang of the blacksmith's hammer.

Quin was laid out like a poorly made wheel, with streets running out from the center like spokes, and the largest, shortest spoke leading to the main gate in the northeast. As she passed rows of houses, Maeve caught sight of the main gate before she reached the center.

Everyone was proud of those gates. Whereas the smaller gates could be boarded over, the main gate was large enough for two tall, wooden doors, through which merchants and clansmen who traded with Quin could ride their strange mounts two abreast. And on either side, supported by smooth stone pillars, stood a large, polished stone chiseled into the shape of an apple. Of the three villages the Patrician governed, Quin might be the smallest, the last structure on the edge of the wild. But here was the orchard of their forefathers, and everyone who rode through the gates knew it.

Maeve was happy to turn her attention away from the stone monuments to the bustle of the village center. People went here and there, visiting shops and going through the business of the day. To reach the Campbells' house north of the village, she'd have to take the spoke that went straight back toward the sheep pastures and farmland.

To her surprise, Katherine stood at the threshold of the smithy, looking into the darkness and tapping her foot with impatience.

The hammering had ceased. Duffy, the blacksmith, must be somewhere in the recesses of his shop. The hot smells of metal and leather reached Maeve's nose, and she said, "Thinking of sneaking inside, Katherine?"

A smile brought out two dimples in Katherine's pretty face. "Only if you're going with me."

Maeve's best friend was a year older than she, with a tall, graceful frame, a head of curly blonde hair tucked into a loose bun, and a smile that made more than one village boy doe-eyed with admiration. Katherine wore the long skirt and composure of a proper woman, but there was a saucy glint in her eye that her mother, Mrs. Campbell, had long given up trying to quell. Maeve loved and hated her friend for it in equal measure.

"It was your idea to steal the horseshoe," Maeve rejoined. "You weren't the one who got punished for it."

Katherine turned and her smile broadened. "But wasn't it a lark? Don't tell me you're still afraid of the blacksmith. He's a perfectly harmless old man. I think he's tied to his smithy with a chain of iron. I've never seen him leave it more than twice."

"Yes, it was fun, but afraid of the blacksmith? Of course not."

Katherine raised her eyebrows but said nothing.

In fact, Maeve was a bit frightened of Duffy. He hardly said a word, but he watched the comings and goings from the depths of the smithy, the light of the forge glowing on his bald head when he worked in view of the street.

"Good. Because I have the memory to make me laugh now that I'm too old and proper for such larks myself. I still say you missed out, Maeve. You never take risks."

Maybe her friend was right, but she had met someone who did take risks. Maeve was about to tell her about the handsome stranger in the orchard when the loud groan of the front gates interrupted her. Voices called and everyone looked to the heavy village gates being dragged open by two guards. A whispering hush fell on the market as the arrivals entered.

One look at the small band of brown-clad guards told Maeve who had arrived. A faint collective murmur rose among the crowd as someone emerged from the center of the group.

The Patrician wore a regal, fur-lined cloak, his gray hair long and smooth to his shoulders. Due to the dangers of the road, he always traveled with a guard, as did others who traveled; permission to travel between villages was granted by him alone. He came three times a year to Quin. This would be his last visit for the year, and he was a day early.

Maeve stood still, her errand forgotten. Usually she was busy working at home when the Patrician arrived. The first time she remembered meeting the Patrician she had been about six years old, and it had happened just here, in the square. She had been playing in the street with some other children, Katherine among them, and when they were done, Maeve alone had gone to speak to the unknown man who had watched their game with a kindly eye.

"Don't worry," said little Maeve, holding up the leather ball. "I never throw this at the apple stones. And anyway, my foster mother says soon I'll be too old to play in the streets."

Her chin quivered at the thought. It was sad to think of growing up, but she had not meant to cry in front of this grand-looking stranger, and she stared unabashedly at him and wondered if he would tell her to stop her tears as Finna often did.

The man only smiled at her kindly. "I should think you don't," he said. "You live with Finna MacGowan, do you not?"

"Yes," Maeve answered. "Sometimes I help in her orchard."

"Ah, yes." He seemed very tall and his hair was only streaked with gray then. He bent down so he was eye to eye with her. "Then you have an extremely important role, child. Finna is lucky to have you."

She had felt herself glow with his words.

When Finna met her in the streets, she had bowed to the Patrician and hurried Maeve home, scolding her until Maeve understood she had spoken to someone extremely important: the ruler of Quin, Ferre, and Dumar, the Patrician himself. He answered to none other than the Lord Protector, explained Finna. The Patrician's grandfather had sworn loyalty to the first Lord Protector, thus providing the three villages with the crown's recognition. Maeve had found the chain of command confusing. But she had understood her mistake in speaking to someone too grand for her. All the same, she wished to see him again and hear him say kind words meant only for her.

Three years later, after a winter of hunger and cold, and no visits from their leader in the warmer months, the Patrician arrived in the fall with food for Quin. Passing by her in the crowd, he winked and tossed her something. Maeve caught a smooth apple the color of a new spring bud. Where did it come from? She had always thought the

Patrician never left his own villages. By then she understood that fear of bandits on the road usually meant fear of wild men with some fear of wild animals mixed in. He must be brave indeed to travel in search of other orchards, for their village owned the only one Maeve knew existed.

Or perhaps he obtained it by magic. She knew the Patrician employed his magic in modest ways, refusing to make a big display. These unique skills, she heard more than one villager say, were more for assistance than for show, and even then he must use them sparingly to avoid depleting the gift altogether.

Magic or not, when Maeve brought the little green apple home to show Finna, her foster mother told her to add it to the apple bucket. It went into applesauce, and Maeve could never say what it tasted like, just as she had never tasted a raw apple from their own trees.

Today the Patrician looked a little older, his face slightly more lined, but he listened to the villagers bold enough to approach him and calmly answered their questions. Two stone-faced guards stood at his side. There were more guards this time than last. Perhaps the wild men grew more violent and necessitated such measures.

The Patrician had turned to her, and with a jolt she realized he must have spoken to her, for he watched her with a kind expectancy. Two or three villagers eyed her with mildly disguised disapproval, and Katherine nudged her in the side.

"Forgive me, sir," Maeve sputtered. "Did you ask me a question?"

The Patrician gave a short, low chuckle, not an unkind sound. "I only asked how Finna's girl could be such a young woman. But then, I am grown old. How are you, child?"

"I am well, thank you." Maeve dropped her friend's arm and briefly bowed her head. Her stomach fluttered at her own rudeness, but the man seemed unperturbed.

He nodded in greeting to Katherine. "I believe congratulations are in order, Miss Campbell," he said. "How are your wedding preparations coming along?"

Katherine smiled and blushed, looking every inch the eager bride. "Well enough, sir," she said, all ease and fair grace. "I'm pleased we'll have the distinction of your company at the ceremony tomorrow."

"And I am honored to witness the occasion." The Patrician smiled and turned back to Maeve. "And tomorrow, the orchard inspection as well. A busy day for Quin. You've yet to be a part of the inspection, haven't you?"

Maeve nodded.

"I think it's time that changed. You've worked alongside Finna all your life; you're old enough now. Would you grant us the honor of your presence tomorrow afternoon?"

If Maeve had been holding anything, she would have dropped it. "Yes," she answered, and could say no more, pride and anxiety a tangle in her stomach.

"Very good." His smile deepened the crinkles around his eyes. "Now I must go to my lodgings. It's been a long journey and my men and I are tired, but the priest must give us his welcome. Until tomorrow." He offered a slight bow before heading for the church, which also housed his adjacent rooms. The guards who followed him would lodge in the inn according to custom.

Maeve turned to her friend, eyes wide with disbelief and joy, and saw that Katherine's expression mirrored her feelings. "Did the Patrician really say that to me?"

"Of course he did. And it's high time, too. You deserve the credit, Maeve. You always have."

Maeve grasped her friend's hand gratefully. Katherine understood her in ways Finna never would.

"Are you able to walk home with me? Or did Finna send you to stare at the smithy?"

"I'd almost forgot. Finna sent me to get the candles your mother promised her."

A shuffling sound drew their attention back to the smithy. Duffy's massive shape lumbered from the shadows, the smell of leather and metal mixing with sweat and growing stronger with his approach. Startled, Maeve drew back, but Katherine extended her hand for the object in the blacksmith's large grip: a knife, small and sleek.

"Thank you," said Katherine, handing him a small coin. "My father claims he can't do anything without his knife. Good day."

Duffy grunted. His narrowed eyes slid to Maeve, unblinking. Without a word, he went back to the forge and took up his hammer, metal striking metal in thunderous music.

Katherine tucked her arm through Maeve's and they strode through the village center and toward the northernmost street, allowing Maeve to shed her brief apprehension. *The blacksmith is just quiet. He's probably forgotten that mishap from years ago.*

Katherine's talk turned to her wedding, and her betrothed Conlan. By the time they reached the Campbell farm some fifteen minutes later, Maeve walked through the noisy yard and into the sprawling kitchen garden with all its sharp fragrances, feeling almost as happy as she did whenever she visited Katherine.

Mrs. Campbell worked alone in the kitchen, her cheeks rosy and streaked with flour. She dusted her hands on her apron and greeted the girls as they entered.

"Maeve! Lovely to see you, dear," she said, pulling her into a hug that smelled of butter and herbs and yeasted bread.

She released her and looked at her daughter. "Katherine, you got the knife, then? Good, good. Your father and brother are storing the last of the peat. And I really need your help with these rolls before your sisters come inside and demand their dinner. I know the neighbors are all helping with the wedding dinner but my, it still feels as though I'm cooking for an army."

"Maeve came for candles, Mother," Katherine said, setting the knife down and donning an apron. "Shall I get last year's beeswax or the tallow ones from Dumar?"

"Finna likes the beeswax best," Maeve put in. Katherine went to fetch them and her mother watched her go, her blue eyes growing watery.

"Well, Maeve," she said, her voice faintly unsteady, "my child married tomorrow. I can scarce believe it."

"Nor can I," Maeve murmured. She looked around the room where she and Katherine had spent many hours together, chasing Katherine's younger sisters, arguing with her older brother, Brody, who'd grown too old for their company in recent years, and playing a game of patterns popular in Quin, its little wooden pieces carved by Mr. Campbell in his spare moments and worn smooth from use.

In years past Katherine had given up their street antics with carelessness, trying to cajole Maeve into a more sedate game of dolls. But Maeve had no interest in such things. In the end they gave up on dolls, but not each other. Any time they had together between their growing responsibilities was spent talking of the future and sharing secrets. Now Katherine spoke most often of Conlan, and after tomorrow there would be no more secrets or games at the Campbells' kitchen table.

The bride-to-be's footsteps sounded her return. "Here, Maeve. Two of the best beeswax candles in all three villages. May Finna's baking be blessed as she works by the light of them." Katherine handed Maeve the slim, creamy yellow sticks and smiled, a hint of the sauciness returned. "You were talking about me behind my back, weren't you? Confess."

"You are awfully self-centered for a bride," Maeve teased. "Shouldn't you be thinking of your betrothed?"

Katherine sank down at the table, a dreamy smile taking over her expression. "It wasn't that long ago, was it," she said, her voice soft, "that we met. His father had just moved their family to Quin from Ferre. I knew the moment I saw him he was the one for me."

Mrs. Campbell, who'd returned to kneading dough, tutted under her breath, a fond smile on her face. She seemed to have forgotten that she'd asked Katherine for help.

"I know," said Maeve, sitting across from her. "You had eyes only for him that day. The only words I got out of you were 'yes' and 'no,' and you mostly mixed them up!" She remembered Katherine's elation when Conlan had declared his intentions, her joy when the betrothal had been approved. Even then it had seemed like some distant event. Now that event had arrived, and their lives would change forever.

"Promise me you'll come visit," Katherine said, leaning forward to grasp Maeve's hand. "Every week, even more, if Finna will spare you."

Something about her expression arrested Maeve's attention. A flicker of discomfort, or something worse, passed over her friend's features. The shift from besotted to unsettled was so brief that when Mrs. Campbell came over with her rolling step it had passed, leaving Maeve to wonder if she'd imagined it.

"I doubt Maeve will want to intrude on your wedded bliss that often," said Mrs. Campbell, one eyebrow lifted high. She set down four rolls wrapped in a scrap of cloth and placed a gentle hand on each girl's shoulder. "Maeve, dear, you'll always be welcome here. Don't forget that."

Maeve smiled up at her and took the rolls. "You didn't have to, Mrs. Campbell."

"Hm," she grunted, and seemed to bite her tongue. Maeve knew she disapproved of Finna's cold nature and had said so, many times, before her daughter chided her for it.

"Mother, the Patrician has invited Maeve to participate in the orchard inspection," Katherine said, looking proud and at ease as usual. "Don't you think that's a wonderful thing?"

"Indeed, I do," said Mrs. Campbell, beaming at Maeve. "And none too soon. Finna won't be able to refuse him, I daresay."

Katherine shrugged and smiled at Maeve, who knew that even this news wouldn't sway Finna's displeasure if she delayed her return any longer. She stood up and smiled, taking the candles and bundle of rolls.

"I'd better go," she said reluctantly.

Mother and daughter accompanied her to the door, and when Maeve flung an arm around Katherine, she felt that strange undercurrent again, as if some unspoken thing wasn't right.

"See you tomorrow, Maeve," Katherine said brightly. "I expect you first thing."

There was no time to ask her what was wrong, not in front of her mother. *Maybe it's just nerves. What bride isn't nervous before her wedding?*

They said their goodbyes, and Maeve looked back at the pair of women standing in the doorway. They looked so alike, the same curly hair, the same smile. Their shared affection had shaped them both. No honor in all of Quin could replicate that. The Campbell home had almost felt like hers, and now with Katherine's departure, it would never be the same.

4. Running

It was only as she left the farmyard that she realized she hadn't told Katherine about the handsome stranger. Tomorrow might not provide an opportunity, either. Loneliness began to curl within her like a leaf withering in winter. On a whim she chose a different route home, one that led along the pasture fence to the shepherd's gate, hoping to see a friendly face.

Unlike the front entrance, the shepherd's gate was a low, wooden fence the height of her waist that spanned much of northern Quin. It allowed people a good view of the shepherds and their flocks as they came down the hills from Dumar and Ferre for the winter. A flock was coming down the nearest hill toward the gate now, distant white and black specks approaching like bleating thunderclouds.

The groan of the wooden gates announced arrivals at the front entrance, but here, the head guard Boyle and his register book received newcomers. To her relief he stood there now, jotting something down in a leatherbound book, then shut it with a snap and stored it in his jacket pocket. He caught sight of her and beamed.

"Good afternoon, Miss Maeve," Boyle said, smiling cheerfully and doffing his cap. He wore the same uniform as the guards who had accompanied the Patrician, though his was slightly more weather-stained. "And how goes the apple harvest?"

She smiled in return as Boyle's steady kindness cheered her a fraction. "Hello, Boyle. It's just begun, but it looks like another good year." Somehow this fixture of Quin always reminded her of Duffy, the blacksmith, but for their opposite manners.

Like most villagers, Boyle and Duffy carried on their fathers' work, as their fathers had carried on from theirs, and the men were as different as the tasks they performed. They were both near Finna's age. And there the similarities ended.

Where Duffy was known for his taciturn manner, Boyle had a kind word for everyone. While Duffy's bald head gleamed in the glow of his forge, a mass of brown and gray curls receded from Boyle's forehead. And while Duffy seemed tied to the smithy as if a chain of iron connected him to the forge, Boyle walked the streets between posts like a cheerful uncle looking out for a multitude of nieces and nephews. How he managed to arrive at this post on time for every shepherd amazed Maeve.

"Yes. Yes indeed." The head guard twiddled his pencil in his hand. Nervous energy aside, no one ever found cause to complain about his work, and the handful of guards who worked under him held him in respect.

Maeve was about to say her farewells when his attention swiveled once again to the approaching flock, and when she followed his gaze, the words died on her lips.

Among the sheep, shouting a good-natured command to the black-and-white dog who nipped the animals' heels, the shepherd reached the gate with the easy motion of one accustomed to spending his days on uneven terrain.

The shepherd was none other than the boy from the orchard wall.

"Good boy, Whistle." He bent down to scratch the dog's ears as the sheep began placidly eating grass around him. Straightening, he went to address Boyle and caught sight of Maeve. Surprise, followed by a smile, flashed across the boy's face. She felt her own face warm and a smile tug at her mouth, pleased that she was the one to surprise him this time, even if it was by accident.

"Come to register?" Boyle said, motioning the brown-eyed boy to his lectern. The shepherd slowly pulled his eyes from Maeve.

"Ah, yes." His voice held the same timber she remembered, though he sounded a little flustered. He leaned over the gate to write his name in the book Boyle held out, then went back to staring at Maeve—this time from the corner of his eye while one hand unconsciously ruffled his dog's ears.

The guard bent over and read his entry. "O'Conner. Not Peter O'Conner's boy, are you?" he asked with interest.

The boy nodded, his expression sobering as a smile broke out over Boyle's rosy face. "Ah, so you would be Liam," he said. "Last I saw you, you were a might shorter."

"I was. I remember you, Boyle. But my father's dead this spring. I had to sell the house. Well, give it over to the town, really." His face tightened briefly, shutting off from the world as if from long practice.

"I'm sorry to hear it, my lad. He was a good man, your father."

Liam nodded once and squared his shoulders. "I'm here to pasture the flock in Quin's hills. Not just for the season, but for good, if Quin will have me."

"I'll pass your request along to the Patrician. Lucky he's here early, isn't it?" Without waiting for an answer, Boyle flipped to a page in his book and referenced a list. "In need of anything, are you? Ah, you have your papers I see, very good. Anything else to declare about the intention of your stay?"

The young shepherd hesitated briefly before answering. "Nothing else."

"You have your lodgings and all?"

"The shepherd's hut is enough for me. A little smelly, but that's nothing new." His face colored slightly at the confession.

Boyle turned to Maeve and put a hand to his heart as if he'd forgotten she was there. "Ah, where are my manners? Let me introduce you. This, young Liam, is Maeve MacGowan. You'll see each other around this autumn and winter, sure enough, and with any favor, in the following spring."

"I'm sure we will," Liam answered. Only his eyes hinted at their previous meeting. His face had regained the mischief and energy from the orchard. "And do you come by the shepherd's gate often, Miss MacGowan?"

Maeve bit the inside of her cheek to keep from grinning. "Almost never," she answered in her most serious voice. "Keeping the orchard safe from intruders leaves me no time for wandering around."

"Intruders!" Boyle shook his head, chuckling. "Don't tease the boy, Maeve. He knows the orchard keeps us safe, don't you, lad? There's nothing to fear despite our proximity to the downs."

Liam's eyes were locked with hers when a flash of understanding crossed his face, an earnest acknowledgment of their previous encounter. Her thoughts went back to his words: *I listen for it, too. What's so wrong with that?*

Just as quickly, he smiled at the head guard. "I'd best get the sheep settled further up the hills. Good day, Boyle. Good day, Maeve. Come, Whistle." He turned and threaded his way through the sheep. The sheepdog leaped to his side and trotted along, panting with a canine grin.

Maeve watched them go, Whistle herding the flock away. They had disappeared behind another little hill when she found herself alternating between relieved and ruffled. Liam was no stranger now, and the thought of seeing him again was more than pleasant, though she hoped he would not try to scale the orchard wall again. It seemed he had enough to keep him busy out on the north hills. And what had made him hesitate to answer Boyle's question?

"Such a shame about his father," Boyle said, tucking the book into his coat and plunging his hands into his pockets. "He was a good man, O'Conner. There's nothing like a shepherd for roaming. But there's another shame: he'll be too busy to join us at the wedding tomorrow. I always say a wedding's a fair time to meet people, wouldn't you say? Oh, you must be thrilled for your friend. Hey, Miss Maeve?"

But Maeve had remembered she was late and felt less than thrilled. "I've got to go," she said. "See you tomorrow, Boyle."

She hurried through the street on the outer rim of Quin. By the time she'd reached her exit, the sun was low enough that Finna would be cross. Maeve ran across the bridge and up the hill.

"Maeve MacGowan, is there a fire at your heels?"

The cold voice stopped Maeve in her tracks. She swallowed, trying to make her dry mouth speak.

"No, Finna," she said, her voice as rough as Finna's was sharp.

"Then why is it so hard for you to observe this one rule?"

Maeve swallowed again. She knew all Quin's rules by heart, which brought her a measure of comfort; yet the relief at knowing what the village expected of her did nothing to stave off Finna's displeasure, which Maeve felt incapable of escaping no matter how hard she tried.

"I don't know, Finna."

It was partly true. But Maeve feared there was something wrong with her. She couldn't recall Katherine getting reprimanded for running, nor any of their other friends, married and moved away since the spring. A heavy stain coiled in her chest, a feeling she knew well. Search as she might, she could never understand why she found restraining her movements to be difficult. *If I knew that, then I could finally stop myself, couldn't I? Ease Finna's disappointment a little?*

Her foster mother sighed wearily. She passed a hand over her face, for a moment looking aged beyond her years. Then she straightened, issuing crisp commands. "Give me those candles before you break them, Maeve, and put those rolls inside. It's a wonder you haven't crushed them."

She went into the kitchen, leaving Maeve to scurry after her. *Will the news of the Patrician's request please her or anger her more?* she wondered. At this point, she feared the latter.

The table was laid for dinner.

"I expected you back earlier. I would appreciate your help in preparing the house. Or perhaps you had more important things to attend to in Quin."

Maybe this is a good time after all. If the Patrician thinks I'm ready to be present at the inspection, will it convince Finna that I'm not completely irresponsible? "I met the Patrician," Maeve said, spooning stew into two tin dishes. "He spoke to me. He was very pleased about the inspection tomorrow." Finna remained silent. "He told me I must attend the inspection this year," Maeve hurried on. "He said it was time I joined everyone."

She brought the dishes to the table and sat down, searching Finna's face. Her foster mother's expression remained cold. She paused for a silent word of thanks before speaking.

"If the Patrician said you must attend, then you must attend."

The knot in Maeve's chest loosened a little. It wasn't the response she'd hoped for, but how could it be, since she'd been caught running?

"However, since you were late this afternoon, you'll need to finish with the cleaning tomorrow morning."

Dismay sent prickling shards through her stomach. "But I've promised Katherine I'd help her prepare for the wedding," she said. "I gave her my word months ago."

"Then you should have been more careful today." Finna took a methodical bite, chewing and swallowing as Maeve waited. "You can leave when you're done. Not a minute sooner."

Hot tears burned Maeve's eyes. *How does making me break my own word teach me not to break a law?* Her throat was too tight to say the words aloud, and anyway, they would hardly sway Finna.

After dinner as she washed the dishes, Maeve's thoughts flicked over the day's events. She repeated Quin's laws in her mind as if doing so would make it easier to follow them.

Going outside the village walls after dark was forbidden. Traveling to another village without the Patrician's approval, impossible. Music was permitted only on certain occasions, and then only Quin's solemn melodies. No dancing, ever. And running outside the village, unless grave danger required it, was too much like dancing to be proper, likely to draw unwanted attention from the wild men of the downs who practiced their dangerous rituals and sacrificed to demon gods.

It was odd, Maeve considered, how the rules trickled down. Women didn't run inside the village for fear or love. And Finna acted as though running was wicked no matter the situation.

I listen for it, too. What's so wrong with that?

Brown eyes and a young man's voice flashed in her memory. She sucked in a breath and bent over the pot, scrubbed harder, and repeated the laws in her mind to silence the other words that lingered there, unbidden as music from the downs.

5. WEDDING

Maeve reached the Campbell farm two hours later than she'd wanted. A small wooden booth sat beyond the sprawling kitchen garden, a traditional element in weddings. A figure in the upstairs window drew Maeve's eye, and she recognized Katherine's face, framed by her long hair. Maeve waved frantically and Katherine waved back. Pressing forward at a rate which would have surely earned her a scolding from Finna, Maeve reached the front door and let herself in.

The kitchen was full of children running about, and the scents of sweet cakes and flowers replaced the usual smells of soap, herbs, and butter. Maeve called greetings to Katherine's younger sisters, Brigid and Mary, as she threaded her way through the noise and up the stairs to Katherine's room.

Mrs. Campbell's eyes widened when she opened the door and ushered Maeve in. She wore a small, ornate broach on her best blouse and her hair was done up tidier than usual. "Maeve, there you are! We were getting worried!"

She hadn't time to answer before Katherine pulled her into an embrace, muffling her in lace and smelling of fresh flowers and nervousness. She pulled back and studied Maeve's face. She must have sensed it had something to do with Finna because she didn't press her. Instead the bride beamed and half-dragged her to the small mirror that hung on the wall beside the window.

Maeve felt grateful and amused, knowing that in her current state, Mrs. Campbell was likely to protest Finna's behavior loudly. Neither Maeve nor Katherine wanted that now.

"I wanted you to do my hair," Katherine said. "Mother helped me dress. What do you think?"

It was a blue gown, a lovely and rare color that set off her friend's pale features and blond hair. Maeve brushed her fingers over the lace on Katherine's arm appreciatively.

"It's beautiful," she said. "It suits you."

"I thought so, too. Mother worked so long on it."

Mrs. Campbell grunted. She was unpicking a delicate, tangled silver chain. "The Monaghans are wealthy. I wouldn't see my daughter disgraced on her wedding day. Ah. There." Maeve moved aside so Mrs. Campbell could secure the necklace around her daughter's neck.

Katherine caught Maeve's eye in the mirror with a searching look. She knew Maeve wanted to tell her something, and that it wasn't something to share in front of her mother. Maeve felt a thrill of excitement. She was eager for one more exchange of secrets before her friend left girlhood behind forever. She went on pinning up Katherine's hair in an elaborate knot.

"Is Conlan here yet?" Katherine asked, breathless.

"Not yet," her mother answered. "Late, the groom! Well, we won't start without them. Beautifully done, Maeve!" she exclaimed over the finished result. She pressed her cheek to Katherine's as her eyes filled with tears. "My girl. We knew this day would come. But—"

The tears spilled over. Maeve stepped back to give them a bit of privacy, yet she could see their reflections in the mirror: the same hair, the same face shape, just as she'd noticed yesterday, full of feeling. Her friend's eyes began to glisten as Mrs. Campbell dashed a hand across her own face.

"Oh, Mother, you've made me cry." Katherine's laugh was between a hiccup and a sob; she turned and buried her face in her mother's shoulder. Mrs. Campbell stroked her shoulders and made shushing noises.

A stab of jealousy broke through Maeve's chest. She couldn't picture a similar scene between her and Finna when her time came, no matter how she tried.

A knock interrupted the quiet sniffling sounds, followed by a familiar male voice.

"Mother? Someone is asking for you downstairs."

Mrs. Campbell sighed. "Coming, Brody." She wiped a hand across her face and kissed Katherine on the cheek, giving her daughter a final smile as she shut the door behind her.

Katherine whirled to Maeve the moment the door shut. "What is it?" she asked, her eyes alight with mischief.

Maeve grinned. She felt a little shy about it suddenly. Katherine had always been the one who flirted and talked about boys. Maeve, who'd felt no abiding interest in boys until yesterday, wasn't sure she wanted to be teased about it. Still, this was her chance. And it felt, deliciously, like getting back at Finna, though the thought made her nervous as well.

She leaned closer and lowered her voice. "I went to the orchard yesterday and someone was already there." She paused for the gratifying look of shock and interest leaping to life in Katherine's eyes and went on: "He didn't come from the town. He climbed over the wall. One minute I was picking apples, and the next, he was just sitting there."

"Was he handsome? Did he say anything? Maeve, who is he?"

She pushed their conversation about the downs from her mind. "He disappeared over the wall before he told me his name," she said, enjoying drawing out the saga. "But I met him again."

"Where? And naturally he's handsome."

"He's a shepherd. He spoke to Boyle about staying in Quin for good."

Triumph lit Katherine's face as she sat back, clasping her hands in excitement. "At last! Promise you'll tell me everything. And I don't care what time it is, when he kisses you, come see me straight away."

Maeve laughed as warmth spread across her face. "Slow down! I doubt Finna will want me to see a shepherd. And besides," she said, sobering, "I'm in no hurry to marry."

Katherine began to speak again when a loud rap on the door interrupted. "He's here, Katherine!" came Mary's shrill voice. "Conlan's here!"

Katherine's eyes widened as she inhaled. "We'll be out in a minute!" she called, but her younger sister went on urgently.

"But everyone's ready, and Mother said it's time! Oh, and here's Father."

At the sound of footsteps and another brief knock, Katherine rushed to her feet. "It's time," she repeated, and Maeve couldn't tell whether it was relief or anxiety in her voice. "Come in, Father."

The door opened and Mr. Campbell, looking uncomfortable in his best suit, came in. He'd not had as much luck as Brody in smoothing his salt-and-pepper hair, but his beard was newly trimmed and neat. "My Katherine," he said, his brown eyes shining with quiet affection. "Hello, Maeve. Thank you for being here for our daughter's wedding."

"Of course, sir." *As if I'd be anywhere else.* She stole a glance at Katherine, who looked like the perfect bride. She sensed again that something was off with her friend, and wished she'd had the chance to ask.

"Finna's asking for you, Maeve," said Mr. Campbell. He held out his arm and Katherine went to him in a rustle of skirts.

"Goodbye, Katherine," Maeve said, trying to smile.

Her time with Katherine was over. No more secrets shared in this room, no more mischief or scheming or giggling about things only they thought were funny.

"Goodbye, Maeve. Oh, god's trees, I'm nervous." Laughing, Katherine pressed a hand to her bodice and slipped her arm through her father's.

Maeve went downstairs. The time for final embraces had passed.

Maeve made her way through the small crowd to Finna, who wore her best dress of deep, dull green and greeted her with a silent nod. Katherine's and Mrs. Campbell's effusive greeting returned to Maeve like a sharp pang. She turned her attention to the wedding party, recalling how it had been several years since she'd attended the last wedding. That day, the solemn affair had made her glad when the ceremony was done and she could stretch her legs among her apple trees and revel in the silence there. The two or three other friends she could claim had crossed the threshold into womanhood last year, and were sent to Ferre or Dumar to marry and begin their new lives. She was the last of the girls her age to remain as she was.

Before the crowd stood a small, raised brazier alight with dancing flame. Conlan stood on the other side of this, beneath the bower of green constructed that morning. His brown hair shining and his face red, he wore a traditional groom's suit of dark green. His family stood behind him while Mrs. Campbell and her other daughters gathered nearby, awaiting the bride and her father.

A murmur ran through the crowd as a man wearing a worn brown uniform bustled through and took his place between the families. Boyle was often the one to marry couples. It was unusual, as Quin had its own priest, but the head guard was so beloved by the community that Katherine had asked for him, and no one had protested or considered it odd. He'd settled his perpetually smiling face into a somber expression for the occasion. As he took his place, he was beaming so wide that Maeve wondered if he'd ever been anything other than pleased with his work and the people he worked for.

Then a door shut and the crowd's murmurs silenced. The bride was approaching; the ceremony had begun.

The solemn feeling deepened as someone began playing a slow, formal tune on a fiddle. Even the audience seemed to hold its breath. Katherine walked toward her betrothed, clutching her father's arm. As she passed, Maeve's heart quickened and reached out to her. Katherine's face was pale and drawn. Her friend was frightened.

As Boyle spoke the words that joined the two together as husband and wife, Maeve kept her eyes on the bride, hardly hearing a word. Katherine followed suit, her voice sounding far away. Then came the binding ritual.

Inwardly, Maeve squirmed. She'd never liked this part, though it was just as much a part of the wedding as anything else. Mrs. Campbell stepped forward with a square of cloth from one of Katherine's old dresses. She handed it to Katherine and Conlan, who each took a corner and pulled. The loud ripping noise made Maeve flinch. Katherine, who now held a strip of fabric smaller than the one in Conlan's hand, gave her piece to Conlan's mother, who tied it to a piece of leather imprinted with Conlan's last name. The groom held his torn piece of fabric up and let it fall into the fire. It sizzled and caught, the smell of burning fabric catching in Maeve's throat and making her cough. Finna glanced at her.

Why did it have to be ripping and burning? It was supposed to resemble the joining of lives. But all she could see was the loss of her friend's dress, the burning of something Katherine had once worn with pride. It was senseless and violent, and a desperation rose up within her, one she struggled to subdue.

Then Boyle pronounced the ritual complete: Katherine was now Mrs. Monaghan. The bride and groom were escorted by their families through the crowd and down the lane, while people began filing quietly behind. Katherine passed in a blur of blue and reddish gold. Maeve tried to dart into the moving crowd, but a hand grabbed her arm.

"Let the Campbells by first, Maeve," Finna scolded. "We are not family. Wait your turn."

With an effort, Maeve checked herself. Her desperation grew thicker until it choked her thoughts. She wanted to move, to reach Katherine and to reassure her that everything was fine.

Or perhaps she needed to reassure herself. Of what, she wasn't sure.

6. Break

The smiling wedding guests, leaving somber ceremony behind, walked down towards the church in a colorful mass that carried Maeve like a tide. Up ahead the large doors swallowed the bride and groom. Delicious smells wafted from within: fresh breads and roasted meat and sweet pies and Finna's second apple cake of the season, baked this morning.

The church was a large building, with a plain sanctuary frequently utilized for meetings and other social events. The loud, cheerful sounds of people exclaiming over food and company rose to the rafters. It pressed against Maeve's head as if she were a skin drum stretched too tight, about to burst. Katherine and Conlan were already seated at the bridal table, where several of Mr. Monaghan's fellow merchants crowded to congratulate the couple. Finally, when Finna allowed her to go and speak to Katherine, a small crowd of people moved in front of Maeve and blocked her view.

"Weddings are tiring affairs, are they not?" said a familiar voice at her shoulder. The Patrician stood next to her, his arms behind his back, watching for the bride and groom.

"Sir," said Maeve, bobbing a greeting. She hadn't seen him at the wedding. He must have been there, yet he seemed almost as out of place as she felt amidst this celebration, which was odd for a man of his prestige. Yet it also made him seem more approachable than he ever had, and her heart warmed to him, grateful for his presence. Here and there a passing guest would nod or bow in greeting to him. But for the most part, the village leader seemed content to observe, as Maeve was. He looked tired, too. His eyes were lined and red, and his posture lacked the usual straightness. "Are you well, sir?" she asked.

"I'm well enough. You're kind to ask. It's only that the journey grows more taxing the older I become." He smiled at her before nodding at the crowd ahead. "The lovely bride and groom. They look quite happy, as they should."

"Yes," murmured Maeve uncertainly. The crowd was at a standstill. A large, well-dressed man was speaking, presumably to Conlan, but his frame blocked the view. Suddenly the crowd shifted and a brown uniformed man slid next to the Patrician.

"Excuse me, Patrician, but you're needed elsewhere."

It was the guard who'd watched Maeve on her way to the Campbells. Maeve pointedly ignored him as the Patrician acknowledged him.

"Very well, Thomas. Excuse me, Maeve. Perhaps I can give my regards to the couple another time. I will see you very soon."

She nodded as he departed through the crowd. She'd almost forgotten about the inspection, but was still too twisted with anxiety to spare either excitement or dread for the upcoming event. At last the crowd moved a little and Maeve could see Katherine. The bride's face shone, but beneath her smile was a fatigue that worried Maeve.

Then she became aware that Thomas hadn't left.

He was standing close behind her. This part of the room was very crowded; he must have gotten stuck, like she was. Maeve glanced at him from the corner of her eye, wishing he would leave, when he bent over her shoulder and spoke in her ear. She stiffened, unable to move.

"You're too pretty to be here all on your own," Thomas said. "Someone will want you for themselves soon enough. You know what a compliment that is, don't you?"

Then he was gone. Maeve still felt him, felt his breath on her neck and the cold where he'd stood too close. The room blurred and the lights shone too brightly. The crowd shifted again, but she couldn't see Katherine. Someone else jostled her, apologized, and left. Maeve stumbled and bumped against someone's table, but no one noticed.

"She'll be next, no doubt," said a matronly voice from somewhere behind her. "Finna's girl. Finna couldn't get a man, but Maeve will have to. Two spinsters in Quin in the same house? That won't do."

"Oh, but will it be easy to find anyone who will marry her?" The other voice was also female, higher and sweet as warm honey, sounding pleased with the direness of her own concerns. Maeve couldn't stop listening even as the words brought something cold creeping up her throat. "The foundling, you know, that's what she is. You know what they say about when she was found, don't you?" The woman's voice lowered to a whisper that pierced Maeve's ears. "Who would leave a child outside of Quin? No one *from* Quin, that's all I'm saying."

"You're not suggesting—" gasped the first woman, her voice dropping to a loud whisper. "You're not saying she's a child of the wild men, are you?"

"All I know is that Finna is the only one who would take in such a creature, having no child of her own. How could she refuse? She has no one else to help her. She must keep a close eye on that one."

"And so lovely," the first woman said sadly. "She doesn't look wild, I must say. Why, anyone would be fooled by that innocent appearance."

"That's just what the wild men do. They fool people. And that is why we stay in here, Margaret, and you know it. If they're out there, they can't do anything to us in here."

Maeve didn't hear the rest of the conversation. The room was too hot, the press of bodies too near. The noise grew to a roar in her ears.

Thomas might come back. And she was—she was what? Unable to avoid him?

A child of the wild men?

Her limbs trembled with the need to flee. The air in the church pressed into her lungs, hot and stifling. She needed fresh air. She had to get outside.

Outside, the chill doused her like a bucket of cold water. She took in gulps of it as she followed streets she could navigate with her eyes closed. Quin blurred around her in smears of pale plaster and dark wood. Nothing mattered but escaping grasping hands, stinging words, and she could barely walk fast enough.

The road dropped away and she found herself on the bridge leading to her house, blinking in sunlight shining from the clear autumn sky. Had she come home so fast? Had she been running? She cast a look back over her shoulder, but no one was coming to scold her. The faint smells of grass and running water rose up to her. The cheerful, constant chuckle of the stream beneath the stones reached out like a welcome companion, and up ahead, the apple tree limbs swayed in a light breeze. Relief spilled over and cleared her mind. The urge to run, long suppressed, pushed her on. This time she didn't care about following propriety. Fueled by desperation and emboldened by solitude, Maeve ran up the hill and into her refuge.

Over her pounding heart and heavy breathing, the faint scratch and rattle of branches sounded like a loving voice. She inhaled deeply. The taste of soil and leaves and the faint, sweet breath of ripe apples calmed her. She rested a trembling hand on the rough skin of a tree and found herself rooted.

Child of the wild men. Finna must keep an eye on that one. The women's words from the church soaked her in dread, bitter and heavy.

A child of the wild men? Is that what I am?

Maeve had always known she was a foundling. She had known, for as long as she could remember, that Finna wasn't her blood mother. Other children grew up with a mother; she had grown up with Finna's last name and the knowledge that the care she received came from necessity rather than warmth of feeling.

She'd tell Katherine. *Katherine always understands. She won't care what I am. What I might be.*

But no—Katherine was married, had entered a new life, and that new life felt like a distance of miles to Maeve.

Her breath came in gulps again.

Her skin tingled. The wind strengthened and pulled, tugging, twisting hair and clothes and branches. Something inside her writhed in distress, seeking an outlet, as if sixteen years of being made to follow rules and walk just so had trapped something inside which sought escape with the energy of a winter storm. Her sprint to the orchard wasn't enough.

She let the feeling burst through her limbs and ran with all her might. Her arms and legs pumped until she reached the wall, her hands seizing the rough stones and hauling herself up until she sat balanced on the edge, looking out over dangerous, forbidden territory.

The downs rolled away in endless green. She saw nothing but grassy hills for miles until they faded into the horizon where the sky took on a cloudy, misty vagueness. Her hair whipped her face and stung her eyes.

And then the green faded to black all around her.

She whirled in a flash of night, suspended beneath star-speckled skies reeling overhead, and grew dizzy and light as a leaf on the air. A smattering of lights broke off and melted like yellow bits of butter scattered on a hot pan. Strains of tempestuous music rose from hidden depths and shook her bones, the melody rising and falling like the craggiest of hills.

The music rang in her ears as the vision faded and the downs stretched before her again. She trembled, blinking in the wind, and the music faded to the ordinary sounds she knew.

Maeve was balanced precariously on the wall. Her foot slipped, and for a terrible moment she wobbled, about to fall onto the grass below.

Instead, she threw herself back. Pain raked its claws down her back and something massive knocked the breath from her lungs. She lay on the earth, looking up at the blue sky and fighting for air.

After her first ragged gasp she struggled upright and looked around, her heartbeat throbbing in her skull. At least she had landed within the walls. Something long and twisted lay on the grass beside her, something she'd broken off in her fall: a tree branch as thick as her leg.

Compelled by horror, Maeve bent for a closer look. She'd never seen a branch that big fall from a tree. Inside the branch, where the wood should have been hale and hearty, a twisting pulpy center oozed.

Something was wrong with the orchard.

Footsteps sounded at the entrance. Maeve looked up and her heart fell again. The Patrician, several guards, and Boyle stood there with expressions of concern and shock as they took in the scene.

"Oh, child." The Patrician's face creased with deep concern. "What has happened?"

Maeve's heart leaped to her throat. Had they seen her standing on the wall, or falling off and bringing the branch with her? Her back throbbed with pain, but it was nothing to the disappointment on the Patrician's face. It was worse than Finna's coldest, most leaden gaze. Maeve struggled to keep her shawl in place as if it would protect her from that disappointment, and waited in the dreadful emptiness while only the wind keened on.

How could I be so foolish at my first orchard inspection?

Another set of footsteps sounded and the crowd moved aside. Finna, her face strangely animated, appeared at the front of the small crowd. When she saw Maeve her face blanched. "What happened?"

The Patrician studied Maeve a moment before turning to Finna, but not before Maeve saw a softening in his eyes. "There seems to be some trouble with the orchard," he said.

Finna took in the scene with pressed lips. Maeve's heart sank. Nothing in the woman's face or ramrod posture suggested compassion or advocacy. She regained her composure and strode over to the branch, bent to inspect it, and stood up. "Some kind of tree rot," she announced, as if the rot had better look out. "I am deeply grieved, Patrician. I don't know how this could have happened."

"I'm sure it was no fault of your own," Boyle put in, but Finna's attention was elsewhere.

"I think it was." Her eyes narrowed in thought. "We are, after all, the orchard guardians. These trees are in our care."

Maeve, racking her brain for a cause, alighted on one just as Finna strode over and seized her arm.

"Maeve," she said slowly, "did you water the orchard yesterday, like I told you?"

Maeve's skin went cold. She wanted to shrink into the earth. *No.* Every day she or Finna sprinkled water from the stream on the orchard ground; it was a sacred ritual, passed down through each generation of orchard protectors. Yesterday she'd gathered the apples as instructed. But someone's unexpected arrival had driven one simple, vitally important task from her mind. Had the tree suffered so much so soon because of her neglect?

Maeve stared at her foster mother, searching her face for any sign of kindness from the woman who had raised her. Why did Finna only show vehemence when Maeve failed? She read nothing in her face but fierce rebuke.

No, not just rebuke. A flicker of fear crossed the woman's thin face like a shadow. Her nails bit into Maeve's arm.

"I—" Maeve stammered, then stopped , unable to admit her failure aloud.

A sting across her cheek brought a cry from her lips. Finna, her anger spent with the slap, continued to stare at her until Maeve's watering eyes dropped and her confession fell from her lips.

"I didn't water the trees," she whispered.

She heard shifts in the crowd as Finna released her grip. From the corner of her eye, she saw the Patrician's gray cloak sweep by as he also bent to examine the fallen branch.

He straightened, but Maeve kept her eyes downcast, her cheek burning.

"We will have to examine the others to see how many are afflicted. But rest assured, we are not without remedy."

Maeve looked up. "There is a remedy?"

"Yes." He smiled kindly at her, lifting some of the dread. "And you, Maeve, will help me make it."

She nodded eagerly. "I will, sir."

Finna began to protest, but the Patrician held up a hand and went on. "It's all right, Finna. Yes, there are two things we must do first—one is determine the cause of this disease.

I doubt very much that one day without the stream water could cause this rot," he said, gesturing at the fallen branch. "There may be some other force at work."

Maeve's heart beat faster. *He means the wild men and their magic.*

"Secondly, we will have to inform Quin. The villagers deserve to know the danger to their sacred trees." He looked to the head guard. "Boyle, please have your men inform the village that we must meet tonight. You have my guards' assistance." He nodded to his closest guards. One of them, Maeve realized with a sickening jolt, was Thomas. At least his attention was on the Patrician. His face was all seriousness, as if his duty was all that mattered.

"Of course, Patrician," Boyle replied, his red face set in determination. "Come, lads," he barked, and the other guards followed him out of the orchard.

"Now, Maeve." The Patrician took her hand gently in his. "I really think you should go home and rest. You have had a trying day, and tonight I must ask you to help me inform the villagers of what has befallen the orchard."

"You want me to . . . ?" Maeve squeaked. The thought of standing before everyone terrified her. Her mind shifted to another question. "Is the inspection over, sir? Or may I stay for the rest of it?"

"We will conclude the inspection once we have completed the remedy." He released her hand and addressed Finna. "I will be staying in Quin until this is finished."

"Of course, you would not abandon Quin in her moment of need," Finna replied. For a moment, Maeve thought she heard something biting in Finna's tone, but the moment was gone.

"You understand." The Patrician bowed. "And now, let us retire. It has been a busy day, and we still have much to attend. Perhaps some of your famed cake for Maeve, hm, Finna? It is most restorative."

Finna's face looked stone-still as the Patrician took his leave. Then, silently, Finna left Maeve alone in the orchard.

She watched her enter the cottage and shut the door.

Had she somehow influenced this disaster? Anxiety at the memory of her strange vision twisted her in a merciless grip. What did it mean? Had she somehow invited danger into the orchard?

A child of the wild men.

She felt heavy with questions, many of them too awful to voice even in thought. Yet they all filled her with determination to see the remedy through.

Maeve hoped she would not get in the way of that.

7. Church

Maeve sat at the kitchen table, a large slice of apple cake before her. She couldn't eat. Through the small kitchen window, the sunset burned red and pink and yellow. The fragrant cake was no substitute for what Finna had denied her. Katherine's wedding feast had ended, and she had missed her chance to say goodbye.

She'd watched Finna and the Patrician walk back into the orchard to gauge the severity of the rot. Forbidden from attending, she'd paced the kitchen, waiting for her foster mother to return with news. But Finna had only brought back the empty bucket and dipper. She had sliced a piece of the cake, set it before Maeve, and gone straight to her bedroom for a rest, saying she had a headache and leaving Maeve no wiser than before. Quiet draped the small house like a shawl. Maeve picked at her food, perplexed and troubled by too many things to name.

She looked up when Finna's quiet step signaled her entrance. The woman's eyes were shadowed and the lines about her mouth were drawn, as if tonight's meeting were a funeral for someone she loved. It might be, if the rot in the orchard spread. *Would she feel the same about me if I were in danger? Does she regret taking me in?* The thoughts were a pang of hunger in Maeve's chest.

Maeve stood, and Finna's eyes met hers.

"I saw what you did. I warned you, Maeve. I have warned you for years."

Maeve's heart sank. She had seen her climb the wall, or maybe seen her run home. Any words of self-defense would be useless. The silence lay thick as apple butter left too long on the fire, sticky and bitter.

"Maeve, why do we protect the orchard?"

The answer came from Maeve's lips easily. "Because the orchard protects us. The wild men have magic and would overtake everything if the trees failed."

Every child in Quin knew the stories of what happened beyond the walls; it was part of the great recital learned in school. But just as easily as the first words came to her, the rest vanished from her mind like smoke. She resisted the urge to rub her cheek which had stopped throbbing not long ago.

"And?" Finna prompted, her voice never rising. "Keep going."

Maeve inhaled slowly. "They don't have the magic of the apple trees. The apple trees were a sacred gift to us from the god of our people who guided us to this place. Those who are responsible for the orchard are responsible for the safety of Quin." She remembered other parts she had learned in school that were not a part of the great recital: The MacGowan family had been entrusted with the orchard since the beginning. It had always been a married couple who took care of it, until Finna.

Finna's direct gaze cut into her thoughts again.

"If anyone proves unworthy of caring for the orchard," Maeve continued, "and thus placing Quin in danger, they will be removed from their post. But the great recital isn't clear on what exactly makes them unworthy, though. Why is that?"

"It's none of your concern, Maeve. The Patrician has Cromwell's law, and he abides by that. Girls have no need to concern themselves with it. What else have I warned you of, about the wild men?"

Maeve frowned, her eyes darting to the window as if she could escape by looking at it. "I remember it, Finna, I promise. Please don't make me—"

"Say it." Finna's voice was almost a whisper. "You must say it to remember it."

Maeve remembered this warning even though it wasn't part of the great recital, even when she wished she could forget it.

When she was thirteen summers old and her blood cycle had begun, Finna's first and only words on the matter had been to warn her not to stray from the village. Maeve had listened, confused; hadn't she been warned against leaving the village since she could remember? Strange and unsettling as this change in her own body was, why did it make Finna think she must warn her again? Did blood make some people forget? She would ask Katherine, whose cycle had begun months earlier.

But Finna's words took a grimmer turn.

"Remember that there are not just wild beasts, but wild men in the southern hills," she had said. "Wild men who will take and give nothing back, for what they take cannot be returned. You are becoming a woman. Now more than ever you must fear them, and shun the music and the downs from beyond these walls, anything that comes from outside the Patrician's three villages."

"What has the music to do with wild men?" Maeve had ventured.

"The music is wild," Finna answered, with a cold intensity that sent shivers down Maeve's spine. The strain of returning Finna's piercing gaze made her eyes water, but she feared that looking away would risk a slap. She let her eyes fill. This seemed to satisfy Finna. Perhaps she mistook her tears for contrition or fear.

Now as she returned Finna's gaze in the darkening kitchen, Maeve was afraid not of the music, but herself.

"The wild men will carry off girls who stray from Quin. We must let ourselves be protected," Finna said.

"But Finna, what if someone inside of Quin doesn't act like he should? What if not everything I need protection from is outside of Quin?"

A muscle twitched in Finna's jaw. "Why do you think I've always told you to walk instead of run, to not draw attention to yourself? Behave as you should, Maeve, and you'll have nothing to fear."

But I wasn't misbehaving at the wedding feast when the guard—

Finna's face was a closed door. No amount of pleading or explanation would get her anywhere now, and Maeve let the thought drop. It was too confusing and uncomfortable to carry on her own. The church had been too crowded. *I'll have no need of being so near that guard again.* She clung to the thought, begging it to allay the sickening feeling in her stomach, but the comfort it offered was like grasping spilled apple butter with her fingers.

Finna turned away and pulled her shawl from its peg. "Come. It's time."

The evening gathered round them and pooled in the village, where lights burned bright against the dark. Her foster mother remained silent during the walk. She seemed to trust that the lecture would serve to keep Maeve silent as well, and she was right. Maeve's thoughts remained on the warning from three years ago.

If the orchard protects us from the wild men, why is it that I am such a threat?

But then, she had failed to water the orchard. Even if the Patrician didn't believe that her mistake had caused the rot, what about her strange vision? She had no answers, only anxieties churning within.

The church glowed with a soft blue light. This was not the usual warm yellow flame of smelly tallow candles. It was the Patrician's light. His was a modest magic, not for grand display but for aid. With the wealth of candles burned for the wedding feast, he must have decided to offer his assistance. Lingering smells of food reached her. Now she regretted not eating, and her stomach ached with hunger.

Villagers entered the church for a quieter event than the afternoon's festivities. She entered behind Finna for a second time that day. The tables were gone, and the usual rows of hard wooden seats had been rearranged to face the front. The blue lights offered little comfort. The crowd was more spread out this time, making the room feel larger, almost too vast, as if she might lose herself in it. *Maybe that wouldn't be so bad.*

The low hum of voices filled the room. Maeve scanned the room, her heart beating faster as she recalled Thomas's behavior this afternoon, and instead found Boyle, greeting people in one corner of the room. But he was too far away and too busy to notice her. The Patrician stood near the front of the room, the place for calling meetings together or dispensing news from the outside world. In his place of honor, he was removed from Maeve's troubles, standing in his leader's role rather than as a sympathetic observer. A guard stood on either side of him against the back wall. Maeve shivered and looked away when she recognized one of them. *Will he return to Dumar, or will he stay with the Patrician?*

The Patrician raised his hand, just as he had done in the orchard, and the room hushed. *Strange that the same motion can silence both a crowd and one person.*

"Thank you all for coming," the Patrician began, smiling at the crowd. "It has been a busy day for Quin, as many of you were at the wedding celebration only hours ago. I won't keep you long. Therefore, I shall be direct. You all know how important the orchard is to Quin."

From somewhere in the room, a tiny voice piped up, "The orchard protects us. The wild men have—" before someone shushed them into silence. A murmur of chuckles rippled along the crowd and even the Patrician smiled.

"Go on," he said patiently, gesturing to the speaker. "Tell us."

A small boy climbed up to stand on his parent's lap. "The wild men have—don't have apple trees," he piped, twisting his shirt with one pudgy hand and trying not to grin. "The trees are blessed. Those who are respons— responsible for the trees are responsible for the safety of Quin." His task done, the little boy gave in to an ear-to-ear grin and clambered back down amidst smiles and sounds of approval.

"Someone is listening well." The Patrician paused long enough for silence to settle again. "I don't want to alarm you, but there is something wrong with our orchard. It's only fitting that those responsible for its care tell us what has occurred. I ask Maeve MacGowan to come up with me and tell us what she found."

Maeve's feet and lungs turned to lead. She knew he'd called her name, but it took Finna's nudging to get her moving, to make her way through the standing crowd until she was side by side with the Patrician, facing a blurred sea of faces.

"Go on, Maeve," he said softly. "Tell us how you discovered what's wrong with the trees."

His dark blue eyes smiled at her kindly, but she could hardly keep his gaze. Her hands tingled. Did he mean her to tell everyone that she'd stood on the wall and practically invited the wild men in? Had he seen her, after all? She tried to take a calming breath. The Patrician and everyone in the church were quiet, and the silence seemed to break her ears.

"What happened to the branch, Maeve?" he asked, still softly, as if they had all the time in the world.

Maeve inhaled again. She faced the crowd now. She could even see their faces, some expectant, some worried. For a moment she searched for one familiar face surrounded by a mass of blonde hair before remembering Katherine wasn't there. She gulped the air again and spoke. "I—I broke a branch from one of the trees by accident," she said, steeling herself against the ripple of murmurs that spread around the hall. "The tree is inflicted with rot. It's eating the core of the tree."

The murmur fell instantly as the Patrician raised his hand once more. "I've examined the trees more thoroughly, and only five of them are diseased," he said in a clear voice. "Five out of forty trees. We can't lose even one. Now I have consulted my grandfather's records and spent much time in thought. Thankfully, there is a cure that can heal our trees and restore safety to our people."

Maeve caught her breath. She'd heard about this cure. It supposedly came from Sir Arthur and his blessed vision, but it had seemed a thing of legend.

The Patrician continued, "I have found this cure, and together with Miss MacGowan's help, we will heal these five trees and prevent such a catastrophe from assailing Quin again."

More murmurs, this time of relief, of surprise, almost of celebration. Maeve blinked as the news settled into her brain.

"Tomorrow, we gather the elements necessary for the cure. My men will assist us."

The Patrician gestured, and the two guards behind him stepped forward. Thomas, who looked as bored as he had in the orchard, slid his gaze away from the crowd and gave her one quick wink.

Her hands clenched to fists at her side. Though nothing had been said outright, something told Maeve that she would not be looking in Mrs. Campbell's kitchen garden for this cure. Why else would she need protection? She was being sent beyond Quin's boundaries without Finna, in the company of guards, and one of them seemed anything but protective.

8. VESSEL

The fire in the Patrician's room blazed cheerfully as Maeve stood alone, waiting for his arrival. Everyone had gone home after the meeting, save Finna. The Patrician had invited them both to wait in his rooms to hear what to expect for Maeve's sudden and unfamiliar journey.

But Finna, who prided herself on keeping an eye on her foster daughter, had looked uncertainly from the village leader to Maeve. "No thank you, Patrician," she said at last. "I will wait for her in the aisles." And she had left briskly, leaving the Patrician to lead Maeve to his quarters before seeing to another task.

One wall of the room was lined with floor-to-ceiling cupboards. A door left of these led to a small bedroom, while the door to the right led to the church sanctuary. Two tall windows faced the dark and quiet streets of Quin. Two worn, brocaded sofas stood on either side of the fireplace, but Maeve didn't feel as though she could sit down.

She felt relieved to know the Patrician had a plan for saving the orchard. Succeeding in her task would mean she and Finna kept their home, their livelihood, their place in Quin. But in this comfortable environment, some of her earlier thoughts had settled enough for her to look at them, and she couldn't get the words she'd overheard at the wedding out of her mind.

Am I the daughter of the wild men?

Did that explain her draw to the downs, when everyone else in Quin seemed to possess their right minds on the matter? Would going into the downs bring out something in her that no one could ignore, something that marked her irrevocably as an outsider, a dangerous person, a threat? Was this brief journey, this necessary, inescapable venture, the very thing that could result in her being cast off even if the orchard was restored?

A door opened and the Patrician entered. "Ah, Maeve. Thank you for waiting. I apologize for the delay." He gestured to the couch. "Seat yourself, please. It's been a long day for all of us." He opened a cupboard and began leafing through papers and a few books. Maeve, realizing he wasn't going to sit yet, reluctantly sat down at last and sank into the cushions. They smelled of herbs and something sweet. The fragrance combined with the warmth made her feel suddenly very sleepy.

"Now, I know this is very sudden. I wish I could give you more time, but I'm afraid creating the cure can't be postponed. With the weather changing, and the severity of the rot, this really is the only time we have. Ah. Here it is." The Patrician took something from the cupboard, shut the doors, and sat on the couch facing hers. "Take a look at this."

Maeve accepted the book hesitantly. It was a leatherbound volume, much smaller and plainer than the Bible in the church sanctuary. The page to which it was open was covered in handwriting: small, neat, yet difficult to read. A large water stain smudged the lower corner, blurring and in some cases obscuring the words altogether.

"'The cure for tree rot,'" Maeve read aloud, and sudden understanding dawned on her. "Am I holding Sir Arthur's book, sir?"

"Indeed." He nodded, looking pleased. "Can you make out the rest of the words?"

Maeve squinted at the page. Under the larger, elaborately scripted title were words she recognized as a prayer; all the prayers Quin prayed had come from their homeland across the sea, or from Sir Arthur's book, which she now held in her hands.

God of our forebears, attend our prayer. God of the sacred orchard, guide our steps. Heal all wrongs, purify impurities, protect our land, which you gave us. Bless our humble efforts to cleanse the trees you gave us. In the name of the god of unity, amen.

Many of the words were familiar. It gave her a sense of comfort.

Under the prayer was a strange list.

"There's a prayer for the cure, which I can read easily, followed by words I don't know." Maeve squinted. "'Star point leaf, dusted dew'—are these plants, sir?"

"Yes. Well done."

"I've never heard of them before."

"Some are herbs we call by different names today. Others are found just outside of Quin."

Just outside? As in, near where the music comes from? But surely Sir Arthur wouldn't have gone that far.

"Excuse me, sir, but if you recognize these plants, why do you need me? I am grateful for the honor," she emphasized. "But I . . . it's all very important."

"And that is why I want your help. My eyes aren't what they used to be. And you are better suited to the task, if you would let yourself believe that."

Maeve ducked her head under the weight of this praise. "Thank you."

"The first thing we need, that star point leaf, is an herb that grows right on the edge of the downs, just west of the peat bogs. The other things we can find from the farmwives' kitchen gardens. I'll send a guard for those. Tomorrow, you and I will go with some of my men to gather the star point leaves. In the meantime, there is something I must give you."

The Patrician rose, went to another of the large cupboards lining the wall, and opened the door. Maeve caught a flash of burnished metal—gold? He closed the cupboard and brought the object back to show her.

It was a replica of a Quin apple, its twin in shape and size. The firelight flickered on the smooth, orange-yellow surface.

"Is it gold?" she ventured, marveling at the beauty of it.

The Patrician smiled. "No. It's a bronze vessel, forged by order of the first Lord Protector himself. I can only imbue it with magic for a night and a day before you must return it to me, but it will help the orchard until the cure is finished."

He cupped it in his hands and shut his eyes, murmuring words under his breath like a prayer. Maeve gasped. A fierce blue light burst from the apple, so bright that it set every line on the Patrician's face into relief. Then the glow dimmed until the apple bore only the faintest light. He sighed deeply and held it out to her.

"Here. Take it, child. It won't hurt you."

It felt heavy and a little warm. She turned it over, weighing it in her hands and marveling at the new object and its purpose.

"As you may have noticed from the page, parts of the cure are obscured by water damage. We cannot say how long this cure will take. If my grandfather ever needed to use it, he left no record of this. And I shall have to write to Lord Protector and tell him about the rot." His forehead creased in thought, as if he did not relish the prospect. Suddenly his face became serious.

"Is there something troubling you, sir?"

He hesitated before answering. "Nothing to worry you at present, Maeve. I have every confidence this cure will work, and so must you."

"The Lord Protector will not be pleased to learn of the trees, will he."

"None of us are, Maeve, and in that sense he is like us. As long as we do our duty, we will have nothing to fear."

That sounded ominous, but Maeve did not want to press if the Patrician would not speak of it. She turned the apple over again. "Where shall I put it?"

When she looked up, the Patrician's face was still deeply lined. *This must have taken a lot of strength.*

He cleared his throat and straightened his cloak. "Put it on the orchard wall. Now, it won't attract the wild men," he said just as the question rose to Maeve's lips. "As surely as my magic is connected to the orchard, it will repel them, or at least help to. But remember to bring this vessel back to me here after we gather the herbs. As I said, it doesn't hold magic for long. Replenishing it on time is vital."

"Yes, sir. Can I ask you something?" Maeve said as he sat back down opposite her. He gestured for her to continue. "Do you feel the damage to the orchard? Does the rot affect your magic?"

He gave a half smile. "I'm gratified by your concern for me. The answer is complicated, I suppose. I don't feel it, like a wound or a weakening, not directly. Yet our magic comes from the same source. Both have a slightly different feel from the dark magic. Oh, yes," he said in response to her surprised look. "It is very difficult to discern, but it is there nonetheless. And this is no surprise. The real differences are where the dark magic comes from and, of course, how it is used."

"From what do they take it?" She'd heard enough about how the wild men used it—for destruction and disorder, without scruples—but its source intrigued her.

A frown creased his face, not of rebuke, but of someone speaking of something deeply disturbing. "They draw their magic from dangerous sources, Maeve. I'm not entirely sure what they are. The darkest night? Demons? The souls of the troubled dead? It is sufficient to know the dangers exist and to keep away from them. The god who brought us here bestowed the blessings of his magic and the sacred apple tree upon us. I am just magic's caretaker, just as you and Finna are caretakers of the orchard, just as all MacGowans have been since the days of her grandparents."

All MacGowans. She realized then that she had referred to the wild men in her question even though the Patrician hadn't. Overheard insinuations settled heavily on her until she lowered her eyes. The couch creaked as the Patrician leaned forward.

"I understand what it is to bear a family responsibility," he said gently. "It is a privilege and yet, sometimes, a great burden." He sighed. The firelight picked out all the gray in his hair and darkened the lines on his face, and he sat not tall and straight as he'd stood in the church, but slightly bent, smaller. "I know it is not always easy, following in the footsteps of those who came before you. But you have all you need for the task, Maeve. I know you do."

His confidence in her sent warmth radiating throughout her. When had Finna acknowledged this burden to her? Never, that she could remember. With Finna, it was infrequent praise for a job well done and cool, withdrawn indifference or scolding for her shortcomings. It would be painful to lose the confidence of this man, who saw her as a person and not a disappointment or liability.

"Something troubles you." His voice remained soft. It struck her that both he and Finna spoke that way to very different effects. Whereas Finna's quietest voice meant that deepest anger and disappointment roiled beneath, Maeve felt something loosen in her shoulders at the Patrician's words. Still, finding a reply was difficult. She kept her eyes on the apple in her lap.

"It's all right if you don't wish to tell me. But you are always welcome to confide in me, Maeve."

Her tongue loosened and the words spilled out. "I overheard people talking at the wedding," she said in a small voice. "They said something . . . Patrician, I am grateful for all Finna's done for me. For my home and being able to take care of the orchard—truly. And I know I shouldn't listen to gossip, but . . ." *Can I even say the words aloud? Would I lose my place if anyone else thought I wasn't from Quin?*

"But someone said something that has caused you grief."

Maeve nodded, swallowed. "I wonder who my parents are."

Something passed across the Patrician's face, an expression she'd never seen him wear before. Perhaps she'd said too much. Finna had told her that many people died of a wasting illness around the time she'd been discovered. People had been visiting from Dumar at the time, and clansmen bringing wares; the sickness had fallen swiftly and prevented anyone from returning for weeks. Many never did. Even being the daughter of a clansman wouldn't have been so bad. They were accepted by villagers and maintained decent behavior, even if they did ride strange deer-like mounts and keep strange customs among themselves. It was understood that her parents, whoever they were, had died during this time. Maeve even cherished the thought that they'd put her away to spare her the illness, as it had.

None of this would mean anything if her parents came from the wild men.

The Patrician's face cleared to his usual fatherly concern. He sat straighter, some of the weariness gone from his features. "You are a young woman now, and will marry in time. You are at a place where many things will change and set the course for the rest of your life. It's only natural that you should be curious about your parents. I may be able to help you discover their identities."

Maeve straightened in her seat too. "Really, sir? How?"

"I can send letters to Dumar and Ferre asking discreetly for information. There are registries in each village. Like Boyle's, but more formal. I will send two of my men tomorrow."

"Thank you." A certain fear rose up and strangled some of her relief. What if he found out she did come from the wild men? *But he knows their magic from his own*, she thought. *If he thought I was wild, he would probably know, and wouldn't help me. I wouldn't even still be in Quin at all. He believes in me.*

He rose and went to the meeting-house door. Maeve followed. Emboldened by his generosity and support, Maeve chanced another question.

"Will we be very close to the downs tomorrow, sir?"

The Patrician shook his head. "Not at all. You've seen the peat bogs, have you not? Very good. Not even a ten-minute walk from Quin in this fine weather. And anyway, we will be there during the daytime, not the realm of night."

"Yes, sir." She gave the apple a little squeeze and smiled at him. "Good night."

"Good night. Keep to the light, Maeve. It will always guide you."

Finna waited for her as promised. The lights had died down in the sanctuary, and only Boyle lingered to put out the last of the blue-lighted candles once the two MacGowans had left. The blue glow was gone save for the two candles burning near the door. The head guard kept his distance, as if sensing they had a good deal to talk about, but smiled and nodded kindly to them from his place across the room.

"Tell me about it as we walk," Finna said. "It's late and you must be hungry."

Maeve nodded, both grateful Finna would have noticed and stung that this was her only greeting. She wondered if Finna felt put out by the Patrician's choice. Had she expected to be the one to find and make the cure? But the woman only walked ramrod straight through the quieting streets lit by the few burning torches that would remain bright all night.

A gruff voice spoke from the darkness.

"All well, Finna?"

Maeve started and tripped to a halt as Finna stopped, looking into the deep shell of the smithy. She recognized the voice, though she'd never heard it speak those words before.

"Yes, Duffy," was Finna's reply.

Heavy footsteps brought the blacksmith to the edge of his shop so that he was half-shielded in shadow. "Your girl has a big task, I hear." He nodded at Maeve.

It struck her that she hadn't seen him at the meeting, and Duffy was the kind of person one didn't miss. But then she'd been so distressed and distracted during the meeting. Looking for a reclusive blacksmith in a crowd of two hundred hadn't been on her mind.

"She does. And we must get our rest, so she can do the Patrician's bidding." There was something in Finna's voice that Maeve recognized, something that had been directed at her many times. *She's warning him*, Maeve thought with surprise, *but why?*

Duffy nodded his bald head and disappeared back into the depths of the smithy.

The air rose chill over the stream as they crossed it, babbling its incessant conversation just as Maeve finished relaying the Patrician's instructions to an expressionless Finna. Rather than the house, her foster mother led Maeve to the orchard.

"Put it where it belongs and be quick about it," she said, nodding at the apple in Maeve's hands.

She obeyed. The Patrician hadn't specified where on the wall to put it, so she placed it nearest the trees with the rot, breathing a little prayer for protection. Not that the Patrician's magic wouldn't hold. But she wanted to add her help, in the hope that her efforts meant something too, and in apology for breaking the branch.

Even in the darkness she could see a band of something wrapped around the trunk of the nearest tree. It was cloth of some kind, and similar markings adorned the trunks of four other trees nearby. *These are the five trees the Patrician mentioned,* she thought. She stole a glance across the downs, where darkness covered everything, and thought of the Patrician's words. It didn't matter where the wild men got their magic, not really; she knew enough to ignore the draw of this place, to keep her head down and keep to her task.

Swiftly she turned back to Finna. The woman nodded, her lips tight, her thin arms wrapped around herself. It might have been a nod of approval, but Maeve wasn't sure.

Then they hurried into the cottage. Finna added another peat brick to the fire and started the water for tea.

"We won't waste that cake. Put some of this on it." Finna went to a cupboard and took out a small plate of butter. She handed that and a knife to Maeve. "You can get the tea things out, Maeve."

Maeve said her thanks and did as she was told. Butter and cake were cold, but with them and the tea, her growling stomach grew quiet. Finna only took tea and watched her eat.

She had to say something to soften the silence. Maybe her foster mother feared she wasn't up to the task; maybe she wished the Patrician had required her aid instead. Either way, she must prove herself, and she was determined to do so. "Finna, I promise I'll help with the harvest, even though I'm to work on the cure, too. You won't lack my help at all."

"I know. You always do." The words came without an edge, without sharpness. Maeve ate in silence, unsure of what else to say and knowing that this was as close to praise as she would get. Finna's response was smaller than the last apple left in a whole orchard of trees, too small to ease the memory of the slap across her face. Finna had never slapped her before. She had made frequent use of the switch when Maeve was young. But the slap stung with a different sharpness that had little to do with the physical pain. Maeve's chest felt like an empty basket forgotten after a meager harvest, grown dusty and brittle with waiting for someone to fill it.

Maeve sat up in darkness, blinking, something soft wrapped around her. Disorientation faded: she was lying in her bed, it was still night, and something had awoken her.

Was it a sound? Her mind flew at once to the orchard and the apple. She flung herself out of bed and pulled on her shoes, lacing the boots with trembling fingers. Finna's room was silent as ever; her foster mother never stirred in her sleep. *Should I wake her? No, it's surely nothing, and then I'll have made her cross for no reason.*

Still, she had to check. She couldn't keep her fingers from trembling as she pulled her shawl from the peg and wrapped it around herself. The door creaked faintly as she opened it, making her wince.

Maeve hurried under cover of darkness to the orchard. The blue-glowing apple shone like a faded star against a quiet night. Once within the walls, Maeve felt she'd returned to some measure of safety. But the trees—she hurried to the one with the broken branch and looked it over, searching for any sign of further damage. All was quiet and still. Yet she couldn't shake the feeling that something was different.

Uncertain as to what harm she could discern without breaking another branch, she still felt compelled to look. She ran gentle fingers over the bark of the next tree, searching for something, anything odd. Over and over again she found nothing besides bark and the rough fabric markers.

Because nothing happened inside *the orchard. Not yet.*

A chill crawled down her back even as she faced away from the downs. Above her, the boughs stirred in the rising wind, her loose hair tangling as her nightdress stirred. Then she heard it. A keening, piercing cry, causing gooseflesh to erupt down her arms. Animal or human, she wasn't sure.

Then came the sound of footsteps.

Something beyond reason compelled her. Maeve spun, crashed into rough stone, and flung her arms out for balance, brushing against something smooth and faintly blue. She was closer to the wall than she thought.

The bronze apple flew from its perch and tumbled down the hill, down into shadows and out of sight.

Her heart skipped and jumped. Then, before she could stop herself, she leaped over the wall and ran down the hill after the errant apple.

9. TEST

The way down was much longer than it had looked from the orchard. As the hill rose up before her, Maeve scoured the ground for the apple. When the hill's shadow swallowed her and she found no sign of it, she began to panic. *It must have caught in a patch of grass somewhere,* she thought, puzzled. It couldn't have gone far; the earth was full of hillocks and small stones that would stop even the roundest object in its trajectory.

It couldn't roll up the hill, could it? But then, it is a vessel for magic; maybe something about it interacts with the magic of the wild men? She couldn't entertain that thought, not if she wanted to keep her wits about her. The thought of Finna's disappointment, of grieving the Patrician yet again, was too much to bear. She had no choice but to climb the hill and keep looking.

Up and down again, and still no sign until Maeve came to a cleft in the earth. She slipped through and gasped.

Here she began to realize just how little she knew the terrain. Before her, the earth dropped steeply away, leading to many low hills that melted into the base of a vast, taller hill beyond. What she had assumed were relatively uniform rises and falls in the ground was really a series of deceptive folds in the earth that could easily hide many secrets.

But did one of them hide the apple? Maeve's eyes were well adjusted to the night. The light of a half-moon shone in a sky brushed with wisps of clouds, between which stars peeked through. If she were on the wrong path, her search could take her all night. She went on picking her way down, keeping her mind on the task at hand. *At least the ground is firm. The peat bogs are far away to my left.*

Still, with every step her worry increased. Getting lost seemed easy in this unfamiliar place full of unknown dangers. The sound of running water reached her, offering a flicker of hope. *The stream is near.* Maybe the shallow water had caught the apple and she could easily pluck it out.

But after another stretch of indefinite time she was no closer to finding the stream. She realized that, too, must be farther away than she'd thought, and a moment later she found herself at the edge of something unexpected.

A cool, earthy scent greeted her, mixed with another smell she didn't recognize, both sharp and sweet. Maeve rounded a low hill and found the source: a mossy-edged basin of water stretched before her, tucked into the curving arms of the hill. Its still surface caught the light of the stars above. It was beautiful in a way she couldn't quite put her finger on. Then she registered two things at once: First, at the bottom of the pool, one star glowed faintest blue. The second thing quelled her elation and doused her in cold fear.

Across the pool, between low scrub grown up and the foot of another craggy hill, a shadow melted into the darkness gathered there. Someone else was here.

Her breathing seemed loud as thunder in her ears. She pressed herself against the hill sheltering the pool, waiting, listening. A memory of the cry she'd heard earlier came back with terrifying clarity. *Was it a person or an animal? And to whom does it belong?*

She tried to calm her breathing. *I can't go home without this apple.* Maybe they were gone. Maybe she'd imagined it. Maeve steeled herself and stepped away from her hiding place, fixing her eyes on the blue light in the pool and forcing herself to get as close as possible.

There was no question; she knew that color of blue like she knew the color of the apples on her trees. It had to be the Patrician's apple, but it was so very tiny. How far down was it? She couldn't swim.

A rustling sounded behind her, sending her heart leaping into her throat. To her left, in the shadow of the hill, gathered a cluster of bushes hiding a small ledge. From there, a voice spoke.

"Maeve MacGowan?"

The voice was as surprised as she was terrified. Yet she recognized it. Even as a whisper, she knew it. Curiosity blossomed so quickly it partially drove away her fear.

Liam rose from behind the bushes and stared at her, an incredulous smile spreading across his face.

"What are you doing here?"

The words flew from her mouth before she realized they'd spoken in unison. The shepherd chuckled.

"When I said I'd see you soon, I didn't think it would be here."

She hazarded a few steps in his direction. The ledge was wider than it looked; it provided an ideal hiding place.

"Was that you, sneaking around?" she asked, relief making her voice shake.

"*I* was sneaking? What were you doing, then? Taking the night air?"

Maeve gave a small laugh. She should be embarrassed, being outside in only her nightdress and shawl, and with this strange boy. His lack of direct answer bothered her a little. Yet of all the people she could imagine, he was the only one she'd want to meet out here. Just as quickly, though, his question brought her dilemma to the forefront of her mind.

She gestured at the pool. "I lost something that I must get back. But I can't swim."

Liam toed the edge of the pool with the same carelessness he'd possessed on the orchard wall and looked down into the dark waters. "What is it?"

"It's a bronze apple, and it holds something very important. You don't swim, do you?"

"Not a stroke." As he shook his head, his mop of dark hair released the smell of damp sheep. Only an arm's length away now, Maeve wrinkled her nose. *Smelly shepherd's hut indeed!*

"What will happen if you don't get it back?" he asked.

The thought made her sag. "I'm afraid to think about it. It's for the protection of the orchard. The trees are . . . sick. The magic is in trouble, weakened. Without this bronze apple, the orchard is in danger from other, unholy magic."

She spoke the last two words in a whisper, as if she were afraid to say *wild men* aloud. *Well, I am afraid.*

Liam kept silent at first, shifting his weight between his legs. "And you want nothing to do with this other magic, do you?" he asked quietly, no trace of his usual self-confidence.

His brown eyes regarded her steadily, but she saw wariness, too. *He's worried,* Maeve thought, and though she didn't quite understand why, she hastened to offer him some kind of reassurance.

She didn't get a chance.

A wild sound rose up behind them, twisting and falling like a nightmare given voice, sending cold fear down her back and arms. Liam seized her hand and a moment later she was crouched behind the bushes elbow to elbow with him, holding her breath and watching through the tangle of leaves and twigs.

An unfamiliar voice spoke, low yet clear. "Something strange happened here, Breena. I know it."

Liam tensed beside her. The voice was male, older, and the accent was different from the one Quin's villagers spoke with. *Is it a clansman? Or someone else?*

From her vantage point, she had a clear view across the water and over to the next low hill, but still the speaker remained hidden. Liam shifted beside her. Maeve put a hand on his arm. If he was considering his next move, maybe he didn't know the potential danger they were in. All of Finna's dire warnings returned to her in a flood of fear, urging her heart to beat so fast she thought it might give their position away.

"Something, is it?" said a young woman in the same accent. "But nothing has happened here, Colm. Not for a long time. You know this." She sounded confident yet curious, this Breena, and a little out of breath. Maeve relaxed her clenched hands; she had not expected to hear a woman, and the casual tone of the newcomer's voice was as much of a surprise as her presence.

Quiet footsteps sounded now, growing nearer. "I'm telling you, something was here. No, not something—some*one*. I feel it in my toes."

"And your toes tell the truth, do they?" Breena teased.

Colm chuckled. "Ah, you know they do. Or you wouldn't have followed me here."

"True. You're right, as usual. And do your venerable digits tell you who it was?"

"No," Colm whispered. "But they're still here."

Maeve held her breath. Liam made no move to brush her off and she could hear his own bated breathing. Beyond that she heard the faint, whispered conversation of the man and woman, but nothing she could understand. If the rustling was any indication, the pair had begun to circle the small pool. She crouched lower, ignoring the sheep smell and hoping desperately that whoever these people were, they would decide to leave before they found her and Liam.

"Then we should tell the chief. Orlenn will need to know if the pool has been disturbed."

The footsteps paused. Something in the way Breena said *Orlenn* sent a shiver along Maeve's spine. Clearly, their chief was not one to be crossed. The last thing she wanted was trouble with another leader.

A touch of warmth pulled her attention to Liam, who was taking her hand off his arm with a questioning look. Then he released her and left the cover of the bushes, walking toward the voices.

Too late to stop him, Maeve bit back a cry.

"Who goes there?" demanded Colm. After more rustling, he appeared, partially obscured from Maeve's sight by the twigs and leaves in front of her. He wore a short cloak of rough stuff that left his wiry forearms exposed to the chill. His garments looked like shepherd's clothes, possibly embroidered with a pattern but difficult to discern in the dark. His wild hair glowed silver in the moonlight. Judging by his stance, his gaze was trained on Liam.

Behind him only the woman's outline was visible. A strange sound reached Maeve's ears: a deep thrumming, unlike anything she'd ever heard, emanated across the pool, and she was certain it came from the woman.

"I mean no harm," said Liam, lifting his hands. "I'm alone. Please, hear me out. I'm looking for someone named Lochlyn. Do you know them?"

Breena emerged from the shadows. She appeared no more than a few years older than Maeve was, barely out of her teens. Over a long tunic and slim leggings, she wore a cloak like Colm's, and she held her hands out at her sides as if carrying something invisible but heavy. Other details of her features were obscured in the night, but the starlight gleamed in her eyes. "Why do you ask?"

Maeve held her breath.

"Because my mother spoke of Lochlyn," Liam said, his voice trembling, "and she's gone. I want to know who that was to her."

"What's your name, lad?" Colm asked. Both he and Breena maintained a polite but wary tone, as if they would know the second Liam said anything untoward.

"Liam O'Conner." He paused. "My mother's name was Leesha. I thought Lochlyn might be her family name."

"And why would a boy from the villages believe she had anything to do with Lochlyn?" Breena asked.

"Because my mother possessed something, a gift. I don't know what it was, I've never seen it in anyone else. But I recognize what you're carrying. It reminds me of her. I don't know how else to describe it. It has to be connected with this Lochlyn."

Maeve could hear nothing but the ghost of night sounds. Breena slowly raised her hands as if preparing to shield herself. "And why do you think that?"

"I never knew where she came from. My father told me that name was connected to her, but he didn't know anything more than what I've told you." He paused again, straightening. "Lochlyn is your name, isn't it?"

Colm folded his arms and tucked his chin in his hand, considering first Liam, then Breena.

"Colm," Breena murmured, "do you think we should—"

"Oh, aye," he said cheerfully, "go ahead."

Breena opened her hand and sent something like a great gust of air rushing toward Liam. The twigs and leaves rustled against Maeve's face.

Rather than step aside, Liam deflected the gust with his hands, sending whatever it was away from the water and shaking the trees in its wake.

Maeve began to breathe again. Liam's back heaved as he panted, as if whatever he had just done had taken a great deal of strength. Breena's jaw dropped, and Colm, whose face Maeve could now see, was grinning ear to ear. He rocked back on his heels and elbowed his young companion. "I told you it was someone like us."

"You said it was someone from the villages," Breena protested, wiping the shock from her face.

"You knew?" Liam asked, voicing Maeve's unspoken question. "Was that whole conversation just for show?"

It was Breena's turn to grin. "Why do you think we let you hear it in the first place, boy? We knew someone was here. Someone with magic. You came looking for us. It's lucky for you we found you here instead of creeping around our haunt."

Maeve's heart shuddered once more as Breena's gaze flicked to the water. *Did she see the apple? What would she make of it?* But Colm spoke again, and Breena said nothing about it. Though Maeve couldn't be sure, she thought the woman's eyes swept by her hiding place as nonchalantly as if she were taking in the scenery. Between her magic and use of the word *haunt* Maeve felt more than a little apprehensive.

"His father is from the villages. His mother, possibly Lochlyn." Colm chuckled gleefully. "He's both!"

"Both." Liam repeated the word as if trying it out, looking down at his hands as if he'd never seen them before. "So what does that make you?"

"Lochlyn is the name of our clan," said Colm. "We're a large one, and we live in many smaller groups. It's possible your mother came from one of these."

Liam inhaled sharply, as if finally absorbing what had happened. "I want to know everything. Why did my mother leave? Does she still have any family alive?"

Colm's grin dissolved into a worried frown.

"Not so fast." Breena had dropped her hands, but she took a step forward, causing Maeve to tense further. "There is a lot you should know, but we aren't the ones to tell you. Not yet."

"We'll have to discuss it with Orlenn first," Colm cut in brightly. "The chief is busy with other matters tonight. You understand, lad."

"Yes," Liam answered reluctantly. Maeve couldn't understand at all, and doubted the shepherd did either.

"We'll bring word of you to the chief," Breena said, waving a hand to silence her companion's protest. "Colm, let me finish, for soul's sake. We haven't heard of anyone like you in a long time, Liam O'Conner. You're the first I've met. No telling what to expect. Meet us here tomorrow evening, when the Fiddler's stars appear. If Orlenn has answers, we can give them to you then."

She turned and marched back into the shadows. Colm shoved his hands into his trouser pockets. "It might not be much, but it'll be a start for you. Farewell till tomorrow, lad."

He'd almost disappeared from sight when Liam called out to him. "Wait."

Colm hesitated mid-stride.

"What if I don't come back?" Liam asked. "If I've gone this long without knowing, what makes you so sure I'll come back? Why trust me if you don't know me?"

Colm turned back to the shepherd. "You came out here, tonight, in secret. You're curious enough to be here in the first place or you wouldn't be here at all." His voice was kind and slightly amused. "I'm sure it's a good thing we've met," he went on, when Liam remained silent. "But don't try to follow us tonight. It doesn't go well for those who try to trick Lochlyn, I can tell you that." Then with a rustling of grass, he too was gone.

The quiet that followed was so complete Maeve thought she could hear the water breathe. Her legs had cramped, but she wasn't yet willing to stand. When Liam turned to face her, all traces of carefree confidence were gone, replaced by vague defiance and an undercurrent of fear.

"Now you know why else I came to Quin," he said.

Maeve stood up shakily and looked around the pool before stepping out from her hiding place. Multiple questions ran through her mind and trampled each other so that she hardly knew where to start. "Why did you tell them you were alone?"

"You didn't want to be found." Liam shrugged as if this was plain as day. "Now you're not the only one with a secret."

He must have as many questions as I do.

"Your secret is safe with me," Maeve promised, gratified to see his shoulders relax at her words.

What did he do back there, she wondered, *with the whatever-it-was that Breena sent toward him?* The clansmen she'd seen had never demonstrated magical abilities. But then why should they do so in Quin, when they were only there to trade? She hadn't interacted with them much, and certainly didn't remember every clan name, or many at all.

She looked at the pool again, wishing the starlight granted more clarity to the obsidian depths, wishing for anything to help her out of the mess she'd gotten herself into. Liam may have found some answers, but she still needed that apple. She circled back around the pond the way she'd come and tried not to think about Finna's reaction when she learned about the lost vessel.

"I can't help you get it out, if that's what you're thinking." Liam nodded at the water, then spread his hands. "I can't swim. And I don't even know what I did back there."

Reluctantly she realized the apple would have to wait for now. She'd lost something important, but the Patrician would come with her tomorrow to look for herbs; she could tell him what happened and hopefully retrieve the apple before its magic wore off. Nothing had happened to her after the Lochlyn clan's arrival, thanks to Liam keeping her presence a secret.

No, she wouldn't tell the Patrician *everything* that happened, would she?

Am I really considering keeping the whole truth from the Patrician?

Since keeping Liam's appearance in the orchard a secret from Finna, the decision to not be completely honest with authority had come easily a second time. This troubled her, like a tiny worm wiggling at the core of her being. She pushed the thought away.

Retrieving the apple was the important thing, and there was plenty of time to do that. *He said the herb was east of the peat bogs. In that case, I can't be very far from where we're going to search tomorrow.*

But tomorrow would arrive swiftly, and she'd been out too long. "I've got to go," she said. "Please, don't let anyone know we met tonight."

The carefree grin returned. "Can't promise. I tell Whistle everything. He's all right, though—it's the sheep I worry about. They're awful gossips."

"I promised I'd keep your secret," she said with a frown. "If this is how you repay me, then I never want to see you again."

With that, Maeve scrambled for the gap in the two hills, only for Liam to follow.

"I was only joking," he said. "Please, Maeve. I'm sorry. It's just that—I didn't know how tonight would go. And it went much better than I'd hoped."

Her own outburst had surprised her. Now something about the way his voice softened with that last sentence made Maeve feel strangely soft and elated.

Yet now I have speaking to a boy at night, outside of Quin, to add to my list of transgressions, she thought, quaking to think of Finna's reaction if she found out. *Are those exact rules? Never mind that. No doubt I've broken more than one.*

She remembered that on top of everything else, she was in her nightdress. The embarrassment, long absent, now returned. Wrapping her shawl around herself more tightly, Maeve strode on without speaking. Even beyond the gap, as she made her way over one hill and to the last ridge, Liam kept at her heels.

"Why are you following me?" she whispered over her shoulder when they reached the base of the final hill. "You know the way to the pastures. You could be seen."

"You can't guess?"

This time the hesitation in his voice was clear. The memory of their first meeting warmed her cheeks. She could guess, all right, though she could hardly believe it. No one had spoken in this tone to her before. Once a boy had followed her and Katherine home from school, her friend wearing a look of cool indifference as his low questions and half smiles became pleas for her attention. Later Katherine told an astonished Maeve that her look only meant that she was hiding her true feelings of disgust. Maeve, who had bought the cool indifference just as much as the disappointed lad, wondered if such attraction was always so confusing and unwelcome, and had little interest in romance since.

Until now.

How strange it was to know someone else's secret, especially one of such significance, and especially when she'd hardly spoken to him before now. That Liam had some magical ability put him in a different place than her, as if he were a kind of ruler disguised as a shepherd, someone of power living in a smelly shepherd's hut. Yet for all his apparent carelessness and self-sufficiency, there was no pretense or lordly arrogance to his manner. Knowing his secret felt like a kind of intimacy and a kind of honor. And added to everything, he seemed to feel a similar interest in her to what she felt toward him.

"How did you lose that thing at the bottom of the pool?" Liam asked, effectively dousing said pleasant feelings on the matter. To her growing annoyance, he trotted up beside her, keeping pace. "You don't seem like the kind of person to wander the downs at night carrying something magical. Especially not in your—" He nodded at her attire, then looked away, blowing out a puff of breath.

Maeve took some comfort in the fact that he sounded as embarrassed as she felt. "I don't really want to talk about it," she whispered.

"Is it really so bad?" His voice wasn't teasing this time.

"It's no worse than sneaking out on purpose and nearly scaring me to death." She didn't really believe this, but saying so gave her a foreign, heady feeling, and that he didn't protest only made it stronger. "Now go your own way, before you get caught. That'd do neither of us any favors."

"Fair enough." Brushing past her in a whiff of damp sheep, Liam turned to walk backward, hands thrust in his pockets. "I'll be seeing you, Maeve MacGowan," he said, keeping his voice low. "You can tell me your terrible deed some other time. Or not. I promise I won't tell a living soul. Not even my dog."

Then he sprinted ahead to the hilltop and disappeared over the ridge. By the time Maeve climbed to the top, she saw only the silent house and the walled orchard, now devoid of its glowing guardian.

Upon entering the house, she breathed a prayer of thanks that Finna kept the door well oiled. She slipped into bed undetected, her mind racing like the stream after a storm. She'd escaped a misadventure with the wild men; Finna was none the wiser and would remain ignorant of her chance encounters. In a few hours, she could redeem herself by retrieving the vessel. By the time she drifted off to sleep, the gray light of dawn had already crept into her room, and Maeve dreamed of a shepherd boy whose smile made her feel a multitude of exciting and confusing things.

10. Cure

Over her porridge the next morning, Maeve tried valiantly to contain her jaw-splitting yawns. She'd woken with a start to find her room flooded with light. The orchard wall stood bare, and the night's events flooded her memory, setting her heart racing again. *The pool. Liam. Colm and Breena. And . . . Liam.*

Now she was blushing over her bowl, shoveling food into her mouth as she tried to collect her thoughts. Every element of her night on the downs competed for attention. Would the Patrician be angry? Or worse, disappointed? Who were Colm and Breena, and why were they out at night?

Yet as much as these things tied her stomach in knots, thoughts of Liam affected her in entirely different ways. It seemed wrong to think of him so much when she had done something as foolish as further endanger the orchard with her carelessness. She glanced up at Finna, worried that somehow she might accidentally lay her thoughts bare with the wrong expression.

But Finna stood at the fire. She pulled the kettle from its hook and poured more hot water for tea. *I should tell Finna about the apple before she finds out on her own. At least I can—should—be honest about that part.*

"We'll harvest apples this morning before you go to the village," Finna said. "You will fetch the water this time."

To atone for my sins?

"Finna," Maeve began. The porridge felt like a lump in her stomach; she couldn't eat anymore. "Something happened last night. I heard a sound in the orchard and I went to investigate."

"You did what?" A crease formed between Finna's eyes.

"I couldn't let something else happen to the orchard," Maeve hurried on. "I worried—after everything—I didn't think. All that happened is another accident. I knocked the bronze apple off the wall and it rolled away till I couldn't see it." She lowered her gaze, relief and guilt pounding through her veins.

I haven't lied. I have only stopped early in the story. Under Finna's silent gaze, she wasn't sure that was enough. Should she have left the apple alone as her words suggested? But it was too late for that now.

Finna exhaled sharply. "You saw nothing else? Heard nothing?"

Maeve thought of the strange cry. "I heard something. I saw only shadows on the downs."

The ease of the lie frightened her. *When did I become so good at it?*

"What did it sound like, this noise?"

"I don't know," she answered truthfully. "An owl? It might have been a wild beast, but . . . I don't know."

She lowered her eyes and waited for Finna to scold her, to say something cold and sparse, sharp as an icicle thrust under the skin. Her muscles bunched to shield herself from the blow.

Instead her foster mother only rose from her seat. "Then we'd best get started. I don't want you to be late for your appointment with the Patrician. The cure won't wait."

Maeve looked up, surprised. Then she hurried to help Finna clean up from breakfast before they set about their chores.

After a dutiful ladleful of water and a prayer under her breath, Maeve set about gathering apples with Finna. Maeve felt a pang of sadness for the diseased trees. The apples growing on their branches would have to be burned, Finna explained; no part of the tree was good for anything but that now, and not even to warm someone's house.

"The Patrician's cure will tell us whether or not the whole trees can be saved," said Finna when they had almost finished. "It must work, if he has faith in it."

Maeve looked at the orchard and the thought of it empty and barren made her heart squeeze with sadness. "What will become of us if the orchard dies?"

Asking Finna was a risk, of course. Asking her almost anything was. But Finna, despite their work, seemed untroubled at the moment. Perhaps being in the orchard had a similar effect on her as it had on Maeve, albeit one that was less obvious to observers. But Maeve had made a study of Finna's moods as long as she could remember. Whatever the reason, the Patrician's unspoken worries came back to her and she had to ask the question burning in her mind for a day now.

"There is a place in Dumar." Finna paused to examine the apple she'd plucked, then held it out to Maeve. Maeve took it obediently and sniffed. She could detect nothing wrong, but could she trust her own nose anymore? She put it in her basket and waited impatiently for Finna to continue.

"It is a place where unmarried women go, or women who no longer have a home." Finna's mouth tightened, as if she tasted something bitter.

"And that is where we would go?"

Finna nodded once, a frown tugging her face.

"What is it like?" Maeve had never wondered about the other towns before. She'd always assumed they were just like Quin, minus the orchard: cobbled streets, houses and shops crammed together, walled and surrounded by rolling hills. But the way Finna spoke led her to believe that this place was far from pleasant.

"Women are made to work all day, scrubbing floors and mending clothes. They are not allowed outside the walls of the place. Cromwell House, that's what they call it. The first Lord Protector ordered it built after some unmarried women fell pregnant. Everyone who goes there becomes faceless, nameless, forgotten. Few who go in ever come out."

Maeve shivered. She didn't dare ask any more questions, though guesses abounded, each of them more horrible than the last. Instead she gave all her attention over to the task. She had always lived with the threat of losing the orchard hanging over her; this Cromwell House, locked away from the open air and rolling hills, was worse than she'd imagined the punishment to be.

Even though she'd already said it, the watering prayer darted through her mind like a rabbit running from a dog. *God of the world, attend my prayer. Make me pure in heart and worthy of this task. In the name of the god who hears and sees all, amen.*

They brought all the apples they'd picked back home and stored them in the kitchen. Finna baked a small batch of pasties stuffed with apple and sausage, then wrapped one in a cloth and handed it to Maeve. "To take with you," she said, "since there's no time to eat lunch."

Maeve followed Finna down to the village just before noon, her insides squirming with all the secrets she had carried over the past few days.

The stone apples stood stark against the gate, reminding Maeve mercilessly of a small bronze apple at the bottom of a pool.

Unbidden, a memory returned. She was small when she attempted to pull one of the stone apples from its perch, wanting to find out if it could replace the lump of leather she and her playmates were using as a ball. Finna caught her before she could touch it. "These are not toys," Finna had scolded, yanking Maeve away so sharply that her neck hurt. "These are the stones of unity and safety. Anyone who disobeys the laws of Quin must suffer punishment, for they have sacrificed both."

Unity and safety, Quin's guiding lights. Which one will be compromised if I cannot retrieve the bronze apple? Or will I sacrifice both?

The gates swung inward with a groan, drawing her attention and everyone else's, and a small procession entered Quin. Five men sat atop large, slender mounts featuring antlers with a span so wide Maeve found it hard to believe they entered the main entrance gates with such grace. Their rough, dark green garb and long beards marked them as belonging to one of the local clans.

The men dismounted in front of a shop. One of their mounts gave a loud cry, half bleat, half growl. A woman with a tiny child started at the sound, and she scooped her child up and hurried on her way. Others gave the men a wide berth as they unloaded bundles of wood and entered the shop, but no one openly commented on them.

Maeve wondered if these men knew the Lochlyn clan. *Have these clansfolk ever seen the wild men? Why do they treat us with respect when the wild men are so feared and avoided?*

Finna was already at the meeting-hall door, summoning Maeve. Inside, the large open room enveloped them in quiet. Sunlight streamed in through the windows; there was no need for candles at this hour.

The guard at the Patrician's door opened it for them. "You're to go straight in, miss," he said, and stood aside.

The smell of sheep greeted Maeve before she saw the person talking with the Patrician.

"It is settled, then. Welcome to Quin." The Patrician stepped aside from the dark-haired young man facing him and gestured to the door with a smile. Maeve averted her eyes and hoped the sudden quickening of her heart would not give anything away.

Despite this, she risked a glance at Liam. But the young shepherd's gaze was fixed straight ahead as he passed her in a cloud of sheep odor, as if she weren't even in the room.

"Ladies." The Patrician smiled at them both as the door shut. "Maeve, we are waiting for Thomas and Declan. They will accompany us to gather the herbs. You brought the bronze apple, I assume?"

Thomas. Maeve realized her breathing had gone shallow at the name. She forced herself to speak, knowing that Finna watched her. "There's been a problem, sir," she said. "I thought I heard something last night. I worried that the orchard was in danger, so I went to investigate and . . . I knocked the apple off the wall. It went out of sight beyond the hills." She dropped her gaze, waiting for more disappointment. *Maybe the Patrician will decide Finna should be the one to help with the cure after all.*

"Finna, thank you for accompanying her, but you may go. I'm sure the orchard keeps you busy this time of year." The Patrician showed Finna to the door. Then she was gone, the door clicking shut behind her. Maeve exhaled slightly.

"I didn't know it could disappear like that," she hurried on. "It must have rolled uphill somehow. And I'm afraid I haven't told you everything that happened last night. I went after the apple."

The Patrician studied her so that she dropped her gaze again. "You could have been gravely injured, Maeve," he said quietly, and this time there was a warning in his voice.

"As much as I appreciate your dedication to the task, your safety is more important." He held out a hand, indicating she should sit down. "The magic I infused that apple with probably behaved strangely so near the downs. In such a small vessel, the proximity to dark magic interacts strangely with it. That would explain why you lost sight of it. Separated from the sympathy of the orchard, it could easily be drawn over long distances, even uphill."

"There's more, sir." Maeve swallowed. The need to divulge everything—or very nearly everything—pressed down on her like a heavy hand steering her by the shoulder. "When I tried to follow it, I did find it. It had fallen into a pool. It was too deep, and I couldn't get it out."

"Ah." The Patrician's brow cleared. "That makes our task easier, Maeve. I believe I know the place—the stream feeds it through an underground branch. The water looks much deeper than it is, especially when obscured by night. Not to worry. Not only do I have a tool to help with this, but the flower we need grows close by that small pool."

He rose from the sofa and went to the cupboard next to the one containing the bronze apples. From this, he took out a long, wooden rod with a cup at the end, and handed it to Maeve. "This should do it," he said cheerfully. "You were right to tell me, Maeve. I suspect you haven't told Finna everything." He looked at her with the same patient kindness she'd seen last night, and she felt herself smiling with timid relief.

"No, sir. I didn't want to let her down. Again."

The Patrician simply nodded. "You should know I've sent two guards to Dumar with letters, as we discussed," he said. "I cannot say when they'll return, but rest assured, Maeve, I will tell you when I receive word about your parents."

"Thank you, sir."

"Now, where are Thomas and Declan? I told them noon, and they aren't late as a rule." He rose and went to the door.

But Maeve, whose relief had swiftly changed to dread, fidgeted in her seat. "I've met Thomas, sort of," she began.

Talking about the orchard was easy. Talking about her daily work, about Quin's laws, about the wild men was easy. There were conversations and experiences, and where there were no experiences, there were stories and scripts. She had no script for this situation, only a firm belief that the Patrician would not want his men speaking the way Thomas had spoken to her at the wedding. The memory of his unwanted nearness, his breath on her neck, made her insides clench. It was too confusing and unpleasant to speak of, like waking from a bad dream that left only a heavy feeling of dread and indistinct images.

"I—I don't feel he is best suited for this task," she said, reaching for the easiest thing to say. "I think the best people for this journey are people who are truly invested in the orchard."

The Patrician paused with the door half opened and regarded her. "But aren't we all invested in the orchard, Maeve? I know I needn't remind you that if part of Quin suffers, we all do."

"Yes, sir, but in the orchard . . . he looked bored," Maeve said, grasping for something that would communicate her worries in a way he would understand.

"People in all three towns and beyond benefit from the harvests. Maybe," he said, a half smile lifting his lips, "you expect others to demonstrate their commitment to Quin the same way you do. You say Thomas looked bored. What would you have had him do? We'd made a long journey that morning and we were all tired. He doesn't know how to look for tree rot any more than Boyle does. It isn't his job. Just as it isn't your job to question your elders. You are wise when it comes to picking apples and making apple butter. You don't know Thomas. Between you and me, he's had a difficult year in his personal life. Trust me to make the decisions I must make, as I am trusting you with this important task."

Chastened, Maeve lowered her eyes and nodded. *I have no right to question him.* While confusion churned within her, the Patrician's advice felt steady, reliable. She must have misread Thomas's actions. Maybe he was paying her a compliment at the wedding. What experience did she have with those? Katherine was always the one to attract attention, not she. It really had been terribly crowded in the church.

And anyway, the Patrician would be with her when the guards accompanied them to the pool. She couldn't be more secure than if she was with him to guide her. Yet the Patrician's assurances felt strangely like medicine that took the edge off the pain but did not address the root of it, leaving a sour taste in her mouth that she couldn't quite swallow.

A noise burst into the church, arresting her attention. The Patrician, who'd been speaking to the guard outside his door, went swiftly into the large room. Maeve followed him.

A pale-haired, drawn-faced man staggered into the sanctuary, carrying a boy of about seven or eight years old who howled in pain and clutched his arm. The Patrician, bending over him, spoke in soothing tones as he examined the arm. The screams rose jagged, then quieted to sniffles and whimpers as the Patrician placed a gentle hand on the boy's head.

"The arm is broken," he confirmed.

Lines deepened on the father's face. "I'm sorry to trouble you, sir, but he's terrified of the blacksmith. I thought it best to bring him here." He looked down at his son, whose small face was almost gray with pain.

"It's nothing to apologize for. Bring him to my rooms."

Maeve stepped back as the three of them swept inside. The Patrician seemed a beacon of calm amidst the boy's whimpering cries and the father's worries. He directed the father to lay the boy on the sofa, then examined his arm again as the child whimpered. As the Patrician whispered words of comfort, Thomas and Declan entered the room.

"Ah. Gentlemen, I'm afraid you'll need to escort Miss MacGowan by yourselves to gather the herb." The village leader kept his eyes fixed on the boy. "I must see to this child."

Maeve stiffened at his words. He looked up and caught her eyes. "You're in good hands, Maeve," he assured her. "You are looking for a small yellow flower that has three pointed petals with a blue center: this is star point leaf. It is the leaves you want, not the flower. Fill one of your apron pockets with them; that will be sufficient. Come back here and I'll help you with the rest." He nodded at the long pole Maeve still clutched, reminding her of the other task, then turned his attention back to the injured child.

The two guards had already left the room. Maeve, her hands sticky with sweat, adjusted her grip on the pole, pressed her misgivings far down, almost out of reach, and hurried after Thomas and Declan.

For most of the walk, the guards acted as though she wasn't there, which didn't trouble her at all. They passed the front gates and followed the main road only briefly. Then the two men abandoned it, treading down a broad, easy slope to the right. Maeve caught her breath at the sight.

A faint path in the grass wended away from Quin. The earth was much flatter here, making it easier to see ahead. To Maeve's left was the black soil of the peat bogs, creased in neat angles from the recent harvest. Behind her and to the right, the orchard was a small cluster of trees in the distance overlooking the place she'd followed the bronze apple. The expanse of earth was deeply wrinkled there, as if visibly retracting from the orchard's power.

The path became a winding trail that soon hid the orchard from sight. *A pocketful of star point leaf. That's not difficult.* Maeve turned her attention to the short, soft grass at her feet, looking for the small yellow flowers. *The sooner I can find what I need, the sooner the trees will be healed, and the sooner our future in Quin is secure.*

"Here. It's down there you want to look," Declan said, pointing to a rocky slope.

Timidly, she edged closer, until she could see a carpet of tiny yellow flowers growing down below. Maeve's eyes scoured the scene. *This must be close to the pool,* she thought. *But what about the guards?* She still didn't feel comfortable with them. Though so far they'd mostly ignored her, she feared they might change their minds and decide to go with her. Being alone beyond Quin with the two of them was almost more disconcerting than being alone in the dark the previous night. Out here the Patrician's words of belief in Thomas felt as thin and comforting as watered gruel.

To her relief, Thomas sat down and took a canteen from his coat. Declan eyed him a moment before accepting it and taking a swig. "You'd better get started," he said to Maeve. She nodded and began picking her way down the rocky slope as quickly as she dared, leaving them to their rest.

The flower was just as the Patrician had described. Carefully, Maeve plucked the thin leaves from the plants and filled her pocket. Finna's sausage and apple pasty filled the other pocket. When she had made certain that the guards remained in their place, she took the rod she'd left on the ground and hurried along a thin, rocky path in search of the pool.

It wasn't hard to find; the path led her straight to it. Half the smooth surface lay in the shadow of the overhanging hill, the other half reflecting the blue sky like a mirror. She could see more clearly how the earth slipped away from it on the side where the two strangers had appeared. The pool itself shone crystalline, the bronze apple easily visible on the uneven stone floor. Already the blue glow was almost gone. Maeve dipped the rod into the water and—

Crack!

Her arm jerked as a sudden whirling current tugged the rod and released it just as quickly. The wood splintered in her hand, piercing her skin with splinters and drawing a cry of pain from her lips.

When she pulled out the rod, she found it had broken in two. The other piece lay useless and small at the bottom of the pool next to the tiny bronze apple. *It isn't salvageable at all. I'll have to ask the Patrician for another one. But what caused it to break?*

"Look at that, Colm. I knew our young friend wasn't telling us the whole truth last night."

Maeve spun around, her heart suddenly in her throat. The young woman Breena stood on the sloping ground behind her, hands open at her sides, expression intent. Colm stood nearby, grinning. She hadn't heard them coming.

In the light of day, she could make out their features more clearly. Breena's face revealed a closed hostility. Colm's was lined with age and his grin belied a fierceness that filled her with dread. Maeve knew with terrible certainty that even if she alerted the guards to danger, these two could do whatever they wished long before the men found them.

"Of course he wasn't. Even I knew that." Colm chuckled. "What does she want, d'you think?"

Maeve remained silent.

"I intend to find out." Breena stepped toward Maeve, her eyes never leaving her face, and nodded. "Now, village girl, I think it's time you told us what you're doing here."

ii. Notes

Maeve wondered if Breena and Colm would view her differently if she had magic. Would magic calm her racing pulse and make her voice strong?

"I've lost something important in this pool," she said, her voice sounding small in her own ears. "The village leader sent me to get it back."

Breena's eyes narrowed. "What else did he send you to get?"

"Just some leaves. The star point leaves. See?" Maeve pulled a handful from her pocket and held them out. "I can get you some, if you like," she offered, grasping at anything that might satisfy the two people who had powers she didn't understand.

"I don't need those." Breena waved a dismissive hand at the leaves. "Why did you hide last night, girl? Why not show yourself?"

"I wasn't supposed to be there at all. I didn't know Liam was coming to meet you, either. I didn't know anyone was here at all. Please, I don't mean any harm."

As she said this, something steeled in Colm's face. A flicker in his eyes, as if a memory stirred. "Mean and do are different things, lass," he said seriously. "Now if you've got your leaves, you'd best be on your way."

"But I don't have the apple. The bronze apple." Maeve glanced at the pool, which was perfectly still again, almost another world. Desperation rose up in her throat and scratched in her voice. "Something broke the rod. Please, can you help me? I'll offer you anything you like."

"Hear that, Colm? The village girl is so polite." Breena's grin twisted and fell as swiftly as the rod had snapped in two. "What makes you so sure we'd want anything you could give us?"

"I have apple seeds." The words seemed to jump from her lips. Maeve pressed them together. *I have just offered seeds from the sacred grove to who knows who.* But no one used the seeds, and so no one would miss them. If the apples only grew on Quin's blessed ground, well, they could hardly blame her for that, could they? To face both Finna and the Patrician as a failure for a second time was too much. She wanted to get the bronze sphere and go back to the orchard, or at least back to where the Patrician could help her with the cure before the rot spread any more. "We're harvesting the apples now. I can bring you some seeds tonight."

Breena's mouth twisted in thought, but Colm spoke first. "Not tonight," he said. "Tomorrow night, lass. For whatever mystery haunts that pool will be weaker then, and will give up your lost trinket."

"But I need it today." Maeve began clasping and unclasping her hands. This was not how she expected—how she needed—today to go. She tried to explain herself to these two from Lochlyn, but dismay grew heavy in her chest and tightened her throat. Her eyes burned dangerously with tears as she looked away from the old man and the fierce girl.

It struck Maeve that she didn't know exactly how this failure would cause her and Finna to lose the orchard, or how close she was to that punishment. *How many chances do I have before we're sent to Cromwell House? Ten? One?* She would just have to tell the Patrician and face the consequences. *Perhaps if I work hard enough on the cure,*

*it will keep us from losing our livelihood. I will do
whatever I must.*

She emerged from her thoughts just enough to see
Colm and Breena whispering. With a grunt, Breena folded
her arms and looked at her.

"Besides those leaves," she said, "what else do you have
to trade?"

Worry threaded down Maeve's back like a hot, stiff wire,
pulling tighter the closer they got to the church and the
Patrician. The star point leaves made one apron pocket puff
out while a heavy object drooped in the other pocket,
knocking against her leg. She was too anxious to even spare
much thought for the brief look Thomas cast her way, even
though that too made her skin crawl.

The village rose up ahead of them. She passed through
the open gates and entered the sounds and smells of Quin,
and in no time at all found herself before the Patrician's
quarters.

But the Patrician wouldn't see her.

His rooms were shut and a note pinned to his door
instructed Maeve to give the leaves to the guards and go
about her day. She was to return tomorrow at her earliest
convenience to start preparing the cure.

Relieved and puzzled, Maeve did as she was told and
hurried away, happy to leave the guards and return to the
familiarity of her orchard. If the weight in her pocket
chided her, at least she had the start of the cure. And as she
passed the village center, a figure emerged from a shop and
made her heart leap with joy.

"Katherine!" she called, and had to stop herself from
running up the road and flinging herself at her best friend.
Katherine wore her hair in the usual way and a new gown of
deep green that set off her pale hair beautifully. Maeve

wondered fleetingly if it was a gift and remembered the torn gown from the wedding. *Something to replace what was lost?*

Katherine saw her and her eyes lit up. "Maeve!" she cried, throwing her arms around her as they had always done. For a moment, all Maeve's worries for her friend vanished. She was still the same Katherine; of course she was. Nothing could change that, and why should it? She was a glowing bride, and married life suited her.

"How is your new house?" Maeve asked.

"How is the orchard?" Katherine asked at the same time, giving her a meaningful look.

Maeve blushed, looking about the streets. She knew Katherine didn't mean the tree rot, and this was not the place for such things.

Her friend made a *tsk* sound. "Come to my house tomorrow afternoon then, and tell me. You will be my first guest of honor." Katherine's husband appeared and slipped an arm around her as she finished, eliciting a little sound of surprise from her.

"I was just inviting Maeve over," Katherine said, looking at Conlan as if he were the only one standing there despite just speaking her friend's name. "You'll be working, of course. We won't pester you with our gossip," she added cheerfully.

Conlan nodded in somber recognition of Maeve. She had never spent much time with him, as Finna didn't socialize with merchants, or rather, merchants never socialized much with Finna. Their wealth and her isolated, oddly privileged position simply did not mix in Quin. The brief time Maeve had spent with Katherine and Conlan was in the company of crowds: at church, a summer feast, a spring meeting, and there was always much to occupy them all.

Now Maeve was struck by how little he seemed to have changed since the wedding too: as if he had always carried the weight of his father's business on his shoulders, not like a burden, but like a crown so rich and heavy that it made turning his head to look at other people difficult.

I wonder why I never noticed that before.

"Of course. We will pay in coin," Conlan said, now looking at Katherine as if he'd already forgotten Maeve existed. "Come on, Katherine. Let's go home." He took her hand and led her up the street. Katherine cast a blushing look over her shoulder and mouthed, *Tomorrow!* before she and her new husband disappeared around a bend in the road.

The house and orchard were empty of Finna, and while it was odd she left no note, the absence didn't bother Maeve much. No doubt the woman was on an errand to gather jars or something similar. A patch of white on the floor caught her eye. Maeve picked it up and saw that it was a slip of paper, stamped with her own footprint. A list of Finna's? Opening it, her curiosity changed from one kind of surprise to another.

Maeve, read the scrawled handwriting, *you were brave last night, and I didn't say so. I haven't known many girls, and none of them would've been as calm and level-headed as you were. Please don't be mad at me for ignoring you at the Patrician's offices. Something happened but I'll tell you later. What I'm trying to say is, I want to make sure you're all right.*

If you want, leave a note for me stuck in the northern orchard wall.

It was signed *Liam.*

Maeve reread the words several times. The words *many girls* and *calm* and *level-headed* glared at her from the page. *How many girls?* She shook her head. *And I wasn't calm, I was scared.* Still, that he thought she was different—better, even—than these others made her feel pleased. Then she wondered what had happened at the Patrician's rooms.

Surely he didn't suspect Liam of being connected with the wild men? Colm and Breena were nothing like the picture she'd been given of those people all her life. They were more like the clans that came and went through the apple-guarded gates, not part of Quin but welcome in trade nonetheless. She'd never interacted with them. She'd never had cause to. But as Conlan and his father had business with them, perhaps she could ask him tomorrow to tell her more about the clans. Maeve remembered his hungry attention on Katherine and reconsidered. She could ask Katherine to ask him instead.

Gone were the days of easy welcome at the Campbells' farm. Perhaps she and Conlan could become friends in time.

Meanwhile, Maeve held a letter from Liam. *He was worried about me.* The warm feeling returned. He hadn't ignored her out of disinterest this morning.

But Finna—*I can't let her find this letter.* Maeve couldn't keep it on her at all times, and she feared no place in her room was safe from Finna's piercing gaze. Stifling a twist of regret, Maeve threw the note into the ashes and stoked them with the fire rod until the paper caught fire. She watched it curl and blacken, knowing that if she left a note tucked into the wall for Liam, as she wanted to, Finna would find that too.

A few minutes later, she left the house. With no one's eyes on her, she picked up her skirts and ran to the orchard. Passing through the gate, she pulled the object from her pocket and placed it on the wall facing the downs, where she studied it intently.

It looked exactly like the bronze apple still waiting at the bottom of the pool.

"It won't last long," Breena had warned earlier, when her magic was spent and she'd handed over the replica she'd created. It weighed warm and smooth in Maeve's palm. "Once you retrieve the real one, this will disappear."

"Please tell me, how will I do that?" She didn't know these two, but they seemed to understand the pool far better than she did. What other choice did she have but to trust them? The bronze apple was as good as in their hands.

"Come tomorrow night, remember?" Breena said. "Midnight, when the moon rises. Bring your seeds. The chief will know what to do."

Maeve shivered and looked out across the rolling hills, whose domes and valleys appeared deceptively shallow from the orchard. *The chief.* Was she to face yet another leader? The Patrician was one thing, when he had known her all her life and was looking out for her. She felt a pang of guilt for the false apple, another lie. *I can't disappoint someone else.* Yet this Lochlyn chief was the only one who could help her get back what the Patrician had entrusted her with, and she wanted that more than anything.

With this in mind, she turned her attention to the diseased trees. Around them lay heaps of apples on the grass, green and sunken with rot, fallen to the earth before they could fully ripen. Even now one fell to join the others with a wet sound, releasing a sickening, sweet smell into the air. She walked among the untouched trees, pressing against the bark, looking for signs of rot on the branches, in their fruit. They smelled whole enough. Many apples had reached ripeness even since she'd last picked the fruit two days ago, signaling the true start of the harvest season.

But she needed seeds. *I should pick them out of the rotten ones while I have the chance.* As she hurried back toward the southern edge of the orchard, she caught sight of a figure walking over the stream. Finna. She, too, caught sight of Maeve, and quickened her pace. Maeve glanced at the slimy mass of apples at her feet. The smell made her choke. *Could I even get the smell off my hands if I touched them? And would seeds from diseased apples provide what Lochlyn needs?*

But her hesitation had cost her. Finna entered the orchard, basket in hand, and went straight to Maeve without sparing a glance for the rotten fruit. "You're back," she said, nodding at the bronze apple on the wall. "Well, come on. Today we begin our baking for Quin."

They picked all the ripe apples they could find on the trees nearest the rotten ones, sparing the good fruit, Maeve hoped, from catching the disease. She wasn't sure exactly how rot spread, but if Quin had taught her anything, it was that proximity to rottenness bred more of the same. She had to fetch a second basket before they'd finished.

Pleased with what they'd gathered, Maeve followed Finna home and fell into the soothing rhythm of baking preparation. She knew the methods and the recipes by heart now. First, she and Finna would bake heavy cakes studded with fruit and soaked in spirits to trade and to keep in the cold cellars for winter. They'd make more flaky pasties, full of tender fruit and savory sausage from the butcher's shop. Some would go into cold cellars around the village to survive the winter. The remains of the harvest, when the apples hung swollen and overripe, would become apple butters and jellies.

All this could disappear if the cure doesn't work. But of course it will. The Patrician believes it will.

They worked in the silence always accompanying these tasks, letting only the resistance and slice of knives through shiny red skin and tender white flesh make their conversation. Then Finna surprised Maeve by saying, "There's a good amount of apples here. Enough to get started with, at least."

"Yes," Maeve answered, wondering if this were indeed true and how it could be, given the current predicament. "That is good, isn't it? The orchard is still mostly healthy?"

"Hm." Finna's knife slipped, shooting an apple across the scrubbed wooden counter. She snatched it back without slowing her pace. Two smooth brown seeds scattered under Maeve's hands like muddy raindrops, sounding like the fallen teeth of some fabled monster. So close, yet she knew better than to take them under Finna's eyes. Even occupied with this task, the woman missed nothing.

"There is no reason to believe the cure will not work. Just do what you're told and everything will return to what it was before, and we will carry on as we always have." Finna, whose voice had begun in a level tone, hardened to something like stubborn bitterness. Maeve was unsure if the bitterness was meant to stem the tide of change or if it arose because change would never come.

"How will I know if I'm doing enough?" Maeve asked in a whisper. Every question felt like a game of chance with Finna: she might offer an answer, or she might close down and scold Maeve for asking.

But I am tired of carrying questions and having to meter them out carefully. I want to let them all go at once and be free of them, but I can't. Whatever happens to Finna happens to me. Why take me in and raise me to care for the orchard, only to act as though the rot threatening the orchard and our livelihoods isn't significant?

She thought of Finna's reaction when she'd accidentally discovered the rot, humiliation burning in her cheeks and simmering in her core. Did Finna care more about Maeve making her family look inept than she cared about the trees themselves? Despite everyone's trust in the cure, the unknown loomed larger than a storm cloud on Maeve's mind, too heavy and dark to ignore.

She thought Finna would not answer her, that the silence would pile back up like the apple cores and seeds and stems in the bucket. "I told you," Finna said. "Do as you're told. It is as simple as it sounds, Maeve."

But is it?

"I have been meaning to speak to you about something," Finna continued. "The wedding brought it to mind, and then the rot and cure drove it away. But it is time we considered your future."

"I thought my future was here," Maeve said, uneasiness creeping into her voice. "I want to stay and tend the orchard." She thought of the Patrician's letters to Dumar and Ferre and wished she could speed the messengers' return.

"I meant your marriage." *Slice, slice,* went Finna's knife. The sound rang in Maeve's ears. "You both would come and live here, of course, after my death, and care for the orchard. I suppose some boys wouldn't like that. But someone will be sensible of the privilege. You are the last of your friends to marry. It isn't seemly for young girls to wait too long for marriage when so much depends on our survival here."

Marriage, my survival? As if I'll die without a husband? And what has become of you, Finna, unmarried and alone? The woman spoke as if she had never been a young girl herself, as if she belonged to a different class entirely. As if she had never thought twice about a small, treasured garment being ripped in two for a man who looked at his wife the same way he might take stock of his possessions.

"You needn't look so distressed." Finna paused in her work and frowned at Maeve. "It's not as though I'd betroth you to the first spotty-faced youth who takes notice of you. There must be someone who's caught your eye."

Lively brown eyes, impudence, *I listen, too*—warmth rose to Maeve's cheeks as she understood something vital. She felt intrigued by and drawn to Liam, but marriage? Too soon, too much, too fast. It was as if life had taken a sharp turn and sped up, giving her no time to adjust to this new pace. *And I doubt Finna would allow me to marry a shepherd.*

Finna was watching her with a gaze so sharp it sliced through her exterior and into her muddied and anxious thoughts. "It's just so soon," Maeve protested. "Please, can we wait a few months? Quin would be taxed, anyway, with another wedding following Katherine's so soon, and the harvest always leaves you tired and ill afterward."

"Hm." Finna still held the knife, an apple half-carved in her other hand. "Your betrothal would last a few months, Maeve."

"But everyone will be preparing for winter soon," Maeve hurried on. "It will take all our energy for that."

"You've made a point. We will discuss this again before spring. No later, mind."

Maeve began slicing again with trembling fingers. *Does she want to rush me out of her house? Am I a burden?* But Maeve already knew the answer. Despite Quin's well-known customs of early marriage, perhaps Finna had tired of caring for her long ago.

I just want to belong in my own home. Will I always be that same abandoned infant, shuffled from place to place?

A frustrated gasp startled Maeve. Finna held an apple full of brown, mushy flesh. One after another, she pierced perfectly good apple skin to reveal a rotten center, until more than a third of their harvest lay exposed on the counter, too many to fit in the waste bucket. Maeve found a good many of hers lost to rot as well.

"I'm going to the orchard for a closer look," Finna announced, wiping her hands on her apron. "Finish preparing what we have for cake until I come back."

Maeve watched her go, wishing she could help. *So the rot has spread.* If the Patrician had not told her to wait until the following day to help with the cure, she would have gone to the church that very afternoon.

But here was her opportunity. Among the rotten mounds of brown apples and discarded cores lay an entire orchard's worth of seeds. Maeve chose seven brown teardrops from the healthy, discarded scraps, wiped them clean, and stowed them in her apron pocket in a scrap of wool.

12. Object

When Maeve brought the ritual bucket of water to the orchard the next morning, she took extra time examining the trees for signs of disease. Finna's own thorough search the day before had uncovered nothing different in the thirty-five trees. But if the apples could turn rotten so quickly, then anything was possible. Maeve paid special attention to the trunks closest to the diseased trees, smelling the bark and unripe apples, feeling the bark here and there.

And there—a softening in the bark of one, a thick, sticky liquid oozing from a small crack. Maeve hurried to return the bucket and ladle, said a quick goodbye to Finna at work in the kitchen, and made her way to the Patrician's rooms with Finna's warning not to run nipping at her heels.

To her relief, the Patrician stood talking to Thomas and Declan in the church. He greeted her with a smile when she entered, and drew her straight into his sitting room. The air smelled pungent and herbal today. Maeve saw her modest offering of star point leaves sitting in an open glass jar next to the fireplace, which contained a cast iron pot on the flames. The cupboard from which the bronze apple came stood shut like the mouth of a secret-keeper. The real bronze apple was still at the bottom of a pool. Her mouth went dry.

"There is something I must show you," the Patrician said, holding up an opened letter. The seal was a luxurious crimson wax, bearing the image of a strange beast standing on hind legs. "The Lord Protector has written to offer warning and aid. It seems the wild men have attacked one of the villages to the northwest of us. He is sending additional soldiers to our three villages once his men have recovered and regrouped.

"It does seem as though the wild men are becoming bolder, more desperate. It is a blessed thing to have begun this cure. I hope it will take no longer than a week, though we cannot be sure."

Maeve nodded, unsure of what else to say.

"We will begin by saying a prayer of our god over these leaves."

The Patrician spoke it slowly once; it was one Maeve had not heard.

God of our forebears, attend our prayer. God of the sacred orchard, guide our hands. Heal all wrongs, purify impurities, protect our land, which you gave us. Bless our humble efforts to cleanse the trees, which you gave us. In the name of the god of unity, amen.

The second time, she joined him.

After a third time, the leaves shivered in the pot, releasing a bruised fragrance.

"We stir it for a quarter of an hour now," the Patrician said.

As she stirred, Maeve watched closely for other signs of change in the cure. She knew better than to ask if the Patrician had heard anything from the messengers he'd sent—it was a two-day journey to Dumar. But the thought of Cromwell House clung to her like burrs to wool. *If I can discover my family, perhaps I'll have a place to go if we lose the orchard.*

"You look quite pensive." The Patrician kept his eyes on the pot as he spoke, his tone casual and gentle at the same time. "Not a leaf you chose bore a spot or a tear. We have spoken the right prayers. This potion will work."

"Finna told me about Cromwell House," she said.

"Ah." He straightened and clasped his hands behind his back, looking a little sad. "I'm sure she told you the truth, plain and unvarnished. I'd hoped to shield you from that a little longer. It is not a place of many comforts, though it does house those with nowhere else to go. But that," he said, "will not be your fate. My confidence remains with you, Maeve, and with our god. And today, I will send you home with a new bronze vessel."

Maeve's burgeoning relief sizzled out in a flicker of confusion. *There is another one? Why did I not know?*

When last she'd been in these rooms, it had seemed the bronze apple was one of a kind, the only one commissioned by the the Lord Protector. This thought had partly driven her to make that desperate offer with Lochlyn to retrieve it.

"In all the business yesterday, I forgot to tell you to bring the bronze apple with you this afternoon."

"I will bring it as soon as I can." Maeve's thoughts worked like fingers at a loom. *Will he be content to wait until tomorrow, when I have the real one back?*

But that didn't concern the village leader.

"No matter. I sent a guard to fetch it. Ah," he said at the knock on the door. "Just in time."

Maeve's heart leaped into her throat. There at the door stood Finna, holding the false vessel in her hand. She nodded to the Patrician and gave it to him. Something passed between them which momentarily arrested Maeve's attention, a secret inscrutable look. Then it was gone before she was sure what had happened. She watched helplessly as the Patrician put the false apple in the cupboard, opened wide to reveal a row of perfectly matching bronze shapes nestled in velvet supports. He chose one and shut the door.

Maeve's throat felt full of wood dust. "Doesn't this leave the orchard unprotected?"

"Remember, the wild men are less powerful in the daytime," the Patrician said. "You have nothing to fear now." He held out the bronze apple and performed the ritual.

Maeve followed Finna home in a daze.

How am I to get Breena's apple back, even if the church is unlocked? Guards must watch this place at night. What if . . . I open a window and drop it through? Or just bring it with me tomorrow and sneak it in when the Patrician's back is turned?

No. Stop being stupid, Maeve. The only way to replace the false apple with the true one is to break into the Patrician's rooms. Inwardly, she groaned.

"Are you even listening, Maeve?" Finna asked as they crossed the village square.

Maeve noted the annoyance in her foster mother's tone, which told her Finna hadn't been waiting too long. When Finna's voice became toneless, that meant real trouble.

They stood at the crossroad in front of the blacksmith shop. The road behind them led to Katherine's house—and Maeve had promised to see her friend this afternoon.

But Finna would not let her go unless she responded with care.

"I'm sorry, Finna," she said. "I was remembering that Katherine invited me to see her this afternoon."

"Well, you can't go, I'm afraid. Aside from getting the Patrician's vessel back to the orchard, we've got to start cleaning the jars for jellies and jams. We'll have to be quick about it, with the way the trees are going."

"And I will help you, I promise. But I also promised Katherine. I won't be gone long. I can ask her what she'd like from the orchard while I'm there, and that's important, isn't it? Please, Finna. She and Conlan haven't established their preferences yet, or told you what they're willing to trade." Though Conlan had promised her money, supposedly instead of the trade.

Finna's mouth pressed thin in thought. Her gray eyes examined Maeve, making her feel like a peeled apple, all exposed and bare.

A deep voice spoke first.

"Finna."

It was Duffy, who'd appeared silently like a giant animal from within his cave.

"I need to speak with you," he said, his voice oddly soft. He cleared his throat and the gruffness returned without lessening the unusual urgency it contained. "Please, Finna, hear me out."

But Finna straightened her shoulders and shook her head. "I can't." Turning to Maeve, she said, "Go and see Katherine. You have half an hour." She held out her hand. Maeve stared at it, uncomprehending, until with a *tsk* and impatient wave of fingers from Finna, Maeve pulled the new bronze apple from her pocket and handed it over.

When Maeve turned from Finna's retreating back to the forge, the blacksmith was gone.

Katherine's house was one of several tall, narrow townhouses with dark wooden beams and fresh whitewash. Children ran by in the street, shouting as they chased a ragged cat. Smoke rose from all the chimneys in the row. It looked snug and tidy, but very close together. Maeve rapped the metal knocker against the smooth wooden door a few times. Barely had she dropped it when the door swung open to reveal Katherine, whose face lit up with a smile.

"Maeve! Come in." She dragged Maeve into the house and shut the door behind her.

The narrow, well-scrubbed hallway led to a well-appointed kitchen twice the size of Finna's. It smelled of tallow wax and something savory from a covered pot simmering over the fire. Katherine bustled around, strands of hair falling down on her shoulders as she pulled something out of the oven.

"I hear you sniffing," Katherine said, turning around and holding out a rather dark loaf cake. "I'm nowhere as good a baker as you or Finna, but I did try."

She looked so pleased and proud that Maeve couldn't help the laugh that escaped her lips. "It does look well done," she said. "But I'm sure you did."

The front door opened and footsteps sounded before Conlan entered the kitchen. Katherine went to greet him with a murmur. His quiet reply was hidden from Maeve, and he nodded in greeting to her.

"I was asking Katherine how many jars of apple preserves she might want," Maeve said, "and if she wanted one of Finna's cakes." Minutes ago, she and Katherine would've giggled over that last comment. But Conlan's seriousness seemed to suck all the humor out of the cheerful kitchen.

"We appreciate that. It's always a good autumn with Finna's baking." Conlan's face softened into a smile, making him look younger, like someone Maeve could be friends with. Her heart lifted. "We would like two jars of preserves," he said. "What else, love?" He turned to Katherine, threading his fingers through hers. He seemed more at ease here in his own home. That, Maeve could understand. The warmth with which he looked at Katherine sent a stab of longing through her, which she quickly pressed down.

"I think at least a jar of jelly and apple butter. And a cake." Katherine's face dimpled with her smile.

"That sounds perfect." Conlan tore his gaze from his wife and addressed Maeve. "Please come back when the food is ready," he said, pulling some coins out of his pocket. They landed like a dead weight in Maeve's hand. *In other words, not before.* Conlan's serious tone had returned. "Thank you for your visit."

Maeve forced a smile, knowing it was time to go.

Katherine walked her to the door and quickly hugged her. "I hope the baking doesn't take long," she said, her blue eyes large with apology. "Thank you for coming, Maeve. Tell Finna I have some lace I want you to have, too. I'm so glad to see you."

Maeve returned the hand squeeze. "You too." Her desire for a longer visit had vanished, somehow. She hurried down the street without waiting for the door to shut behind her, sidestepping the children and a woman pushing a cart. The only thing she heard over the foot traffic and rattling wheels was the frantic meowing of a cat caught at last.

The church is full of hushed conversation and a scattering of blue candles as Finna and I make our way to our seats. My insides squirm, thinking of the last meeting where the Patrician called me up to tell everyone what was wrong with the trees. We sit at the edge of a pew with Mrs. Campbell on Finna's other side, and the two of them exchange a crisp, polite greeting. I look for Katherine before remembering again that she must be sitting with Conlan's family. Where is she? There, I see her, several rows ahead of us, her golden head bent close to her husband's. They are laughing about something. A secret joke, perhaps. My heart squeezes.

Once during service, Finna allowed us to sit together. We amused ourselves by repeating the priest's droning sermon and changing words here and there, until we couldn't keep our laughter silent and Finna's steel gaze turned to us. She never allowed me to sit near Katherine again. But no one would stop a wife and a husband from conversing, even if an old woman or two sends disapproving looks their way.

The hum of conversation quiets as the priest steps to the front of the church. I notice a guard on either side of him, almost hidden in the shadows, but I can't make out their faces. Then the priest steps forward to speak of the Orchard of Lights.

In a ringing, nasally voice, he speaks of Sir Arthur, who had recently established Quin when the wild men attacked. He prayed for help. At that instant, the orchard glowed blue and formed a wall of protection around the village, and Sir Arthur experienced a vision. He saw not one but three villages, all safe and thriving, with the blessing of God upon them. Soon after, he oversaw the settlements of Dumar and Ferre.

My thoughts wander to the vision I had in the orchard not three days ago. It feels all angles and spikes, as if it doesn't fit me. But Sir Arthur possessed a certainty that paved the way for our existence here, which is fitting for a ruler and not a young girl.

The Patrician steps to the front and nods at the priest, who returns the gesture ingratiatingly and backs his thin form out of the center, standing just so that the meager light illuminates his austere yet fine clothing. He no longer leads the ceremony, but we can't ignore him, either.

"Our god brought us to the land long ago," the Patrician begins, as if we've completely forgotten the priest's words from moments ago. It strikes me as strange, that our village leader speaks as if he were a priest, though I never questioned this before. "He gave Sir Arthur the vision and the miracle of the apple trees. Just as those trees glowed as a reminder of the light in darkness, we cling to the light today, and we let it chase away the darkness of the land and in our hearts."

All around us, the room has grown brighter as the Patrician speaks. Candles hidden in shadow spring to life until the room is bathed in a cold, pure light.

The Patrician continues to speak of light and darkness, of our responsibility in this land to carry on the faith and protect the blessing brought by Sir Arthur. It is the strangest thing. As every candle casts its light, a familiar, heavy weight presses down on my chest, as if darkness had a form, until I am gasping for a breath. Old fears drag at me and tug my attention from the Patrician's words until his voice is no more than a droning in the background.

All around me are the people of Quin, law-abiding citizens who play their part. They look serene, content, confident. They have not threatened the safety of our community with their foolishness.

They are not hiding secrets.

Suddenly the need to tell the Patrician everything eclipses all. I must tell him where the real bronze apple is, before he discovers that I have lied. His trust in me cannot be broken. His words still sound far away, as if they are underwater, yet his words about darkness in our hearts ring in my ears and my body trembles.

I barely notice the rest of the ceremony. Before I know it I've risen, Finna is prodding me, and we are filing toward the front to receive the piece of apple bread that she has been preparing for the past couple of days. The priest places it in my hand. The bread feels like coarse wool in my mouth. It seems odd to call this a feast day, when we only taste this piece of the apple tree's bounty, but it's also called a feast of lights. We remember the light surrounding us as it pierces every soul and seeks out hidden things.

The ceremony is over, but the urgency tightens around my rib cage. Now everyone is moving about the room and speaking to each other, satisfied with another year commemorating our shared past and our key to the future. I slip away and press toward the front, but the Patrician is gone. Perhaps he has gone to his rooms? To my great relief, no guard stands watch outside his door, and I knock once, twice. No one answers. Worried Finna will come and take me home before I have the chance to speak and rid myself of my burden, I open the door and slip inside.

The fire is dead in the grate. The room is dark save for one yellow-flamed candle sitting in a wall recess, and the lightest trace of herbs lingers in the air. The pot with the cure stands over faintly glowing coals. I suddenly remember the false apple in the cupboard and run my eyes over the rich wooden door. There appears to be no lock. Then the sound of voices reaches me.

Someone is talking outside the door leading to the courtyard behind the church, and the urgency I hear is familiar. Without thinking why, I walk forward to listen.

"We need the wool and wood," says an accented male voice thick with pleading. One of the Ragad clansmen, I think. I move close enough to peek through the door and see one of the men who rode on the giant, horned mount, his face twisted in a desperation that seems to make him small. Another man stands obscured in shadow with his back to me. I can't see who it is. A faint, pale light from the stars above shines down on the cobblestones and the pleading man's hair. "We have caused you no harm," he continues. "Always we bring our goods on time. Why are you doing this?"

"You and your wife brought your filthy talismans into Quin." I recognize Thomas's voice, hard with careless malice. "You know the rules. None of your pagan nonsense here."

"What harm have they ever done to you?" A new voice speaks up, a woman's, and the clansman turns to look at someone outside my line of vision. I can see worry lines marking his face as he whispers something in a different tongue.

"You shouldn't be asking the questions," Thomas says. I shiver at the tone of his voice. "You are lucky the Patrician is letting you go with merely losing our business. You could have lost so much more."

The woman says something in a string of her language, something fierce that makes me both fear for and admire her. There is a scuffle, and the sound of a fist hitting flesh and bone. I can't see what happened, but scattering footsteps signal that the man and woman are leaving. Someone is whimpering as they go. I know I should leave too, but I am frozen to the floor, my mind spinning.

What has Thomas done? Surely the Patrician wouldn't condone violence? He has always stood like a figure of peace. Once I saw a scuffle break out between a clansman and one of ours. The Patrician merely walked over to them. His presence alone was enough to stop it. I've never seen him lift a hand in my life. The very thought is absurd.

But he didn't tell me the truth about the bronze apple, and that fact freezes the weight on my chest that only moments ago propelled me into this room. Now I'm hovering between doubts.

Another sound outside the door alerts me. I hold my breath as footsteps approach from the courtyard.

"Do you think it's safe, being outside at this time?" Thomas says, torn between what seems to be concern, incredulity, and respect.

Someone takes a deep, slow breath, and even before he speaks, I know who it is. "I know the risk." His voice is low, but firm. He doesn't need to lift a hand or his voice to make his point. "You gave them the message, then?"

"Yes, Patrician. They took it as well as I thought they would." The scorn in his voice is so thick a paring knife could cut it.

"Do not be quick to judge them harshly, Thomas. They have not the benefits we have. Their lives are more rugged and sparse and so we must expect their manners to be, as well."

Thomas grumbles something I cannot hear. The thought occurs to me that maybe Thomas is keeping too much from the Patrician. Is Thomas craftier than the Patrician knows, because Thomas is deft at hiding it? Perhaps it is the older man's desire to see the good in his men that keeps him from seeing the truth?

Perhaps it is the Patrician's desire to see the good in me that keeps him from seeing the truth I hide?

I shake my head. If he trusts me, why didn't he tell me about there being more than one bronze apple?

The pattern of thoughts shatters some indecision within me. Breena and Colm helped me, and they are part of a clan. I have just seen how easily clans can be dismissed. I think of the broaches on both of their cloaks and wonder what terrible things those would be in the eyes of the Lord Protector's laws. Though I hardly know them, I do not want to endanger them, and they certainly don't deserve punishment over a trinket. In a way, they are helping Quin, and nothing but good can come of that. I no longer want to tell the Patrician about my errand tonight, either.

So I won't.

I feel dizzy, strange with this decision. But the footsteps are heading toward the door, and I flee through the Patrician's room, through the blue glow of the church sanctuary and out into the evening.

It is only halfway home with Finna that I remember something else: I will have to break back into the Patrician's rooms later tonight to replace the false bronze apple before it vanishes.

13. Feral

It seemed forever until Finna fell asleep. Maeve could not sleep if she wanted to; her whole body felt alert, tight with nerves. When at last she could wait no more, she padded quietly out of bed, dressed, and threw her shawl over her shoulders. Breathing a prayer of thanks that Finna had oiled the kitchen door again the day before, Maeve left the cottage as silently as darkness itself.

Out of habit, she made way back to the pool through the orchard. The stars hid behind tattered clouds, and with every light out in the cottage and the spiny mass of Quin, the darkness was almost complete. The hills before her rose and fell like lumps in the worst porridge she'd ever made, but from there, she knew where to go.

Moments later Maeve was running down the hill, the wind streaming through her hair. Rather than afraid, she felt light, warm, happy. Something more than that. She was too surprised to name it as the hills rose up to greet her until she remembered Mrs. Campbell's cat.

The orange tom used to eye her whenever she went to the farm. Once when she tried to pet him, he had leaped off the wall and streaked away from the farmyard, as if he only pleased himself. Maeve had imagined it could go almost anywhere it wanted. No one would dare stop this creature. *Feral.* That's what Finna had called it; something wild, no doubt, by the curl of disapproval in her voice. Mrs. Campbell frowned her own disapproval at this indictment of her pet.

Now as Maeve flew down the slope, Finna's warning flashed across her mind only a moment before the thrill of freedom took over. If she was feral this one night, she could leave her feral-ness behind on the hills when she came back with the bronze apple.

Soon she found the niche between the rocks that took her down to the pool. The water looked still as glass, impenetrable in the darkness save for the faint glow of bronze at the bottom. She could still hear movement, though. The grass and few shrubs rustled in a faint breeze, and even the water seemed to have a voice, quiet yet insistent. She wondered if the bronze apple would disturb the pool when it left and how she would retrieve it with the clan's help.

She slipped a hand into her pocket and ran a finger over the seeds there, smooth and warm with her body heat. *I wonder what they need them for. What if I disappoint them by bringing something they can't use? I must tell them that the seeds won't grow on any other soil. I should have told them from the start.*

The grass rustled somewhere nearby. "Who is it?" Maeve asked, her voice little more than a whisper, fear suddenly gripping her throat as she remembered the strange howl on the night she lost the bronze apple. What if something else found her first?

"It's only me, Maeve."

Maeve felt a lurch of recognition that left her both relieved and flustered. "Liam?"

He stepped into view from across the water, the way she'd come the other day looking for star point leaves. His hair was tangled as ever, but she could hear the grin in his voice better than she could see it.

"They told me you'd be coming too," he said, sounding pleased. "Are you ready?"

"Ready? For what? They told me to wait here."

Liam shuffled from one foot to the other. "Last night, when I met the clan, Breena asked me to bring you to them," he said. "She and Colm can't meet you here because it's their feast night."

"Oh." Feast night. All the warnings Maeve had grown up with clanged loudly in her head. *Dark magic. Tortured souls. Wickedness in the night.*

"We've got to hurry," Liam said, though he sounded less insistent and more puzzled, as if he sensed her uncertainty and wondered over it. A sudden, strange anger washed over Maeve. What must it be like to live without the expectations of a community? What must it be like to be able to choose?

She ran her fingers through the seeds again, as if they held the answer to her questions, and anger fizzled into vague confusion. A confusion, Maeve realized, she'd carried for so long that she couldn't remember living without it.

"I wanted to get word to you before tonight, but I wasn't able to. I'm sorry," Liam said, his voice softening. His sincerity loosened a knot in Maeve's stomach that had formed without her knowing it. He was different from anyone she'd met in Quin. He saw the world differently, but he believed her story. He'd never shied away from her, even asking after her when Finna had not. Being around him stirred up so many feelings, many of them new and strange. But among them, she recognized for the first time a sense of ease so rare it was no surprise she hadn't identified it before. Could she trust this feeling?

The stories of the wild men were vague and threatening. Even the Patrician didn't claim to understand how they got or used their magic. Despite the widely held belief that the wild men possessed strange powers, the members of the Lochlyn clan she'd met hadn't used them against her, though they could have. Against all expectations, they had even helped her. Liam, teasing and audacious as he might be, was real and demonstrated consideration for her. She remembered again Thomas's treatment of the Ragad man and anger prickled along her arms. Those people were real, and their punishment deeply unjust.

Should the old stories really dictate her choices, when before her stood a person who was in many ways not so different from her?

"I wanted to leave you a note," she confessed, "when you sent me one. But I was afraid Finna might find it."

"It's all right," he said carelessly, shrugging.

"Why did you ignore me the other day, when I saw you leaving the Patrician's rooms?"

The question escaped before she could stop it.

"He had sent for me that day," Liam replied softly. "He wanted to ask me if I knew anyone here. He asked me a lot of questions about my parents. I think he suspects I'm half Lochlyn, but I didn't tell him. It was hard not to; he can be very persuasive. I didn't understand what he was doing until much later." His face twisted into a grimace at the memory. "I didn't tell him about you being at the pool, either, though he wanted to know where I've been since arriving at Quin." He looked at her, and there was something vaguely pleading in his voice.

No wonder he'd ignored her that afternoon in the Patrician's room. Maeve was not the only one taking a risk by being here. *He knows more about risking expectations than I thought.*

"Yesterday I trusted the Patrician more than anyone I'd ever met," she said, leaning against the rock and looking up at the black and gray-clouded sky. "Now I don't know whom to trust. I'm afraid if I look too closely at everything, everything around me will fall apart. All I know is that I must save the orchard."

Her survival depended on it. Finna's, too. She could not bear to be sent away from her beloved trees, to never see Katherine again or hear the wind soughing over the hills or walk the crooked cobbled streets she knew by heart. She had to protect her trees, and she was here, defying who knew how many of Quin's rules to do so.

Still, she hesitated. Making a choice and acting on it were two very different things, especially when she had been taught so effectively to do one thing and made to fear the outcome if she failed.

"We've both kept each other's secrets," he said. Maeve pulled her gaze from the clouds. Liam had stepped closer, close enough for her to see faint starlight illuminating his eyes and the scar on his cheek. He reached out a hand and let it drop. "The Patrician's not here now. He won't know what you're doing tonight. I'd really like it if you came with me, Maeve."

The simple honesty of his request made her feel warm and clear headed. There was no one to scold her and no one to disappoint. In the vast, lonely night, she and Liam could be the only two people awake in the whole world. The sky was clear and the joy of it came back to her, the wide openness of everything that felt thrilling and terrifying all at once, and it belonged just to them. She pushed away from the rock and stepped around Liam, gratified to see his eyes light up and a grin begin to lift his mouth.

"Then let's go," she said, skipping from one foot to the other in a barely contained excitement, giddy and dizzy with her own swiftly changing decisions. She wanted to, without doubt or question. "Come on, quick! Before I change my mind!" And Liam, his grin widening, turned down a little path between two trees that Maeve had not noticed before, looking back once to see that she followed.

They laughed as they went along the twisting little path through birch and yew trees. Maeve felt his hand brush hers, sending a shock of warmth through her. She wasn't sure if he noticed. Their swift footsteps along the unfamiliar terrain provided enough for her to focus on, but all the same, Maeve wished he had felt her touch and that she knew what he thought of it.

After several minutes, they left the shelter of branches and wandered along a little ridge. The moon appeared whole and bright in the sky, shedding silvery light across everything, and Maeve found she didn't care about looking behind her. When they reached a level part of the trail, Liam looked back over his shoulder and spoke.

"If I'm not prying, can I ask you something?"

"Yes." Out here, she could answer anything.

"Why is that thing in the pool important to you?"

To me? The words surprised her. Finna never asked her that question. The Patrician had told her he knew the orchard was important to her, even seemed to act as if he knew everything about her. But everything she loved was for someone else. The trees really belonged to Quin, and really, she supposed, to the Patrician. Katherine belonged to Conlan and their friendship spoke of the difference in silence and absence.

"You must know about Quin's orchard," she said. "Do you know the trees are rotting?"

"No. I mean, I know about the orchard. My dad and I lived outside Ferre before I came here, and you can't escape hearing about what happened to Sir Arthur's blessed apples." Maeve could almost hear Liam's eyes rolling. Apparently he didn't hold much respect for the villages' revered forefather. "But no one up on the hills here talks about what goes on in the village."

So Maeve told him about the rot and the cure, and of Breena's temporary substitute that Maeve had to replace before morning if she didn't want to face the consequences. She didn't mention the threat of Cromwell House.

"The Patrician said he would have to write to the Lord Protector about everything. I thought at the time he was doing everything he could to protect me and Finna, but now . . ." Maeve's voice trailed away. She shivered and clutched her shawl tighter. "Tell me about Lochlyn," she said, turning the conversation. "Have you heard the music, Liam? The kind good villagers aren't supposed to hear?"

"I've heard Colm whining on a whistle." Liam sounded mildly pained. "Breena was instructing me while he made that racket. I asked him what the instrument was made of and he said, 'from the bones of a lad who wouldn't shut his mouth and listen to his elders.'"

Maeve suppressed a laugh, both at his indignant impersonation of the clansman and the use of the term *elder* when Breena was only a handful of years older than he. "What were you supposed to listen to? If . . . if it's all right for you to tell an outsider," she added, not wanting to pry into places she didn't belong.

"Breena was telling me about magic." Liam fell silent. He didn't sound as thrilled as Maeve would have expected, especially remembering his enthusiasm the night he met Breena and Colm at the pool. Perhaps she had pried too much, after all. Perhaps the forbidden music belonged to the clan alone, as she had always thought.

"Have you learned more about your mother?" she ventured, picking her way over a small cluster of jagged rocks.

"She was Lochlyn," he said softly, his back to her. "From another group that lives not far south of here. She used to sing me a tune. It's the only thing I remember about her. When I hummed the tune, Breena and Colm recognized it as one of theirs."

So his mother had given him something from the downs. She wanted to ask him if he recognized it as the music he'd heard before, the music he mentioned that day he'd perched carelessly on the orchard wall and distracted her from her task.

"It's the same tune I've heard before." Liam answered her unspoken question, and Maeve felt as if everything in her strained to listen. "Once, I came with my dad to Quin with the sheep. He wouldn't answer my questions about the night music I heard from the downs that sounded like Mother's song."

The sorrow in his voice was so raw that Maeve kept silent. The music spurned and ignored in her village was the very thing keeping Liam connected to a beloved parent he'd never see again. Her heart squeezed with sadness for both of them, even as conflicting fears battled for attention.

Grief won out, at least for the moment. Had her mother ever sung to her? Had she lived long enough to see her child? Had she given her up as one passes on an outgrown garment?

"Here, watch out." Liam paused to point out a sharp rock jutting up from the hill, then waited for them both to navigate around it.

"Liam," Maeve said, "why did you come to the orchard that day? I didn't hear any music playing, and yet you came all the way around Quin in search of it."

Liam stopped abruptly. Over his shoulder, Maeve could see a little overhang where the hill dropped away in a rugged shelf of bald rock. Beyond that the scattered trees thinned and disappeared altogether. He jumped down, then turned around and, grinning, lifted his arms toward her.

"I'll catch you."

Liam's words began in certainty and ended as a question. While the thought was something more than attractive, Maeve, suddenly shy, declined his offer by jumping down herself. Her feet slipped on worn rock and she pitched forward and collided with him. With an *oof!* they landed on a smooth patch of grass.

If his grunt was any indication, Maeve had slammed her head against his chin when she landed on top of him.

She scrambled to push herself upright. Liam was looking up at her, half raised on one elbow and rubbing his chin. The smarting on her head was nothing to the pounding of her heart as it danced with the bated breath in her lungs.

"You didn't answer my question," she whispered. Her mouth felt dry and fuzzy. But that, she realized, was because she was speaking around a mouthful of hair. Puffing and spluttering in an undignified attempt to disentangle herself, she stopped when Liam reached up and brushed it away from her face. If a spark from a fire could feel pleasant, it must feel like this.

"Huh." With Liam's breathless chuckle, his wide-eyed expression faded into something else. Maeve was suddenly aware of the sweet smell of grass and the warmth of him beneath her. Blushing furiously, she struggled to her feet, feeling his warmth ebb away. She brushed her hair back from her face, which had come loose with a vengeance upon her hasty ascent and now tumbled freely around her shoulders.

Liam scrambled to his feet and cleared his throat. "The orchard, hm. I don't know," he said abruptly with a shrug. He shoved the dirt with his boot. "All right, then. I was looking for the music, though I didn't hear it either that day. Where else would it be? But then I saw something over the orchard wall that made me forget it a moment." He glanced at her from the corner of his eye as if afraid to face her.

"Oh." Maeve could not find a response for that beyond the warmth rising to her scalp.

This shepherd made her feel more flustered and pleased than she had thought possible, but it was a combination she found herself drawn more and more to, just as she was drawn to him. How on earth did Katherine make it all look so easy?

"Ah!" a deep voice broke in. "We feared you might not be coming, Liam, but it seems I've interrupted you!"

Colm appeared from just below them, beaming in the light of a flickering torch. His impish expression turned to concern. "Miss Maeve. I've made a terrible mistake, telling you to come on a night like this. I'm sorry, lass. Neither Breena nor I could escape to meet you at the pool, we had that many preparations. But I'm not sure it's wise for you to be here." Worry lines deepened on his forehead and pushed his wild gray hair back, like folds of the earth bunching into hills.

"I'm sorry. I didn't know what else to do." That sickening feeling of being out of place thickened Maeve's throat as she dug into her pocket for the seeds. "Here are the seeds, like I promised. But I must tell you that they won't—"

"Maeve!" Breena appeared, hands on her hips, a grin on her face. "You found Liam. Good."

"They worked it out, in more ways than one! Smart thing, Liam, bathing all the fust off you."

"Ah, stop it, Colm," Liam protested, his face pink in the light, but he was grinning ear to ear. Maeve turned to hide a chuckle. Now that Colm mentioned it, she had noticed the distinct lack of wet sheep smell.

But Breena, Colm, and Liam were suddenly going on, walking to the top of the low, broad hill before them. Sounds of people talking reached Maeve's ears. When the trio reached the ridge, firelight gilded their faces and hair.

"Wait!" Maeve called, hurrying to catch up. She tried to shove the seeds into Colm's hand. "I still haven't told—"

"Walk now, talk later. The chief wants to see you before the dance begins." Breena caught her elbow and steered her down the hill.

The chief! "Can I not simply make the trade and go?"

A wild grin lit Breena's face. "Tonight is the Midnight Feast, Maeve. Do your village tales speak of that? More than food and wine flows when the sky is dark and the first moon of autumn is new."

"Time stops!" Colm crowed, jumping in what seemed to be a frantic dance as he followed her down. "We glimpse the invisible, and the invisible glimpses us."

"But that isn't possible," Maeve protested, trying and failing to make sense of his nonsensical claims. Then she saw Lochlyn and her protests fell away.

The light came from a large bonfire in the middle of a cluster of earthen huts. People of all ages bustled about in a hive of activity. The air of celebration was palpable. Maeve's feeling of being terribly out of place intensified.

"Remember, Colm," said Liam, laughter in his voice, "she's from Quin."

That caught her attention. "You don't understand this any more than I do," Maeve snapped, but Colm laughed.

"Don't worry, lass," he said. "We haven't forgotten the trade. But first, the chief awaits."

14. Dance

Breena steered her to one of the huts, Colm and Liam trailing in their wake. The old man entered first, leaving Maeve outside with the other two. *Why didn't I ask Liam about the chief? Has he even met him?* Images flashed in her mind of a severe man who alternately looked like the Patrician and an angry version of the Ragad clansman, neither one better nor more assuring than the other.

A terrible cry from behind Maeve made her shriek and spin around. "What is it?" she cried, unable to stop herself from stumbling backward into Liam at the sight before her.

A towering shadow had emerged from between the chief's hut and the next. Not a shadow, Maeve realized with growing terror, but an animal on four legs. It was the size of the Ragad's horned mounts, but instead of a deer-like head, this creature looked like a great dog with smooth pointed ears that lay back against its skull. It was black as a starless night. Pointed teeth protruded from its closed mouth, but a low, earth-deep growl emanated from the creature. Its eyes were a fearsome red and it turned them on Maeve.

"Now, Aodh." A tall woman stepped forward, placing her hand on the animal's neck. "It wouldn't do to petrify a guest on her first night here, would it?" Cooing to it as one might a child, she scratched the smooth, dark fur, and the animal's mouth hung open as if it were panting.

Maeve blinked. The woman was dressed similarly to Breena, in leggings and a tunic. Over both she wore a cloak clasped with a yellow broach of a beautiful interwoven shape that glimmered like gold.

The woman turned to Maeve. "You're here with Breena and Colm, so he won't likely hurt you. But Aodh and his kind can smell fear. You'd best straighten up."

Maeve swallowed and did as she was told. The woman's stare was almost as formidable as the creature's.

"His kind?" Maeve blurted out.

The woman didn't answer. Instead she turned fully toward Maeve and clasped her hands together. Behind her, Aodh flopped down with such force that Maeve braced for the expected impact. The creature snuffled in what must have been a sigh, lowered its massive head onto its paws, and shut its bloodred eyes.

"Now," the woman said to Maeve. "I hear you have something to show me."

You? The woman must be a representative, then. Somehow the thought didn't reassure Maeve all that much. She wanted to look to Liam for support, but he, Colm, and Breena remained out of sight, and she didn't think it would be acceptable to turn away from anyone sent on the chief's business.

"I've brought apple seeds from Quin's orchard in exchange for the bronze apple I lost at the bottom of a pool," Maeve said. "Only I wasn't completely honest." She drew a shaking breath. The woman's gaze was unflinching, and Maeve found it difficult to maintain eye contact, though in a very different way than it was sometimes difficult to maintain eye contact with Finna.

"These seeds won't grow anywhere but in Quin's orchard," she said, twisting a corner of her shawl. Her other hand clutched the seeds so hard that their tiny points bit into her palm like teeth. "I should have told them earlier, but I was so desperate to get the bronze apple back. I thought it was the only one, you see, and its magic is protecting the orchard, which is rotting—dying. I couldn't let Finna and I get sent to the home for misbehaved women, and—" She stopped, suddenly appalled at herself.

Liam stood next to her now, his face twisted into a look of confusion that approached horror. But the woman drew her attention like a spark to dry wood. How could she be so disrespectful, especially when meeting someone of obvious rank for the first time? She had never talked on and on like this, like a babbling stream, like an idiot.

But another shock came to her when she realized that her questioner watched her without anger. The only expression on the formidable woman's face was one of mild amusement.

And suddenly Maeve felt a wave of anger. She was tired of not being taken seriously by those who said they needed her help but didn't trust her with all the facts. She was tired of not being told the whole truth. When she released the crumpled corner of her shawl and straightened, this time it was to look the woman defiantly in the eye.

"Take me to your chief," Maeve said. "I was told the apple seeds would make an acceptable trade, and he must be able to do something with them. I've come all this way on behalf of my village. I will get the apple one way or another, and I can't wait any longer."

"My apologies—" said Colm behind her, but the woman silenced him with a lifted hand.

"My bold guest," she said, addressing Maeve. "I am afraid your errand must wait a little longer. But come, show me these seeds you speak of, before our midnight celebration begins. And as chief, I welcome you to join us."

Her words sank into Maeve like cold water poured over her skin. "Oh—you—" she sputtered.

"I am Chief Orlenn," the woman said, smiling. In the firelight, her smile held a hint of the feral, too. "We do not often welcome outsiders to our camp, and few seek us out. But we are honored with your presence."

A woman chief? It was strange, unheard of. It was wonderful. Maeve felt a nudge at her elbow and realized she was still staring and holding the seeds. She stepped forward and held them out. The seeds fell like drops of rain into Orlenn's outstretched hand.

"I should have told Breena and Colm sooner," Maeve said.

A thought hit her like a green wave of nausea: she'd behaved no differently than the Patrician, by withholding information to get something from someone. *Never again,* she promised herself. *I will not allow myself to become like him, no matter the cost.* What exactly had he hoped to gain by withholding information from her?

"It's true there must be a trade, if the pool has claimed something of yours," Orlenn said, "and offering something of personal value is wise. But it needn't have been magical." She returned the seeds to a bewildered Maeve. "Keep these for now. I will help you retrieve your bronze apple from the pool after tonight's feast."

Numerous questions about the nature of the pool swirled in Maeve's head like water in a bucket, but everyone was walking toward the bonfire.

"*Maith an buachaill,*" Liam said under his breath to the creature as they passed. Aodh opened one red eye and growled, a deep timber Maeve felt in her feet.

"We get on better than he shows. He really does like me," Liam told her, tiptoeing past and keeping his arms outstretched between her and the giant animal. "It's his mate who isn't so sure of me."

Maeve happily left the creature's proximity–and thoughts of his mate–behind. Colm and Breena laughed up ahead as they followed the chief. Laughter erupted from around the bonfire, and a child darted past Maeve into her mother's arms. Everyone beamed, called to friends. One or two called a greeting to Liam, who returned it with a wave and an almost bashful reply in the same tongue.

Then, from the other side of the fire and bustle, came a sinuous, scraping noise that arrested Maeve's attention and made her heart skip. The sound flowed into a melody, warm and liquid as summer sunlight, and other sounds joined it: the rhythmic beating of a drum, trilling notes that sounded like someone blowing through something. The excitement prickled in the air like invisible bolts of lightning.

"Let the dance begin!" called Orlenn, and all around Maeve people began joining hands, calling out to one another, gathering in formation. Maeve found herself outside a ring of clansfolk of all ages circling the bonfire. Different music notes scattered and rushed together, and the musicians, now visible, struck up a tune that filled Maeve with a longing so big and vast she had no room for anything else.

So this was the music she'd been warned against, the music she'd heard once in a while from the safety of the orchard. Not the tune Liam had shared, but a vast, intricate melody that changed the very atmosphere. It didn't make any sense. What the villagers feared and shunned was the loveliest, most thrilling thing she'd ever witnessed. Tears squeezed in her throat at the beauty of it. She felt desperate to join as she pressed back against the shadows, watching hungrily, unable to make sense of the steps. If she had felt feral on the hill, then this was a wildness far beyond anything she could ever claim as her own.

"Come on, Maeve!" Colm took her hand and pulled her into the throng. A short, stout woman took her other hand and smiled before Maeve gave herself to the movement. The music, the light, the dancers swept her up and brought her in; she found the dance much simpler on this side of it.

Everyone kept the circle formation going one way, then the other, round the fire, and someone sang in a voice eerie, sad, and fierce, words Maeve could not understand.

Faster, faster they went, around the fire again and again as sparks leaped into the sky in a dance all their own. Back and forth, side to side, always linked by hands or arms, the circle curling into lines that flowed like water. Between the other dancers Maeve fumbled with the steps. She tripped and jostled, but that did not bother anyone. The music swelled and swirled around them and continued as if stopping were impossible. Maeve felt it in the hands of those she danced with and in the soles of her feet. She caught sight of Liam, a few rows of dancers ahead of her, looking almost as bewildered as she felt. He caught her eye and they both laughed.

Then something—everything—changed.

A breeze like the freshest summer wind, hot and cool at once, whistled around the group, lifting Maeve's hair off her neck. It seemed to fill her lungs with more air than she'd ever taken in one breath, as if she'd never really breathed until now.

A different sound rose from somewhere. Whether it came from the dancers' throats or from the ground or the air, Maeve could not be sure. It was the sound of water roaring and fire burning, the sound of trees growing and soil decaying and flowers opening. The sound seemed to come from within her, too, and yet it was all around her, and she felt light as the wind and rooted as the trees. The dark sky swallowed everyone and her with them. The lightness in her limbs became a painless burning, as if she were rising into the vastness of stars. Her feet tread a brightly speckled darkness. She never lost her grasp on Colm's or the woman's hands. They were dancing among the stars, Maeve with all the clan, threading their way throughout a deep and endless corridor of sky, her limbs light and fire.

Then the stars fell away and her stomach rose, trying to escape her throat. The earth swallowed them in a warm embrace. Maeve heard ancient voices twining in song with the lone singer. These other voices, old as memory, reminded her of the apple trees. She felt as though she danced deep within the heart of the world, among decay and roots, the smell of death and rebirth, always with the same fluid movements and ease.

The music gathered itself and stopped. Beneath a dark and star-scattered sky the dancers released one another's hands and cheered. Maeve found herself before the bonfire again, trembling and laughing, and saw faces she recognized. Colm, his face transformed into a warrior's, fierce and reverent as he wiped a tear from his face. Orlenn laughed, picked up a child and spun him around. Maeve felt as if she were still spinning and tried to catch her breath as a laugh escaped her lips, too.

Then everyone began to form a new configuration as dancers claimed specific partners. A smiling Breena joined hands with a flaxen-haired girl, Colm found a smiling, gray-haired woman, and Orlenn took a tall, somber man by the waist. Two dancers together, arms looped around waists, the outside arms free to move. Maeve fumbled with her hands until someone tapped her on the shoulder.

It was Liam, his face flushed and shining. He gestured vaguely with his hands and let them drop as the music started again.

"You're the only other person who doesn't know this dance," he said. "Dance with me."

"We'll trip on each other's toes." Maeve tried to sound indifferent and gave up. She had hoped he would ask her. They each put an arm around the other and everyone began at once, laughing and fumbling at first, then struggling to catch up with the others. The movements were a mixture of spinning, switching sides, kicking out and short steps. Before long, they were both laughing wildly as they lurched and bobbed like laundry left out in a fierce gale.

"We keep hitting people!" Maeve shouted as her hand smacked another dancer's head for the third time. The music itself seemed to lead them on, offering wordless instructions, and yet it was so new it felt like learning to walk again. The strange ease that overcame her in the last dance was gone.

Liam steered them toward the edge of the crowd. The music was just as loud, but there was less chance of injuring someone. After a few minutes of following the steps, Maeve's confidence grew. Now the dance began to feel like a memory.

"I think we're getting the hang of it!" Liam shouted, his voice cracking on the final word. She lifted her eyes from her feet and saw his demeanor had changed, his laughter softening into a complex and familiar expression. Maeve tripped lightly and stopped altogether, her attention fixed solely on him. She waited, breathless, hoping, and still he held her hand.

As the music swirled around them, Liam gently pulled her nearer. His breath feathered against her cheek. Blood pounded in her veins. She leaned in until she felt his warmth against hers, and shut her eyes.

The music leaped to a halt and hung suspended in the air. Cheers and whistles erupted around them. Maeve pulled her hand back and stepped away, cheeks burning furiously, and glanced around, trying to make herself small. But there was no need. No one seemed to care, and everything was a celebration.

15. Pool

The feasting that followed was the happiest, most boisterous feasting Maeve had ever experienced. She and Liam found seats side by side at one of the long tables. There was mutton and rabbit stew and hearty bread with honey, cream and late berries, fish from the streams, mead and wine, herbs and roots and curling, leafy greens, and not a single thing made with apples.

Aodh plodded into view along the edge of the crowded tables with a gray version of himself at his side. Maeve almost choked. The sight of the animal still terrified her, and seeing two did not exactly help, even though no one else seemed bothered by them. The creatures didn't seem to notice the existence of the clan. They walked with purpose, their red eyes fixed on something she couldn't see, though what that purpose was, Maeve couldn't guess. When they disappeared from sight, she asked Liam why he hadn't warned her about them before their arrival. Looking sheepish, he replied that he was distracted.

Breena appeared at that moment to fetch Liam for the chief. "For training," she said, and Maeve knew better than to ask to go with them.

Now it seemed a long time since he had left, and though the others at her table were kind and generous, Liam's absence was another thing that made enjoying the feast difficult.

The bite of fish melted on her tongue as she thought of Finna. She had to get home. This was a dream of a place, wonderful and far more welcoming than she'd expected, with a dance so full of things she couldn't begin to make sense of. Surely daylight would arrive in mere hours. She had to get the bronze apple, and she had to go home.

Still there was no sign of Liam. Hesitant to interrupt whatever he might be doing, she rose from the table and went in search of Colm.

She felt shy around Orlenn, but that was who she found first. The chief conversed with her dancing partner. When Maeve approached, the man gave her a smile and touched Orlenn on the shoulder. Turning to look, the chief waved her over. The man whispered something to her and left.

"Are you in need of something, Maeve?" Orlenn asked.

It struck Maeve that the Patrician had never asked her that. Nor had she ever heard him ask anyone else, even after the lean, thin winter, where small children and the aged had died of hunger. He simply told everyone what they needed and provided it.

"Thank you so much for your hospitality," Maeve said, "but I must go home. I don't understand how time can stand still, and I'm afraid I've been away too long." She twisted her hands in her skirt and looked down at her feet. Any levity she'd felt was gone, replaced by a weight that tied her all the way to the pool, and to Quin's rules and the orchard and to Finna and the Patrician.

Orlenn did not speak at first. "I understand," she said at last. "We are all connected, Maeve, even to those who would not acknowledge it."

The answer struck Maeve as odd. She'd hoped for something simple and direct, an announcement that they would leave immediately for the pool. In the discomfort grew questions she'd long tried to stuff down. So long, in fact, she feared it was no longer possible to ignore them.

In spite of herself, or perhaps to quiet these thoughts, a puerile question escaped her lips. "Chief Orlenn, can I ask you something?"

The chief nodded.

"Forgive me, but are you familiar with the clan known among the villages as the wild men?"

A smile flickered across the woman's face. "You might say we are they," she said. "I believe your history bestows the title upon anyone who fails to abide by the rules your people brought with them from across the sea."

Not long ago, such a revelation would have elicited many feelings from Maeve. Fear. Shock. Shame. The urge to flee back to the safety of what she had always known. And while the last impulse simmered just under her skin, the Ragad man's face, pained and pleading, taunted Maeve for her simplicity and naivete in thinking the world was as simple as she'd been told.

I have kept many secrets, doing whatever I could to save the orchard and protect Quin from the world beyond, only to find that the world beyond Quin's walls are far more complicated and beautiful than I thought.

Still, the urge to defend herself demanded voice. "I only want to protect my foster mother and I from being sent away."

To this, Orlenn offered no answer. Colm, Breena, and Liam appeared then, and both clanswoman and village girl turned their attention to them.

"Well, Liam?" the chief said, looking from her sentries to the young shepherd. "How does your evening go?"

Liam squared his shoulders. He looked grave, as if he had left boyhood behind for good within the last hour. "It goes well," he answered. The carefully constructed, nonchalant confidence on his face dissolved, though he maintained his posture. "That is, I'm trying, Orlenn. This magic I have, it doesn't always make sense. I don't like that. I don't like possessing something I barely understand."

"Then think of it not as a possession, but as a gift. None of us own it, Liam. I know you have been working hard, but you have only just begun. Remember this: what you have is a gift that includes time to embrace and understand it."

"Breena and Colm have told me that I may live with the clan when my training is complete." Liam looked almost defiant.

Orlenn nodded. "And what is your decision?"

"Can I beg your patience, Chief Orlenn? For time to make my choice."

Again the chief nodded. "That is wise. You have until your training ends."

Liam bowed his head in acknowledgment.

"The night draws to a close for both of you." Orlenn rose from her seat. "I will take you to the pool myself and help you retrieve the bronze apple. You began an exchange. It is time to complete it."

Maeve exhaled a breath she didn't know she'd held, but her relief was mixed with a strange sadness. A low growl at her elbow made her start. Turning, she came face-to-face with a large black muzzle beneath fearsome red eyes. Head bent to her level, the creature sniffed at her. Its breath wafted warm and brushed her hair from her face. Then, as if ascertaining something that satisfied it, the giant dog raised its head and sat down, never taking its eyes from her.

Somewhere in the frozen landscape of her mind a thought shrieked: *Is this our escort?*

Colm's chuckle broke through her terror, but Breena guffawed without shame. Maeve realized she'd shrieked aloud. At the other end of Orlenn's table, clansfolk smiled or watched with open amusement. Maeve backed away, trying to hide the scarlet rising in her cheeks.

"We don't ride the Cú Sidhe like pack animals," Breena said, wiping her eye. "Oh, your face, Maeve! You should have seen it!"

Orlenn said a few words to Aodh. He growled again, shook his head, and bounded away from the circle around the fire. Maeve heard the pounding of many large footsteps, as if a whole pack of the Cú Sidhe had taken shape in the shadows and were fleeing in search of someplace darker.

Colm stepped forward, smiling at her. "I'll be thinking of you, lass. We'll meet again, of that I've no doubt." Maeve only smiled. She could not risk coming back to this wild and wondrous place, but Colm's kindness warmed her heart, and she could not bring herself to contradict him.

"Goodbye, Maeve." Breena squeezed her shoulder. "I pronounce you not so bad, for a villager."

Maeve returned her grin, thinking of the light in Breena's hands and failing yet again to find the right words. "Goodbye."

Liam stood a little apart from them, looking small and uncertain, his courage deflated now that he had spoken his piece. What kind of test had he undergone?

Maeve offered him a warm smile, and he returned it gratefully.

Orlenn led them swiftly over the hills. She said nothing, only glanced now and again at the stars as she turned down one trail, then onto another so narrow Maeve would have never seen it. The downs had never seemed so vast as they did now.

Maeve wanted to speak to Liam and ask him about what he'd undergone after the dance, but now was not the time. And Liam, walking quietly beside her, seemed busy sifting through his own experience, perhaps forming an answer for Orlenn.

Maeve kept alert for any sounds of the Cú Sidhe. Their existence raised even more questions on a night already replete with them. The giant hounds didn't seem to belong to the clan, but lived close to them. The sight of Aodh would cause any shepherd from Quin to break out their knife—or break into a run. Despite having survived an encounter with one, she found the creatures more terrifying than anything she'd ever imagined roaming the downs at night. She gathered the courage to ask Orlenn another question.

"Chief." She had to repeat the title multiple times while gasping for breath during the climb. At last Orlenn heard her. "Can you tell me more about the Cú Sidhe? What purpose do they serve?"

"They live," Orlenn answered. "They are bound to no one. They respect us, some love us even, but if something disturbs or threatens their kin or clan, their first instinct is to defend."

"Do they attack?"

"If you are asking whether or not they will trouble the good citizens of Quin, then you are probably safe. As long as no one wanders too far from the safety of your walls."

Orlenn's tone was inscrutable, and she offered no other answer.

Maeve wasn't sure if the way was shorter than it had seemed on the way there or if time really had stopped. But sooner than expected, they climbed the last gentle rise to the pool. The trees rustled in a chill night wind, and the pool glowed and rippled, catching starlight and dashing it into hundreds of dazzling shards.

Orlenn bade Maeve add the seeds to the pool. They fell with barely a sound and were lost in the dark. The surface of the pool trembled once, but it might have been from a slight breeze.

"You will have no trouble retrieving it now," Orlenn said. "It must be you, Maeve. I leave you to it." She laid a hand on Maeve's shoulder and smiled at her. "You were bold tonight, and I suspect that boldness came at a great cost. Remember this: before you can belong anywhere, you must first belong to yourself." She withdrew her hand and nodded at Liam. "Farewell for now." With these final words, the Lochlyn chief departed.

Liam nodded at the sky. "It's almost sunrise." The black arc above them was fading to gray at the edges, and the stars were winking out. They did not have much time. Liam glanced at the pool, then back at her. "I wish I could help."

"I wish Orlenn had explained what I am supposed to do." Maeve straightened. "But I lost the apple. It's only right I should get it out."

The bronze shape sat at the bottom, taunting, the depths bending and twisting its shape in the faint and scattered light.

Maeve pulled off her shoes, inhaled sharply, and stepped in. The cold burned with a white-hot intensity. She bit back squeals of protest as it rose past her ankles, knees, and thighs, dragging at her skirts and underclothes. Taking her time would only prolong the agony. *Don't think about it, just do it. Do it!* Drawing in a deeper breath, she shut her eyes and plunged beneath the surface.

What shocked her was not the cold. The water swirled around her like heavy yet mild summer air. In the surprisingly beautiful crystalline depths, she pressed ahead, wondering how long it would last. She almost laughed with surprise. This time, without fear to hinder her, it was an astounding experience. If she had no pressing task, she imagined she could play for hours, limbs suspended and gliding through liquid no longer biting into her bones with cold. Almost as astounding was how quickly she reached the bottom. With just a few pushes of her legs, her outstretched hands met with resistance.

She opened her eyes.

The water rippled with an emerald and sky-blue light, obscuring the bottom like colorful smoke. Her fingers brushed something smooth and round: the apple. She pried it up, its weight insignificant underwater. She spun around, kicked behind her and her foot struck wildly at nothing, leaving her to wave wildly in a bid for purchase. Trying again, her feet found a smooth indentation in the rock floor, and she pushed with all her might. Maeve broke the surface of the water in a shower of luminescent droplets. Only then did she realize that she'd never stopped breathing.

Liam's hands gripped her arm and pulled. She blinked water from her eyes and scrambled onto the bank with his help. The cold returned with vengeance, shaking her limbs and teeth.

"All right?" Liam asked.

"I've got it," she said with a breathless, shivery laugh, and held out the bronze apple. Liam placed his hands on her arms, and her clothes dried almost instantly, the sensation so pleasant that she laughed again. How good it felt to be warm!

"Huh. It worked." Liam looked pleased, then shrugged, his face turning pink again. "I asked Breena to give me something that would help you dry off."

"It feels lovely," Maeve replied.

But the urgency of her task wouldn't let her get distracted for long, and she reluctantly stepped away. "I have to replace this in the Patrician's room before the false one disappears," she said, hurrying up the trail. Liam followed.

Quin's wall and gate came into view. *That'll use precious time we don't have. I'll have to go in through the break in the wall.* "You don't have to come with me," she said, pausing to look over her shoulder.

"I'm going with you." He gave her his first cocky grin since they'd left Lochlyn, and she was close enough to see his scar bend in response. "You'll need someone to cause a distraction."

Grateful and nervous, Maeve hurried along the wall. It was strange to be outside the village in such enveloping quiet, aside from the babbling stream. There was the orchard, and there was Finna's lone cottage above the old, broken ones, scattered like rotten apples.

Soon she scurried through the break in the wall and ran toward the church, with Liam keeping pace. She tried to make her footfalls as quiet as possible on the flagstone streets. She thought about going into the Patrician's rooms through the courtyard door but didn't know whether it was oiled regularly or not.

Through the church it was. The sky overhead was nearly gray.

When they reached the smithy, Maeve stopped and ducked inside, grabbing Liam's arm and pointing. "Look," she whispered.

Outside the church doors stood a figure. Judging by the silhouette, it was a man in a guard's uniform.

Panic rose in Maeve's throat. *I didn't know it would be guarded!*

"I see them," whispered Liam. "If I cut through the smithy and keep in the shadows, I'll distract them so you can get inside."

Maeve hesitated, unwilling to put him at risk of being caught. "Are you sure?"

"What other ideas do you have?" His voice grew insistent. "Maeve, I'll reach the hills before they even see me. It'll be all right."

Gratitude welled up within her. "Thank you," she said. "But be careful."

"Hey." He threw his arms out in a gesture of careless defiance. "I know what I'm offering."

The sky seemed to brighten by the second, highlighting every hole in the cobbled streets and every joint where the wooden building frames met. Even so, she couldn't see Liam as he slipped through the smithy and up the street as planned. The soldier's features became clearer, too, and Maeve suppressed a shiver as she recognized the long face and broad shoulders.

Thomas.

A shrill cry pierced the air, sending an arrow of panic through Maeve's limbs. *Liam.* The noise seemed to come from right next to the church, but Thomas, whose head had jerked up, dashed up the street with a muttered curse. Maeve seized her chance and darted to the door. To her great relief, it opened without protest or hindrance, and she slipped into the quiet church.

It felt like walking into a tomb. The middle aisle seemed to run on forever, and her feet sounded loud against the long carpet, which muffled her steps less than she remembered. At last she reached the door to the Patrician's rooms.

Her heart pounded loudly in her ears, as if she were the blood of a terrified animal moving in a frozen heart. The smell of the cure longered stronger than ever. Though the window, pink tinged the gray dawn. The door to what she assumed was the Patrician's sleeping quarters stood shut, and next to it was the cupboard.

That, too, opened without a sound. Maeve pulled the bronze apple from her hand and inhaled at the sight it illuminated: at least a dozen bronze apples sat nestled in pools of velvet. Whereas the object in her hand glowed faintly blue, these were dull, waiting for the Patrician to instill them with magic and light.

Except one. The apple Maeve had returned glowed faintly, no longer blue but a pale yellow. The moment she reached for it, it fell apart and vanished, leaving no trace it had ever existed.

All this took less than a heartbeat to register. In the space of the next, Maeve had returned the real bronze apple, shut the cabinet, and turned to go.

A creak sounded behind her.

"Maeve?"

Her building elation shattered into a million pieces. Years of habit bid her turn around to face the owner of the familiar voice.

There stood the Patrician, wearing a burgundy dressing gown instead of his familiar robes and holding a gold-flamed candle aloft.

16. Prayer

Despite the Patrician's disheveled appearance and lines about his face, his eyes were alert and his voice the same low, calm one he always used. He waited, not asking why she was in his rooms before dawn. Time seemed to stretch forever.

"I thought I heard something," Maeve said, the lie escaping her lips with unsettling ease. "I feared the wild men would try something bad . . . and . . ."

"And you came to check on the cure," he finished. Maeve nodded, begging her heart to stop galloping and let her take a full breath before the truth escaped her lips.

The Patrician walked to the cure, set down his candle, and gave the mixture one slow stir. He observed it carefully, as if someone had tampered with it and he was searching for evidence. "I see nothing wrong with it," he said, straightening up. "But surely Thomas would have seen something?"

"He wasn't here." Maeve almost choked on the words and swallowed with difficulty.

"Hm." The Patrician stroked his beard thoughtfully. "I wonder what could have alerted you to a possible threat. In the still of the night, you should have been sleeping. Did something draw you here?"

Now he turned to Maeve. For a moment the concern on his face faltered, revealing something sharper, deep enough to lose one's footing and break a toe on.

"No." She straightened, as she had facing the chief hours ago. Never had she realized how much of her life she spent hunched over, staying small, trying to go unnoticed save for the most important things. It was like something in that pool had washed her cloudy vision away.

You want me to tell you everything. Why? So you can write letters to the Lord Protector? So you can watch as your guards take me and Finna from our home and take us somewhere to live out our days in misery? I will never tell you anything again.

The Patrician looked at her a long minute, his face betraying nothing but fatigue. "I can only imagine that something good prompted you to come here. It was the night of the wild men's irreverent celebration, after all, and they could have had plans to breach the orchard and damage Quin's protection. You may have saved us."

She bowed her head, trying to hide the tempest swirling inside her.

"You said there was no guard?" Rustling fabric signaled the Patrician's slow steps.

Maeve nodded. "Yes, sir."

"There will be consequences for that, unfortunately. I cannot have people failing their commitments. You understand."

The door from the sanctuary burst open. "Patrician. Someone tried to get into the church," Declan said, panting. "Thomas just alerted me."

"I see." The Patrician's voice was clipped. "And were you not also posted last night? Or am I confused about which of my men was on duty?"

Declan's face reddened. "I was relieving myself, sir."

"And did Thomas catch the miscreant?"

"No. Whoever it was got away."

The Patrician sighed heavily. "I am dismayed to hear it. And our citizens will be troubled to learn about this breach in safety. Thankfully, Miss MacGowan warded off danger with her quick thinking and devotion to Quin's safety."

Declan nodded in one sharp motion, his gaze fixed ahead. "Yes, Patrician."

"Escort the young lady home, Declan. And Maeve, we will continue caring for the cure at noon today."

Maeve nodded again, her throat sticking like it was full of sawdust. "Yes, sir."

She had almost left behind Declan when the Patrician spoke again. "And Declan."

"Sir?"

"When you see Thomas again, tell him to report to me at once. You will accompany him so both of you may face the consequences for your breach of duty."

"Yes, Patrician."

The guard turned smartly and strode from the room, a muscle jumping in his jaw.

Word of the supposed breach of the wild men must have spread rapidly throughout Quin. When Maeve walked back to the church in the bright midday sun, she saw people clustered in groups of twos and threes speaking in hushed tones. Although one particular group, made up of the priest and Katherine's two little sisters, wasn't speaking in hushed tones at all. As Maeve passed by, she heard a fragment of the priest's one-sided sermon.

"You'd best slow down and behave like young ladies," he scolded in his thin voice. It warbled with barely suppressed anger. "Doesn't your mother teach you how to walk properly? Or do you girls want to draw the attention of the wild men, who were here only last night?"

The priest caught sight of Maeve as the last words faded from his thin lips, and his eyes narrowed. "And you, Miss MacGowan," he said. "Do you think you are above such admonitions, just because you may have stopped those heathens from breaking into our holy sanctuary? Or were you perhaps waiting for wicked things in the dark?"

A gobbet of spittle flew off the priest's lips and landed on Maeve's shawl. But her attention was drawn to Brigid and Mary, who looked at her with scared, pleading eyes. Brigid, the eldest, clutched a basket of yarn, and Mary clutched her sister's arm while her big eyes welled with tears. A mix of tenderness and anger swelled within Maeve's chest. With such a kind mother as Mrs. Campbell, the priest's warning must come as a terrible shock. *And they are so young. Why must Quin subject girls to this terror at so young an age?*

Maeve stepped forward and gently took Mary by the hand. "What pretty colors the dyers have made your yarn," she said gently as she led them away from the priest's glare. The man wasn't pleased.

"You mustn't ignore your elders, girl," he warned. The girls shrank against Maeve's skirt.

"Leave them alone." She didn't say it very loud, and her voice shook, and she didn't dare look the priest in the eye. But Maeve said it with all the fire that burned in her throat, and it felt fiercely good to march away without sparing him so much as a backward glance.

"Now run home," she said when they were safely up the street. They'd passed the church entrance, but Maeve wanted to be sure to accompany the girls out of the scolding priest's hearing range.

"Maeve, you sounded almost like Katherine," Mary said in a wondrous tone.

"No," Brigid said with a sigh, "Katherine is much saucier. That's why Mother says it's good she's married."

"Have you seen her much lately?" Maeve asked, looking up the street toward her friend's house. She wondered how long she'd have to wait before there were enough apples to make what Katherine and Conlan had asked for. They wouldn't be the only residents of Quin waiting for Finna's apple goods. This morning she had found another tree rotten through and through, marking seven dying trees in total. She and Finna had to put off some of their baking and prioritize as best as they could. An old, familiar anxiety clenched in her stomach. If she couldn't finish the cure, there would be far more than apple butter and pies at stake.

"She's much too busy keeping house." Brigid flipped her blonde hair over her shoulder in a very Katherine-like way. Maeve instinctively cast her gaze in search of someone ready to pounce on the motion and pronounce it unladylike. "Come on, Mary," Brigid said, tugging her sister by the hand. "We have to go."

Maeve reached the church door. For a moment she remembered running down a slope steeped in darkness, the feel of the wind tugging her hair and her legs running as fast as they ever had. *But that was last night and I don't belong out on the hills. I belong here. Today, I must focus on the cure. That is all that matters.*

New guards stood at the church doors. Two more polished the large stone apples at the village gate, which was shut and barred. More soldiers than usual had arrived with the Patrician, but they were everywhere today, as if they'd multiplied overnight. It seemed very few of them were allowed to remain at the inn today. All were at work, showing Quin that they took seriously a threat to their safety.

Maeve smiled to herself. The threat was only a boy who somehow found footing in two worlds at odds with each other. Last night she had seen him falter, question. *How strange it must be to have to choose, when all I have ever known is within these walls.*

Until last night. Until I breached these walls in order to protect them . . .

It was confusing, disorienting, if she let herself think about the last several days too much. Still, her path ahead was clear. Maeve nodded politely and blandly to the guard who let her in and went straight to the Patrician's rooms.

At the Patrician's words, she entered. The room smelled more strongly of herbs than ever, and the mixture simmered with renewed vigor over the little brazier. The room was silent save for the faint bubbling of the pot.

"Good afternoon, Maeve. I hope I haven't kept you waiting long."

Maeve pasted a smile on her face as the Patrician swept into the room.

"I had to inspect the new soldiers. What a relief that they've come at last. Not only is this good news for all of Quin, but it bears special significance for you, do you understand?"

Maeve felt as though her face had frozen as she shook her head.

"It means the guards I sent to look into your parentage will return at any time now. You haven't long to wait."

Of course. Her muscles relaxed a little in genuine relief. "That is good news, sir. I'd almost forgotten, with the—" She gestured to the pot.

"Yes. It's been quite a night." He put a gentle hand on her shoulder that felt like the weight of the world. "I am tired, and you must be too. I won't keep you long this time. Would you like to say the prayer on your own today?"

"Doesn't it need more than one person, sir?"

"We're both here, Maeve, and that is what matters. You are more than capable. I think it's an honor you've proven yourself worthy of."

I swallow and try to paste the smile back on my face, but I can't find it.

Not long ago this would have been the greatest honor I could imagine: taking the primary role in saving the orchard, being given this task by the Patrician himself. But all I know is the jagged weight of the familiar words in my throat. I must force them out.

God of our forebears, attend our prayer.

Lochlyn lived here before we arrived.

God of the sacred orchard, guide our steps.

This god has always felt distant—the Patrician used to make him feel near. And I used to accept that, as I used to accept so much.

Heal all wrongs, purify impurities, protect our land, which you gave us.

Fear on the Ragad man's face

Bless our humble efforts to cleanse the trees you gave us.

Trees which Lochlyn helped me save

In the name of the god of unity, amen.

What is unity?

If the Patrician notices how my throat sticks to the words more with each line, he says nothing. In fact, by the time I'm done, I'm quite certain that I've managed to hide the unease squirming within my chest like a worm in an apple. But he looks wearier than ever. As if he has just performed a great feat of strength. When he smiles kindly at me, it's as if he thinks he's done it in the presence of a worthy companion, and a wave of confusion sweeps through me like nausea.

"Well done, Maeve," he says. "Thomas will take you home now."

It's only after he's retreated, leaving me to wait for the guard, that I notice the contents of the cure haven't changed at all.

Thomas strode ahead of her so quickly she almost had to run to keep up with him. For that, and for his lack of attention or acknowledgment, she was grateful. After leaving the village, they crossed the little bridge, and Maeve smelled apples cooking, mixed with the warm scent of cinnamon. Smoke rose from Finna's house.

Maeve began to breathe freely when Thomas turned abruptly and frowned at her. She tried to step back to avoid running into him. But they were still on the bridge, and she had nowhere to go.

"You think you're something precious, don't you?" he said.

Maeve was too startled to respond.

"I don't know what you were playing at last night. But you're too close with the Patrician, Miss MacGowan. Thanks to your wide-eyed antics, I'm in trouble."

He bent closer. Maeve's eyes flickered to the cottage, for once begging Finna to spy and insert herself into an unwanted situation.

"Keep your mouth shut and your eyes down. If I find the heathen filth who broke into Quin, I'll have a question or two for him about what you did that night. And I won't forget who I have to thank for tattling on me."

His hand swung to his hip in a motion that made Maeve flinch. But Thomas paused, his hand landing on nothing but his belt. He pushed past her and stalked off, leaving Maeve alone and shaking.

The orchard smelled of sweet, crisp apples and sour rot. Familiar and new, comforting and threatening. She dragged in a few slow, steadying breaths. Looking toward Quin, she could no longer see Thomas's retreating form, but his words wouldn't leave her head. She remembered his hand at his belt and understood: his hip flask was missing. That must've been the Patrician's punishment.

Now that he was gone, she had no desire to see Finna. She placed the new bronze apple on the wall. A familiar bark sounded behind her. Maeve ran to the back wall in time to see a black and white dog dashing toward the orchard with something in his mouth.

She smiled. "Whistle!"

The dog leaped up, placing his forepaws on the wall so that Maeve could retrieve the scrap of paper from his mouth. It was soggier than Liam's last note, but that didn't stop it from lifting Maeve's spirits. "Good boy," she said, ruffling the dog's curly head with a free hand. He gave one short, happy bark. Then he sprang down and darted around the wall, vanishing into the downs before Maeve could see him go.

I'll be in the orchard tomorrow afternoon, read the note. *Heard from Mr. Campbell that Finna is visiting his wife tomorrow. Will I see you?*

Maeve looked after her energetic messenger, wishing she could reply. No chance of that. But if Finna would be gone tomorrow, she knew what she wanted to do.

17. Visits

The whole village felt on edge after the supposed attempt by the wild men. Not only did the Patrician post more guards around the entrance, but he sent Declan to bring Maeve to work on the cure every day at noon. She did not see much of Thomas for the next two days.

While the cure slowly turned from the brown of early stages to the gray of its final readiness, Finna kept Maeve at home all other times. Her foster mother was more taciturn and short with her than ever. She wouldn't allow her to deliver the few apple loaves they'd already baked. Maeve kept her head down and attended her tasks without complaint, knowing from experience that this mood of Finna's meant the woman was preoccupied with something and more prone to withdraw her already slim supply of support from Maeve. A dropped dish would mean a meager serving of dinner. Too many questions would mean she'd be sent to her room rather than allowed to seek solace in the orchard. Though Maeve wished she could see Katherine, she knew better than to press the matter with Finna.

And she was too happy with another thing that Finna's absences made possible: Liam's visits to her in the orchard.

Today was his second visit in three days. They sat among the healthiest trees and played with Whistle, whose exuberance made them laugh. Liam tossed a ball made from ancient animal hides—not unlike the one Maeve and her companions had played with years ago—back and forth between them while Whistle leaped and barked in his attempts to catch it. He always caught it before long. Then, as if tired of the game, the little terrier would drop his ball beside Liam, bark in victory or farewell, and leap over the wall to go speeding over the hills. The silence that followed filled with unspoken things that quickened Maeve's heart and made her shy.

Liam flung himself down on the grass and looked up at the blue sky interlaced with apple tree branches full of the last ripening fruit. He tucked one hand under his head and let the other stretch out, seemingly relaxed, though his fingertips brushed Maeve's. It felt deliciously scandalous.

She cleared her throat. "Does Whistle go to see the clan alone?" Her knitting needles and a half-finished scarf lay forgotten in her lap.

"Yes. He seems to love it there as much as any of the clansfolk." He plucked a blade of grass to spin between his thumb and forefinger. Then he caught sight of Maeve's puzzled face. "You're thinking that I'm a terrible shepherd for leaving my sheep so often," he said, tossing her an amused smile.

"You do leave them often," Maeve said. "Not just during the day, but at night to see Lochlyn."

He shrugged. "We shepherds watch each other's flocks when one of us needs time for other tasks. Danby and Pike owe me for helping them with hoof rot," he said. "I'd rather be here. Unless you'd rather I wasn't."

He grinned, sending Maeve's stomach into a series of somersaults.

She refused to respond to this tease. Being around Liam was so very strange. On the one hand, it now felt as natural as anything. She hated to consider it, but the ease of being with him rivaled the ease she'd shared with Katherine, who was now so preoccupied with her home and husband that she felt like a different person when Maeve thought of her.

It was a relief to have Liam's company, especially as they'd shared a secret visit to the clan and could talk about it without fear of censure. This freedom felt like a gasp for air after holding her breath for so long she could hardly remember doing otherwise.

But thinking clearly around him was becoming more difficult every time she saw him. This made her worry. Maeve assuaged her anxiety by creating a list in her mind, which she went over every time she caught sight of the brown-haired young shepherd descending the north hills in the afternoon sunlight.

One, I have swept the kitchen and helped with the harvest and baking, and I'm knitting the scarf Finna told me to complete as we speak, so I'm not neglecting my chores.

Or at least, she tried to knit. When she didn't forget about it, as she had today.

Two—because the mention of harvest drew the tightness in her chest the sharpest—*I have already worked on the cure today, and it is progressing as it should. I am doing all I can.*

Three, I know Finna is collecting jars from several people today, including Mrs. O'Neil, who will talk for an hour if you ask her one question.

We have time.

And every morning as she brought the bucketful of water from the stream for the ritual, she prayed her usual prayer: *God of the world, attend my prayer. Make me pure in heart and worthy of this task. In the name of the god who hears and sees all, amen.* If she hurried through it with less attention these days, she hardly noticed, and when she left off the final sentence of the prayer, she told herself later it was because she was distracted by the rot in her dear trees. This was true, at least in part.

They looked so bad that it made her heart squeeze. Silver crepuscules now dotted the bark. The rot hadn't yet spread to any new trees, but the sick ones oozed more and more each day and the fallen apples moldered in stinking piles. Finna had been warned against burning them, even if the damp weather allowed for it.

Liam, on his first visit, asked if she would show him the orchard, which made her heart tighten in a different way. He'd listened attentively when she showed him each of the diseased trunks and their rotten, never-ripened fruit. He'd even offered to ask Orlenn for some kind of spell to help them, but this Maeve refused.

"Breena already helped with the look-alike, and the chief with the bronze apple," she'd said. "I wouldn't want to ask for anything else from them." But she couldn't bring herself to voice aloud the other reason. She feared that help from any clan, but especially Lochlyn, would alert the Patrician to their presence and cause trouble she didn't want to think about. Liam, after her response, didn't offer assistance again.

If Liam also noted the similarities between the Patrician's methods and Lochlyn magic, he said nothing of it. He said very little on the topic of magic altogether. Maeve sensed this might be more because of some reluctance on his part rather than a clan rule against talking with outsiders. She bit down her own curiosity on the matter. When asked about Whistle's escapades, Liam provided colorful illustrations of his little dog's interactions with the grand and terrifying Cú Sidhe, and did so again today.

"I've seen at least a dozen of the Cú Sidhe," he said. Whistle, who lay panting in the grass, looked at him when he said the name, then rolled and stretched on his back, waving his legs in the air and making Maeve and Liam laugh. "You know who I mean, boy?" He reached over and ruffled Whistle's fur affectionately while the dog nipped at his fingers. "The silver one you saw is Aodh's mate, Neemh," Liam went on. "I've asked some of the clan how many there are, but no one knows. They don't keep an eye on them like that. When I asked Colm, he laughed and asked if I worried that a rogue sheep might carry them off in the night?" Liam chuckled and shook his head. "Sometimes I don't understand these people at all. But Colm did teach me something. Look." He sat up suddenly, grinning, and pulled something from his pocket. "It's a bone flute. He made it for me. Maeve, listen to this."

He held the small, slender instrument to his lips. A faint, breathy music emanated from it. A catch snagged at the tune, then recovered, smooth as an untangled thread. The sound lifted the hairs on Maeve's arms and filled her with wonder and fear.

"Liam!" she whispered hoarsely. "You cannot play the wild men's music *in the orchard!*"

A grin cut off the music, and his eyes darted to hers. "Are you going to stop me?"

Maeve lunged forward to grab the flute, but he held the instrument out of her reach. Deftly, he switched the flute to his other hand and grabbed hers. "Not so fast."

But Maeve had ideas of her own. She leaned close, looking him in the eye, and allowed a slow smile to spread across her face. The hitch in his breathing sent a jolt of wicked triumph through her.

A small, furry body jostled into her and began covering her face with wet, stinky licks. "Whistle!" she shrieked, laughing, as the dog wiggled its way between them and attacked them both with affection.

"Bad timing, boy!" Liam laughed, wiping his cheek with his hand. "Go find your friends, will you?"

And Whistle, his mission accomplished, hurtled over the wall and ran for the hills, as he did every day.

"Maybe the Cú Sidhe are giving him lessons of their own," said Maeve. In the orchard, it was easy to joke about such things, when in person the creatures terrified her.

Liam chuckled at the thought, flipping the flute through his fingers. "Maybe."

"And your studies," Maeve said. "They're going well?"

"I suppose. Yeah, well enough. The magic, it's strange, though. I can't understand it."

"Neither can I," Maeve admitted. "Here we are in the sacred orchard which is said to protect us from the dark magic of the wild men. Yet here you are, half wild yourself. I've met Lochlyn and seen their magic." She shifted, images of stars and roots flashing across her mind, too vast and deep to be comfortable despite their immense beauty. "Everything is upside down. If it weren't for that wretched house for wayward women in Dumar, I would be very confused who the enemy is supposed to be."

"Do you need an enemy?" Liam rolled over to his side and tucked the flute into his pocket. He plucked a blade of grass and chewed it. His shirt sleeves were rolled up to the elbow despite the chill, and the faint, ever-present breeze ruffled his tangle of hair. His face puckered in thought. "And if you do, why pin it on a place? Why not this Lord Protector? He's the one behind all of this." He waved a hand, encompassing not just Quin or Dumar and Ferre, but all the settlements sent by the Lord Protector's forefathers in the history of the Great Crossing.

He's right. The Patrician answered to the Lord Protector and carried out his orders. "He's never been more than a distant figure," Maeve said. "I have never seen him. I don't think he's ever even been to Quin. The Patrician used to seem distant, too, but he saw me, and I used to long for his approval. But even that's turned sour." She stabbed a knitting needle into the soft earth.

"He doesn't bother with the shepherds. It's like he's forgotten I exist now. You say the Lord Protector is distant, but the Patrician has been here for a week, and has he ever set foot on our hills? No."

"Do you wish he would, Liam? After he questioned you when you arrived? You are the cause of the wild men's disturbance, after all."

Maeve almost expected Liam to reply with a grin. Instead, he pulled the grass from his mouth and tossed it away, his face serious. "Orlenn is one of her people. She works alongside them, listens to them. The clan is so . . . close to one another."

Maeve pondered this and his change in demeanor. "That seems to bother you as much as the Patrician's distance," she said softly.

Liam rolled onto his back again and plucked at the grass in agitation. Maeve almost reached out to touch him, to comfort him for something that clearly bothered him, but refrained.

"I don't know if I want it," he said, his voice sharp. "Being so close to a group. It was always just me and Dad, and his mind was more often than not with Mother. Even the shepherds here. We watch out for each other, but they've got their own lives. And so do I." He sat up and leaned against the tree nearest Maeve's, now pulling a fistful of grass to shreds. "I don't know if I believe in magic."

"What?" Maeve frowned, perplexed.

"I mean, I've seen Orlenn and Breena use it. There was the dance." He waved a hand in the air like the right words would fly out of his fingers if he shook them hard enough. "But . . . what if doing magic and the source of magic are completely different? Do I have to believe in a magic source just because I can or can't do strange things? They won't take my freedom," he burst out, trying to sound fierce but succeeding only in sounding tired. "I'd rather be alone than be told what to do."

"Really?" She could not quite follow Liam's rapidly changing directions, but the thought of living a life of solitude was horrible to Maeve. Every day was an attempt to stem the tide of loneliness which sometimes overwhelmed her. Even when she and Katherine had been close, her friend always went home to a warm, loud house full of people who had chosen, and kept choosing, each other.

At home, Maeve had the impression that Finna tolerated her at best most of the time. Now, there was Liam. Now, what replaced that loneliness felt sometimes like comfort, sometimes like a dizziness that fizzed deep in her belly and spun in her head, and it distracted her from the hollowed-out places within her. "You'd rather live your whole life with no one but a dog and some sheep for your friends?"

"Not . . . just them." His face lost some of its guardedness. His hand, fisted around a tuft of grass, relaxed and let the green shreds fall, before stretching haltingly toward her. Without thinking, Maeve mirrored the gesture. Liam wrapped his fingers around hers. His hand was warm and smooth, the little calluses on his palms brushing her knuckles.

"Maeve," he said.

That one word held a multitude of things Maeve could barely let herself think of. His eyes flicked to her lips before she looked away, a tumult of conflicting desires within her.

Finna's face shattered her thoughts. It was bad enough toying with the *idea* of kissing Liam. If she gave in to her desires, would Finna know just by looking at her? Maeve had done so many things behind her back. What if a kiss was the thing that exposed her, brought a more severe punishment down on her head than she could bear?

It sometimes felt as if Finna lived in her head, larger than Maeve herself. *As if I live in the shadows, hiding like a mouse in the hollows of my own space. I could almost curse Finna for it.*

She withdrew her hand and returned to her knitting. "Are you going back to Lochlyn tonight?"

"Tonight?" Liam sounded confused, mild frustration lacing his voice. Maeve refused to look at him. "Oh, yeah. Probably. I'd better go."

Fabric rustling against grass drew her attention up. "Already?"

He was looking out over the northern hills, rubbing the back of his neck. Was that a faint flush on his cheeks? "Yeah, I . . . Danby's grumpy if I don't come back on time."

Maeve stood as he strode for the wall. She wanted to say something, to take back what she'd said, but no words came to her. *And I don't even know if I can give him what he wants.*

By the time she reached the wall, he'd already leaped onto it. "You're coming tomorrow?" she asked, looking up at him, painfully eager to make him stay just a little longer. "Finna will be gone again. And I . . . I want to see you."

His face brightened. "I'll see you tomorrow then," he said, and then leaped over the wall and was gone.

When Finna came home later, sour-faced and silent, Maeve was diligently knitting her scarf in the kitchen and only had to remove five rows of her work.

"I worry about this cure, Maeve."

It was the following afternoon. Maeve stood in the Patrician's rooms, stirring the pot as the pungent smell engulfed her. She had said the prayer with him as always. She had tried to put everything of her into the words, as if doing so would help her to believe, help to speed up the process and hasten the cure. But the color stayed the dull, flat brown of yesterday, and hearing the Patrician's words brought up a new worry much bigger than the size of the pot itself.

"Is something wrong with it, sir?"

He stood over the brew and rubbed a hand over his trim beard. "I'm not truly sure," he said. "The parchment detailing the cure is very old. As you have seen, parts of it are worn away, and we have had to make our best guesses. But you see that the cure itself hasn't consistently changed for the past few days."

This was true, though Maeve had been too distracted to really notice recently. *Stupid Maeve, letting yourself be distracted. How could you not see?*

"I think it is time we bring our cure elsewhere," he said.

"What do you mean?"

"All this time we have worked inside. Perhaps we need to bring this cure, from nature and with the help of God, nearer to the place we are trying to heal. The blessing of God is still upon the trees, though they suffer. We shall bring the cure to the orchard."

Dismay wriggled down her throat. "What about the elements?" she protested. "How will we keep it warm?"

"We will build a shelter. Between your and Finna's attentions, I trust it will be well looked after. I will still join you every afternoon, for the prayer and the additional tasks," he said, smiling gently. "I wouldn't leave you alone in this task, Maeve. And think of how helpful this will be. You needn't leave the orchard during harvest, and I needn't send Declan from his duties. I wonder that I didn't think of this solution earlier. We will start this afternoon, as soon as the supplies are gathered."

Maeve drew a smile across her face, but her insides churned. *Will he sense Liam has been there? I can't let him find out—*

A knock on the door cut into her thoughts. Before the Patrician had finished saying "Come in," the door opened to reveal a man and child standing in the church. Maeve recognized them as the father and injured son from the day she went picking star point leaves.

With a quick, apologetic glance at Maeve, the Patrician turned to greet the arrivals. "How are you recovering, my good man?" he asked, bending low enough to address the boy eye to eye. The child held out his splinted arm proudly.

"Doesn't hurt," he said. "Is it going to be weak?"

The Patrician felt gently along the arm while the boy stood proudly, his chest thrust forward and his young face stoic. "You'll need to recover your strength when it comes off. But I have every faith you will be a strong lad very soon."

A smile revealed a missing front tooth. "That's what Dad said," the boy replied, beaming up at his father.

"Run along and wait for me in the church," the man said, "and mind you don't touch anything."

"I'll ask Thomas to show me his sword," the boy said with big eyes.

"You'll do no such thing," his father said. "You've no business asking about guards' affairs, and you're none too handy with sharp things, as you well know." He nodded at the boy's arm, and his son's face fell.

"I'm sure Thomas would be happy to show you the sword," the Patrician said, as the man frowned. "As long as you listen, you've nothing to worry about." The boy's face brightened. With a searching look at his dad, which was met with a curt nod, he went out obediently with a spring in his step.

"He's only a child," the Patrician said. "You needn't be too hard on him. I am sure he wants you to know that he's only doing his best."

Maeve stopped herself from laughing wryly. Had the Patrician never noticed Finna's subtle cruelty toward her? Even Katherine, raised indulgently by Quin's standards, had lived with a father unafraid to raise a hand against their wayward child when they saw fit.

The man stood looking at the brazier, hands thrust in his pockets. McKinnon, his name was; one of the farmers near the Campbells. His wife was a short, round woman who always bartered for apple butter.

"I don't mean to be rude, sir," Mr. McKinnon said, nodding at the cure bubbling away over its coals. "But we're still uneasy since the break-in. My wife won't leave the house unless I go with her or she can snag one of the guards to escort her. I see the new ones've arrived. Can you tell us anything new?" he asked hopefully.

"They have arrived, and we shall be well protected. Meanwhile we have a new development for the cure. I mean to have Boyle write it out and post it in the town center this very day. Don't worry." He put a hand on the farmer's shoulder. "There's been no sign of trouble up on those hills, and there never has been. With my guards about, we've nothing to worry over. Our god will heal these trees and see our safety restored soon."

This seemed to put the younger man at ease. McKinnon exhaled and nodded.

"Yes, sir, thank you. That's good to hear, sir. We don't need trouble from outsiders when all we want to do is live our lives in peace."

He doesn't know about Ragad, then. Does anyone? Maeve studied the Patrician's face and saw only the fatherly regard she knew well. What else did the expression hide?

"I'll sound like an old fool, Maeve, but that little boy reminds me of myself." He had offered McKinnon assurances and sent him out almost as bright as his son. Now the Patrician shut the door behind him with a half smile, his eyes fixed on something unseen. "When I was his age, I could not control my magic at all. It did not please my father, but he kept me safe and taught me how to manage it. I value his lessons. Come to think of it, I'm not so different from the young father, either. I see people like McKinnon and they are looking for that same safety. What kind of man would I be if I cannot keep my own children safe?"

His face was so earnest. But wasn't it always? *He may truly believe his own words, but I do not like the price he is willing to pay for that safety, especially when he himself does not pay it.*

Sudden grief coiled within her. She had recently spent every afternoon with the closest thing to a father she'd ever known. Months ago, this would have made her happier than anything, the fulfillment of a lifelong dream. Only recently had she begun to see beneath his meticulously curated appearance of concern to his duplicity, and the dull, deep weight of loss pulled at her with a sudden strength that she had to fight against. *Is anyone I know as true as they seem? Must a change in perspective always be so painful?*

Even before she crossed the bridge, Maeve could see a shape detach from one of the trees. With no one to see her run—Finna was in the village—Maeve bolted the rest of the way to the orchard and nearly collided with Liam.

"Steady." He put both hands on her arms, a perplexed and amused smile on his face. Something looked different about him. Maeve realized absently that he'd made an attempt to comb his hair. "What is it?"

Her breath came in great gasps and she must have looked worried, but the warning couldn't wait. "The Patrician is coming here," she panted. "The cure. It isn't working so he's bringing it here. He'll be here every day. I don't want you to get caught."

"Well he won't be here at once, will he?" Liam didn't take his eyes from her. No nervous glance toward Quin, no sign of his smile faltering.

"The guards are coming any minute to build a shelter. Thomas—" She choked on the name.

"Maeve, I can get away if I have to," he said. "I know how to hide. You're holding on to me like you fear I'll float away. What's wrong? Why are you so worried?"

Her hands were white-knuckled, clutching his sleeves. Probably digging into his arms. "I don't want him to hurt you."

Silence. She couldn't relax her grip on him, didn't want to. *Will he laugh at my fears? Dismiss them? Feel insulted by them?* Thomas stood a good head taller than Liam. He was older, bulkier, and had probably seen training that Liam never would. Maeve could never forget his warning when he'd walked her home, and sensed he could be ruthless in a desperate kind of way. He had the guards on his side, too, or at least Declan, who was almost as tall and considerably broader.

"You really care about me?"

The vulnerability in his voice drew her gaze to his. His brown eyes were soft and deep.

"Of course." Her shoulders uncoiled, and something ignited deep within her. "Did you think I was risking Finna's punishment just because of your scintillating conversation?"

His eyes narrowed as a smile quirked his lips. "Scintillating. Such a big word sounds like you're insulting me."

"I'm not!" A half-choked laugh escaped before she realized he was teasing her. "I do care about you, you big oaf, and I wish you would take me seriously."

That was when he kissed me.

What had I expected? I'd tried *not* to think about it when I was with Liam, tried to forget the times I'd lain awake at night unable to sleep for thinking shameful, burning thoughts. But I could never forget this. He's so slow and soft that when our noses collide it doesn't do more than give us time to pause for half a breath, and I shiver when he pulls me closer to him. His lips are soft and warm. I'm uncertain. Hesitant, having never done this before. So is he, I can tell, but only for a moment. Then the air between us crackles like lightning and I forget everything else.

I break away first, but not because I feel the tightening coil of fear. It's because this kiss feels so good and alive and new, and I am afraid that what it means will shatter between us like thin ice before a deep freeze. I want it to last. I want to store it for later. I want to live long enough to kiss him over and over again.

"I take you very seriously." He leans his forehead against mine, his voice breathless. Then: "Am I still a big oaf?"

I laugh, as breathless as he is, and gently push him away. I am grinning ear to ear as I watch him almost fall over the wall and stagger up the hills, leaping once into the air and shouting like a lunatic. I am grinning for minutes or hours, until footsteps catch my ear and I see Finna, Thomas, and Declan crossing the bridge toward me, carrying loads of things for the orchard and reminding me of the task I must never forget even for a moment.

18. Shelter

Thomas and Declan built the structure in a few hours, and then stayed in the orchard.

Eventually Finna marched under the archway to speak with them. Maeve couldn't hear anything, but the young men's faces didn't look promising. The moment Finna left the orchard, her nostrils flared and mouth pressed thin, Declan rolled his eyes and Thomas made a rude gesture at her back.

"Stupid boys," Finna muttered in a rare show of vociferousness. She began scrubbing the already-clean kitchen counter with enough force to shave off a layer of wood. "They've been ordered to stay overnight, or so they say. Well then. We'll have a few words with our good Patrician tomorrow. They won't stay in my orchard for long."

Maeve remained silent, secretly hoping Finna would win this fight. It felt wrong to see them lounging against the wall of her favorite, safest place. She wondered if their bedrolls would leave permanent dents in the grass overnight or if they would leave a mess. And she had two other worries: What if they saw Whistle streak past on one of his visits to the Cú Sidhe? Or worse, if Liam was foolhardy enough to try and visit and came face-to-face with them? The last thing she wanted was for anything connected to them or Lochlyn to arouse Thomas and Declan's curiosity.

She tried to pray for Liam's safety, wondering if this god, whom she felt less certain of every day, could bring himself to care for someone who didn't follow his ways. *Would he hear prayers on behalf of someone who belongs to two different peoples? Or would he even listen to any prayer not written years ago in the first place, no matter how heartfelt, no matter who it is for?*

Her anxiety had not lessened the following rainy morning, when Finna forbade her from performing the ritual watering. Having to stay inside at this time of day made her feel itchy and restless. Her foster mother held her sharp chin high and pointedly ignored the "boys" for the duration of the task. Only when the Patrician stood in front of the shelter the next afternoon, watching as two accompanying guards arranged the pot, brazier, and several other accoutrements beneath it, did Finna allow Maeve to set foot outside the cottage.

Finna made an announcement to the Patrician without preamble. "I want them gone."

"They are here for your protection, Finna. Surely you can see that."

"I don't need these boys around with Maeve in the house."

Maeve, who kept her eyes downcast during this whole exchange, stopped herself from looking at Finna. *Perhaps she is wiser about Thomas than I first thought.*

"With the cure here, I wouldn't like to leave anything or anyone open to surprise outside interference, which my men are more than capable of fighting, should the need arise. You needn't fear a lack of their integrity." The Patrician's tone suggested a carefully suppressed impatience.

"And your bronze vessel?" Finna said. "Is the integrity of your magic insufficient?"

It was the fourth vessel in as many days.

The Patrician gave a long, slow sigh. "I understand that this has been your domain for all your life. Give me two days, I beg of you. If the cure has progressed sufficiently by tomorrow afternoon, I will recall these fine soldiers to other posts, and you can go about your affairs unhindered."

Now Maeve could not help looking up to watch the two adults. A muscle twitched in Finna's lean jaw. The Patrician looked wearier than ever. For a moment, some of her old sympathy for him leaped into her heart before she could strangle it back down.

"Very well." Finna spared a glance for Maeve. "Come home directly after," she commanded, then left. In the silence that followed, the door latch falling into place sounded loud and displeased.

The Patrician's tired smile did not quite reach his eyes. "Shall we begin? I would hate to keep your foster mother waiting any longer than she expects."

She performed the prayer, focusing all her energy on the words while trying to block out the discomfort of four soldiers standing nearby. When she was done, her eyes flew open to study the cure.

As the day was fine, it sat in the shadow of the structure rather than inside it. The wooden shelter was just big enough for the brazier and pot. Its sides were enclosed, and the guards had built a removable, flat roof of wooden slats for enclosing the whole thing off in the event of rain. The steam simmered from it and disappeared into the still-blue sky. Maeve pretended to study the smoke, though she was really searching the hills for any sign of Liam or Whistle.

My last words to him should have been "Don't forget to stay away."

The kiss had rather made her forget. *Now is not the time!* Maeve fought the rising warmth in her cheeks and turned her attention back to the Patrician.

"Do you really think it will improve by tomorrow, sir?"

"I do believe it will." The Patrician pointed at the contents of the pot. "Can you smell it? It is sweeter already. This was the right thing to do."

He left soon after, leaving the two new guards as relief for Declan and Thomas. Maeve watched him go. His steps seemed slower than ever, his back almost bent. Was he ill? *Perhaps he will die and I'll never have to see him again. Perhaps—*

Alarmed, Maeve sucked in a breath. Where did such a terrible thought come from? She wanted him gone, not dead. Though she had lost her trust in the Patrician, years of being made to respect her elders would not disappear in a matter of days. She walked back home, reciting her usual prayer under her breath so quickly she'd repeated it three times before crossing the threshold.

Maeve could hardly believe it: Finna was sending her to Katherine's house at last.

The Patrician's prediction of the cure proved true, first of all. The brew had lightened from the color of a stormy sky to ashen gray, and despite its pale, weak appearance, he declared it as following the cure's description. He pronounced the change sufficient and removed both soldiers from the orchard.

Secondly, Maeve suspected that Finna had grown tired of having Maeve always underfoot. The house had never been so well scrubbed as it had the past few days, and Finna had temporarily run out of errands for herself. So when the Patrician departed and Finna announced there were enough loaves of apple bread for the Monaghan household and Maeve may as well take them now, Maeve didn't question it. She accepted the loaves, threw her shawl around her, and schooled her steps into a sedate but brisk pace.

The village hummed with nervous energy. New soldiers stood at Quin's gates on either side of the stone apples, at nearly every street corner, and at the doors of the church. The ludicrousness of how fortified everything was compared to the orchard struck her. *So much faith in a bronze apple and a pot of stewing herbs.* Would she share this faith so ardently if she hadn't met those deemed wild and unsafe? She felt a quickening of gratitude that Orlenn and the clan were wise enough to keep away. Even so, she couldn't help but wonder: *Did their ancestors attack Quin? Why would they? I wish it wasn't so hard to separate the past from lies.*

Soon, though, she stood before Katherine's house, breathing a sigh of relief and anticipation.

But the look on Katherine's face when she answered the door sent that relief away.

"Oh," Kate said. "It's you." She stood aside for Maeve to enter.

At first Maeve was too surprised and perplexed to speak. Katherine's hair sprang from her low knot and her apron looked rumpled and stained, something that never would have happened to the girl Maeve knew. Katherine led the way into the kitchen and stood there, clasping and unclasping her hands.

"I brought your bread," Maeve said. "Finna is happy for the lace you'd promised."

Katherine looked from the window she'd been staring out of. "Lace," she said, distractedly. "If those Ragad folks hadn't decided to stop trading with us, we'd have lace."

Maeve knew little of trading, but she knew enough to say with confidence that the Ragad did not trade in that textile. This was not the time to point that out, however. Worry expanded as she watched her friend, so anxious and unlike her usual happy, elusive self. "Katherine, what's wrong?"

"Nothing. Nothing. Here." Moving past Maeve's outstretched hand, Katherine brushed down the hallway.

In a snug sitting room at the back of her house, she rifled through a basket of sewing notions before abandoning that and turning to a shelf of knickknacks and books. Maeve had little time to take in the elaborately carved wooden chairs, the woven rug in shades of red, black, green, and blue on the stone floor, the upholstered couch. It would have been the room of Katherine's dreams. But wrinkles bunched up a corner of the rug and a thin layer of dust filmed the contents of the shelves. The sewing notions appeared to have fallen over and left on the couch and floor.

"Katherine." Maeve put a hand on her friend's arm. "We don't need the lace, if it's any bother. Conlan paid us enough. Just tell me. What is troubling you? Is it Conlan's business?"

Katherine's frantic search stopped and a line formed between her eyebrows. She dropped the notions on the sofa and seized Maeve's hands, meeting her gaze at last. "Maeve," she said, sounding as if she hadn't known her best friend stood in her house until this exact moment. "Maeve, you are still my friend, aren't you?"

"Whyever wouldn't I be?" *Please, please tell me what's wrong. This isn't like you.* "I will always be your friend, as long as we live."

Katherine released her and glanced down, biting her lip. "Another time, I'd ask you about the orchard, and the boy, and everything else. I wish things didn't have to change." Her pretty face puckered as if she were about to cry. These words would have brought Maeve such relief in other circumstances. Hearing her friend voice her own wishes and acknowledge things had changed, should have meant a return to their old jokes and secrets, to running errands and mending clothes together. But Maeve waited tensely as if Katherine were a frightened horse she didn't want to spook.

"Everything is—" A sound arrested Katherine's attention, and her eyes went wide. "You have to go," she whispered. She seized Maeve's hand and almost dragged her to a door at the back of the room.

"Katherine, what's wrong? Tell me!" Maeve cried. "Who are you afraid of?"

But Katherine, suddenly strong, flung open the door and shoved Maeve through it. "Go, Maeve. I mean it."

Maeve stared at the back of Katherine's house until boots sounded on the narrow back alley. She didn't wait to see if it was a soldier. There was nothing else for her to do but go home.

"What's got you looking like a drowned rat?" Finna asked.

The sappy, syrupy smell of boiled apples filled the kitchen. Maeve stirred the pot over the kitchen fire and hoped she hadn't scorched the apple butter. Finna had gathered the last of the apples while she was at Katherine's, and the smaller harvest was painfully evident. There wouldn't be enough for another batch if she ruined this one.

"Katherine doesn't seem like herself," Maeve said. Was there a prayer for apple butter, like a prayer for the cure? Or was it too mundane a task despite the apples' source?

Who is my friend afraid of? Was it really Conlan?

"Hm." Finna was drying the jars they'd gathered most recently from the villagers eager for this last taste of Quin's precious apples. She held one up at the kitchen window and squinted at it as if polishing a fine lady's looking glass. "Just a newlywed tiff. They'll probably sort it out." Her sardonic tone suggested she didn't think much of the tiff or their methods of resolving it.

"I don't think it was." Maeve was too preoccupied to be surprised at herself for contradicting Finna.

Do all marriages turn sour? And why did you never marry?

If it was Conlan Katherine feared, the marriage hadn't just turned sour. She watched her foster mother set down the last jar and begin cutting the handful of apples on the counter. *Perhaps she was wise not to marry. But I still wonder why.*

"I think it's time we consider your betrothal." *Slip, slip* went Finna's knife.

"What?" Despite her train of thought, the change in conversation was so sudden that at first Maeve wasn't sure she'd heard correctly. "I thought you said we could wait until the spring."

"Surely someone's caught your eye. The Campbell lad, perhaps."

If Maeve hadn't been so distraught, she would have had to hide a smile at the thought. Brody Campbell was thin, serious, and had probably forgotten she existed once they'd both left school two springs ago. Maeve's grip tightened on the spoon handle, panic bubbling up within her like the contents of the pot.

"There's no one in Quin, Finna. I promise." *Not entirely a lie, but still—*

"We might look beyond Quin. Ferre or Dumar. Or even another village."

"But why now? And besides, who marries anyone beyond the Patrician's rule? I thought it wasn't done."

"Sometimes it is done."

"But the other villages are so far away," Maeve said. How far away, she had no idea. She had always known that marriage was inevitable. But so soon! Fear of being sent to Cromwell House, of failing her beloved trees had occupied her—when she wasn't thinking of Liam. She wasn't sure she could bear to leave the orchard when it was the only place of safety she had ever truly known. The present and the future suddenly felt so tangled and overwhelming, like a giant ball of rough yarn pressing against her whole being.

She tried to pull solace from the heat of the flames as she swallowed back tears.

"There is someone here. I've seen the look on your face, Maeve." Finna cast her a glance. "Don't deny it."

Of course she knew. *Stupid, stupid Maeve! Thinking I could escape her hawk-sharp eyes!*

She sputtered, "I do like him, but—but does that mean I have to marry him? Finna, I'm too young!"

"If you like him, you could do worse. Tell me who it is. I will speak with his parents."

"No." Maeve's limbs felt heavy, her whole body imprisoned in an all-too-familiar stiff sensation. But her voice had loosed itself. The deeply ingrained practice of accepting what had been given to her was no longer possible: her restraint was vanishing, dissolving like the false apple in its cupboard.

Finna's hand with the knife stilled. "What?"

"I said I won't tell you his name." She stood shaking, eyes wide against Finna's steel-edged voice.

Finna turned to face her with icy calm. "You, girl, will do as I say."

"All my life I've done as you say, but it's never enough!" The words poured through Maeve, fire melting years of ice. Her arms tingled with a rising anger that was foreign and satisfying. Perhaps it had always been there; she had never let herself look. She watched Finna's profile become even stiffer with shock and forged ahead. "You're trying to get rid of me, aren't you? I've always been a burden to you! You gave me your name but never your love. You're afraid I'll turn out just like you, bitter and alone. But I won't. I will never be like you!"

Ferocity exploded across Finna's features. "What do you know of me?" she hissed, a cornered animal, a fire spitting fat and sparks. "How do you know what is good for you? Do you think it is easy to be unmarried in this town? Do you think I would enjoy a shred of respect if my family had not left me with the guardianship of this orchard? Do you think love will protect you when you are my age and alone, or will it be my family name that keeps you safe?"

"The Patrician is looking for my real family. And when he finds them, even if the orchard dies, I will have a place to go. And do you know, I don't have to bring you with me."

"Is that so?" Finna's nostrils flared and her eyes flashed. "Then I hope they welcome you, Maeve, even knowing you refuse to live by the principles of the very village that took you in. I hope your shared blood is enough to cover your defiance. You will need every ounce of it."

The anger drained from Maeve like warmth from a dying hearth, leaving her cold and hollow.

Finna couldn't know about her secret night meetings, or Maeve would have paid for it long ago. She wasn't sure whether that made her words better or worse. Because even if Finna remained ignorant, her outburst proved what Maeve had already known: that even doing her best would never be enough.

Finna sighed. She turned back to the counter and hunched over it. "Go see if Duffy has his jars ready yet. He's had enough time."

"Now? I thought—"

"Just go, Maeve." Finna's voice lacked her earlier ferocity. It was so quiet that Maeve, who felt a leap of bitter triumph at the sound, struggled with a secondary, odd sensation as she pulled on her shawl and left.

She did not want to feel any sadness for this hard, changeable woman who had raised her without the one thing she wanted more than anything in the world.

19. Attacks

Maeve could reach the blacksmith in a quarter hour or less and be back in just as little time, if Duffy was not busy with a task. But the sharp taste of her own words sat on her tongue like the first bite of food after growing weak from hunger. She did not want to go where Finna told her to go just yet.

She had refused to name Liam not just for his connection to Lochlyn. Just for once, she wanted to keep something secret and delicious for herself, something her foster mother could not sift through and extract.

Liam might not be here much longer if he goes with Lochlyn. The thought was uncharacteristically future-oriented and she did not like it. She pushed it away as she passed the smithy and turned up the street leading toward Boyle's post and the shepherd's gate. She didn't entertain the possibility that Liam was somewhere else, didn't spare a thought for the fact that she had no idea where he kept his flock, just as she pointedly ignored the church on her way past. She avoided Katherine's street easily, though not without a brief, sharp pang of worry and grief.

But there were some things she could not ignore: Finna's words burned in her mind, repeating over and over like lashings that left her bruised and dissolved her own triumph into ash. *You refuse to live by the principles of the very village that took you in. Defiance.*

She may have just as well said, "There is something not right with you and everyone knows it."

I never meant to be defiant. I just wanted to be loved. Can't you see that, Finna? I just want to be seen for who I am and loved in spite of that. But whether I do good or bad, it doesn't seem to make a difference. It's never enough to draw love close and it is always out of my reach.

She reached the top of the street feeling heavy as an anvil, her longing so amplified that even Boyle's cheerful greeting wouldn't have lifted her spirits.

Boyle wasn't in sight, at his post or otherwise. But Liam was. And everything else settled into the back of her mind.

He was leading his flock down the hill, Whistle yipping and darting round the sheep, much like she'd seen them the first time. She drew up to the fence and waited for him to reach her. The hum of activity in the street behind her, the bleating of sheep, and the intermittent yapping of dogs hidden among the hills, all seemed to fall away.

Liam gripped the railing with one hand and ruffled Whistle's ears with the other. The sheep accepted their new place and began pulling at the short grass.

"Maeve." His grin flashed and faltered. "What is it?"

Maeve felt too many things to name at once: relief and tender fear and a flash of longing. It was too much to contain or speak of. Without finding the latch in the gate she set the basket down and climbed over the fence, stumbling into the green pasture. She threw her arms around Liam with such force that the two of them swung around, a surprised sound of delight escaping him as they found their footing. Maeve rested her head against his neck and brushed away strands of hair that most definitely smelled of sheep and green grass and clean air.

"Hm." His arms closed around her. It was the most glorious feeling she'd ever experienced.

"I'm glad you stayed away," she said.

He chuckled. "You're welcome, I suppose. And I'm glad you're here."

Liam's arms tightened around her, but Maeve heard voices again. People still walked the streets. Over Liam's shoulder, she could see rows of houses spilled down the hill toward the village center, and a handful of businesses, too. Most folks didn't pay attention to the shepherd's gate unless they were looking for Boyle, but the wooden fence left them exposed. She didn't want anyone tattling to Finna. She leaned back and stepped out of his arms, searching his face.

The moment shifted. Liam's expression lacked his usual boldness, though it was hardly evident. Maeve, who had grown up sensitive to the faintest changes in Finna's moods, could see something was troubling him by the way his grin had already faded. "What is it?"

"There's been several attacks on the animals since yesterday," he replied. He sounded reluctant to speak of it or believe his own words. "The shepherds are fine. My sheep are fine. But they're scared, human and animal. Danby lost three sheep, almost from under his nose. He'd fallen asleep on a hill and woke up to chaos and blood. But even he didn't see anything. This creature doesn't seem interested in humans."

"Or just didn't have time for a sneak attack," Maeve countered.

Liam's brow furrowed and he glanced down the street, the way Maeve had come. "They sent me to wait for the Patrician."

"Why?"

"He sent word earlier today that he'd come to the hills and look around. Probably set out some protections." Faint disgust curled his lip. "I drew the short straw."

"There has never been an attack on the sheep before. What could it be?"

"Not the Cú Sidhe," came his answer, quick and almost sharp.

"I want to believe you, Liam. But how can you be sure?"

"You don't believe me? Two nights ago, Maeve, Aodh fought with another creature. It must've escaped. The noise woke up half the clan, who found evidence of a scuffle. I wasn't there when it happened, but Orlenn looked grim when she told me about it."

"But if the rotten apples are weakening Quin's defenses . . ." Maeve shifted uncomfortably. "I don't believe the Cú Sidhe are evil. But they are wild. They are animals who must eat and Orlenn said the clan doesn't control them."

She had a sudden thought. *Does Orlenn know of all wild beasts living on the downs?* But even the chief had given her the impression that whatever else lived out there on the hills belonged to their own set of rules and Lochlyn had little to do with them. If they were connected, as Orlenn had said at the night of the dance, then it was a connection held together by mutual respect and leaving one another alone for the most part.

"You'd better go before he gets here." Liam dropped his voice. "We should find out what's attacking the flocks."

Maeve looked around, worried someone would overhear. "Tonight?" she whispered. Liam nodded. "Go to Lochlyn with this unknown animal roaming? I thought they don't know what it is."

Liam shrugged. "What if they do by now? I was going tomorrow night anyway. We can go tonight instead. It's better than sitting up here doing nothing."

"I don't think . . ." Maeve began, but she trailed off at the image of her and Liam running through the night, alone and full of purpose. But more pressing matters reinserted themselves in her mind. "Is it safe?"

"I have some . . . things I can do. To protect us. Breena taught me some skills and made me practice until I could do them perfectly before I left." He stifled a yawn suddenly, as if remembering how long the practice had kept him from his bed. "I wouldn't let anything happen to you, Maeve."

It was a lovely offer, one she wanted with all her heart to believe. "You do believe in magic, then?" she said. "Enough to trust it would keep us from getting eaten?"

He looked away and ruffled his hair, oddly silent.

"I'll go." *Because I trust him. And I miss him.* What other reasons did she need?

At her reply, Liam's face brightened. "Tonight, then," he said. Leaning in, he took her hands in his and whispered, "Then will you kiss me again?"

Without waiting for an answer, he ran back up the hill, Whistle trotting at his heels. It was not the giddy stagger from the orchard, but Maeve felt as if her chest expanded with lightness to know that, despite these dire new developments, she was still the cause of his elation.

The smithy was strangely quiet.

The smoke from the fire billowed up through the chimney like a troubled spirit seeking escape, but otherwise, all was still. Maeve looked timidly around the darkened interior. *Perhaps he's left the jars out somewhere while he's on an errand. Duffy would not mind if I took them and left without speaking to him, would he?*

Difficult as it was to imagine the taciturn blacksmith as anything other than relieved to avoid conversation, Maeve felt reticent to scour the depths of the shop. The bellows lay on the anvil near the fire, and various tools hung from the walls: tongs, hammers, a large axe, two or three punches, and numerous other things Maeve did not know the names of. There were a handful of picks and chisels, which she had seen Duffy use on replacement stones for the walls beyond the orchard. He had never used it directly on the orchard wall.

The light dimmed behind her. Maeve turned to see the hulking blacksmith standing in the doorway leading to another street, his tremendous arms filled with delicate jars.

"Oh, yes," Maeve said, trying not to appear as startled as she felt. "The jars. Finna sent me. Thank you. I'll take them now."

She watched as one by one, Duffy set them down on the table with great care, all the while watching her beneath jutting brows. Maeve felt like she had swallowed all the soot in the air. She carefully placed the jars in her basket, gritting her teeth as they rattled against one another. "We'll bring the jellies soon, if you want."

"Sauce." The one word rumbled from the massive chest, then another. "Please."

"Of course," Maeve stuttered. "Good day."

To her leaping alarm, Duffy blocked her exit in a movement surprisingly fluid for one of his size. He bent down until he was looking her square in the eye and spoke in a voice that was softer but no less terrifying. "Be careful."

"Well, Maeve!" Boyle said, peeking over the blacksmith's shoulder. The sight was comical as Boyle was a head shorter. "It's good to see you both, though I heartily wish I had better news to bring." The head guard's usually smiling eyes were lined and his broad smile didn't quite lift his whole face.

"Here're the knives, Duffy," Boyle continued. He stepped round and deposited a heavy, bulging sack near the forge, and dusted off his hands. "Patrician brought 'em out himself. Wants them sharpened so the shepherds all have an extra blade between them and—" He blustered a moment.

"I heard about the attacks, Boyle," Maeve said, putting him out of his misery. *Please don't ask how, though.*

"You did? Saints. Word travels fast. Makes my job easier, at least." He didn't look relieved, though.

"What animal do you think it is? Is the Patrician really coming to set protections around the pastures?" Maeve asked, reminding herself silently to ask Liam what that entailed.

"We're too far from the forests for it to be a wolf. It's something else. Some monster of the wild men." Boyle's face darkened.

"Has anyone ever seen a creature from the downs?"

"Not that I know of. I suppose those horned beasts of the Ragad don't count." He chuckled nervously. Duffy, who had gone back to the forge, began pumping the bellows, but seemed to still be listening. "What makes you ask all these questions today, eh, Maeve?"

Her heart began beating quickly. Despite this, she pressed on. "There is so much we have been told about but never seen. Has anyone seen the wild men or their beasts?" *What are you doing, Maeve? What are you getting at?*

"We've heard them." This, from Duffy.

Both Maeve and Boyle regarded him as he continued, "no one has seen them for fifty years or more. But we know."

The Lord Protector's letter came to her mind. What really happened in Dumar? Did wild men really lay siege to that village, or was it all fabricated to put the Lord Protector's rule in a good light?

Maeve thought she wouldn't be able to fall asleep that night. But a tapping at her window roused her, bringing temporary confusion as she stared up at her bedroom ceiling. *Is it the apple? Wild beasts, the downs—*

There was another noise outside, and it took her a moment to recognize Liam's voice and remember their plans. She could just barely see his silhouetted form below. She waved frantically through the glass. *Stay there, I'll meet you.*

Half a minute later she was dressed and through the door, listening as always for any sound of Finna stirring in her sleep. The night air greeted her, chill and damp and smelling of rain, as she scurried around the cottage and found Liam.

"I want to show you something before we go," he whispered without preamble. Up close, she could see him smile at the sight of her, and she wondered if he would make good on his last question then and there. But his stance was taut, ready to run. The smile became a look of concentration. With a few spoken words, Liam held out his hands. Suddenly the air vibrated with a sound so deep and so high that Maeve thought she'd lost her hearing inside the church bell.

"There. I've just alerted Lochlyn we're coming. If we don't get there in good timing, someone will come fetch us."

Maeve shook her head. The ringing sensation in her ears subsided to the whine of a fly's wings.

If Lochlyn heard it, then probably only Lochlyn could hear it.

"Let's go," Liam said. "I don't think we should be out till sunrise tonight."

She hardly disagreed on that point. And when he put out his hand, she took it firmly and followed him down to the nearest slope with the niche leading down to the little pool.

The aftereffects of Liam's "device," as he called it, had worn off, but the night seemed full of strange sounds humming in the shadows. Maeve took Liam's apparent calm as a good sign and tried to keep her thoughts on the task ahead.

"I've been thinking," she whispered as they made their way across a thin ridge before plunging into the shadows again. "Could the Ragad clan be behind this somehow? Has Orlenn or the others ever spoken about them?"

"They visited the camp, once."

"And what happened?"

"I wasn't privy to it. But—" He froze suddenly and backed against a rock, pulling her with him. Maeve was wise enough to remain quiet. Still, the shadow that emerged a short distance away made her heart leap into her throat.

A tall creature on four legs stood before them, its massive head lifted, listening. Even as she desperately hoped it was one of the Cú Sidhe, she knew there was little chance of that. It was bristling with horns, for one thing; and when the half-moon came out from behind a cloud, it illuminated large, liquid eyes and a short, stiff coat.

One of the Ragad's mounts. She began to relax. But Liam's arm remained tight around her. She was on the verge of growing annoyed with him when a snarl tangled in the air.

A great, hulking shadow emerged from behind a clump of bushes. It, too, stood on all fours, but it was crouched low and the moonlight did not illuminate its other features. It circled the first animal, a low, thrumming growl in its throat, and Maeve and Liam pressed even closer against the rock. Whatever this newcomer was, it seemed intent on attacking. She hoped the horned creature would flee in time, but it just stood there dumbly.

Then the horned creature's lips curled back to reveal red gums and pointed teeth. With a high, keening cry, it leaped forward. Before it could move at all, the smaller creature gave a twisted yelp of pain as sharp teeth sank into its hide.

The sound was horrific. Maeve shut her eyes tight against the bloodbath. The keening cry was gone, but the tortured cries and yelps of the prey mingled with the sound of ripping and shredding and growling.

Liam was tugging on her arm, dragging her away. She bolted blindly. When they had slipped between two bushes she hazarded a glance back and immediately wished she hadn't. Images of teeth and horns worrying bloodied flesh brought the gorge into her throat. The sound followed Maeve and Liam long after they'd rounded the next rising hill.

Unlike on the night of the dance, quiet blanketed the camp. A fire burned low at the center of the huts, and only one or two people stood guard. Or so Maeve thought. Whenever she turned to look at them directly, the shadows seemed to quiver and melt, leaving her wondering if she'd imagined seeing someone. There was no sign of the Cú Sidhe, though she scanned the spaces between the huts with the fervency of a saint seeking her benefactor.

Was that a Cú Sidhe that died just now? The question sat on her tongue in this slumbering place. Liam released her hand as they approached Orlenn's hut and knocked on the door. He knew so much more about this world they'd stepped into than she did, and she wondered if she would ever understand it. *Life is far more confusing since I crossed the orchard wall.*

The door opened to reveal Orlenn. "You are hours too early," she said, although her voice sounded just as alert as if they had arrived at noon. Her long braid slung over one shoulder and the broach glistening on her other, she looked like a queen despite her humble clothes. The chief took note of Maeve. "And you have brought a visitor again. I can see by your faces that something unpleasant brought you here." She turned, leaving the door open. Liam, who seemed to understand this was an unspoken invitation, beckoned for Maeve to follow him into the stone hut.

A fire in the hearth cast a warm, golden glow about the place. It was small and comfortably, if sparsely, furnished.

Orlenn set down two steaming drinks and remained standing, her hands settling behind her back. The light flickered in her brown eyes. "You're here about the Cú Sidhe, aren't you?"

"How did you know?" Liam asked, not even noticing the drink.

"I'm surprised you came all this way just to hear my thoughts, Liam, with the Cú Sidhe so restless of late. Has your faith in magic suddenly grown?"

Liam was silent, but a look of barely quelled defiance passed across his face. The chief sent him a piercing glance.

"I know no more than you about what is happening on the downs, save that you would do well to respect it. I had planned to send you a message, but I will tell you here: do not endanger yourself by coming here again at night. You are welcome to join us in the daytime. I am aware of the difficulties that poses. But you cannot be so foolish again. The same goes for you." She glanced at Maeve, who nodded obediently in reply.

The walk back was quiet and tense. Maeve put her hand in Liam's, both wanting his support and knowing he needed hers. She thought of the defiance in his face when the chief had asked him about his faith in magic, and she wondered again why he seemed so closed-lipped about it. Surely he would have spoken to the chief about his uncertainty regarding such an integral part of Lochlyn life, yet he was clearly anything but resolved.

Though they watched carefully, the only sign of animals they saw were footprints at the base of one hill. Liam led them far around the place where the attack had occurred, and Maeve shuddered to remember it.

At last the village came into view. Maeve tugged on his hand and steered him toward the cottage rather than through the orchard, wanting to keep in the shadow cast there by the moonlight. With their backs to the southern wall of her house they stood side by side and looked out over the downs, their hands tightly clasped. *So many lies told about the people who live there. They are strange, but not bad. They are different, but they are only people.*

"Liam," she whispered, "what did the chief mean, about your faith in magic?"

She felt him shrug. "I don't like not understanding things, Maeve. You know what I think about magic. I know one thing: if I choose Lochlyn, there's no going back. No one in Quin will accept a Lochlyn shepherd on their hills. Not even good old Boyle."

"And what would you—"

A sound cut her off, a low growl that made the hairs on her neck stand up. *Has a wild creature followed us?* She gripped Liam's hand tighter and dropped her voice until it was barely audible. "Did you hear that?"

He nodded in response. A series of furious head shaking and gestures between them followed, in which Maeve refused to release his hand despite his attempts to push her around the corner of the cottage.

I'm not sneaking back into my cottage and leaving you alone if something dangerous is this close to you and my trees. If you need to use your magic, now is the time to do it.

Liam may not have understood all of her silent protestations, but after running his other hand through his wild hair in frustration, he conceded in keeping her hand in his. A faint light burned once in his palm and melted away, leaving a faint, bitter taste in the air. He wasn't approaching the unknown unprepared.

They neared the babbling stream by way of the old cottages, with the bridge some distance above them to their left. When Maeve cast a look down the hill on her right, the moonlight revealed the hollow in the earth into which the stream disappeared.

But she stopped at the same time Liam did.

The form lay near a pile of fallen stones, so close and shadow-riddled that at first she'd mistaken it for part of the landscape. It wasn't an animal. A person lay on the earth. As Maeve hesitated for a moment, Liam released her and darted forward. She heard his sharp intake of breath.

"Come here. Hurry."

Maeve stifled her own gasp at the sight. "Duffy?"

The blacksmith groaned again as Liam knelt to get a closer look.

But Maeve saw enough from her position: dark liquid ran down the man's broad chest and side, welling from a vicious wound.

"He needs help now." Liam tore his sleeve off and pressed it to the wound. "Run, Maeve. He might not make it if you don't."

20. Duress

The stream was too wide for Maeve to cross. Her feet carried her back toward the cottage and up the rise, until she skidded to a halt at the bridge, remembering the newly-stationed guard at the village entrance. *Would the guard have seen me come from beneath the bridge rather than my home?* She shook her head. *It doesn't matter. Duffy is dying, and there is only one other person with the skill to save a life.*

She tore over the bridge, her shod feet ringing against wood in the quiet night, and almost tripped over something in the doorway.

"Steady!" A male voice, fuzzy with sleep, slurred as long legs picked themselves off the cobblestones. A tall, thin guard Maeve couldn't recognize towered over her. His face was half obscured in shadow, but she could see his youthful features and hear the suspicion in his voice. He wasn't a guard she recognized, but at least he wasn't Thomas. "What're you doing at this time of night? That's against the rules."

"A man's been attacked," she said breathlessly. "He needs help at once. I was going to get it."

"I'll repeat my question, miss. What were you doing outside at this time of night?"

"I heard a noise and went to make sure the orchard was safe." Maeve fisted her trembling hands at her side.

"Right. I'm alerting the Patrician." Long, rough fingers seized her arm. "You're coming with me."

But Maeve jerked away, aided by the rush of urgency and fearing for Liam's discovery if she couldn't warn him. "Alert the Patrician, as you should," she replied. "The blacksmith has been attacked by a wild beast, do you understand? He'll bleed to death!"

"The blacksmith?" repeated the guard, still groggy. He craned his neck as if trying to see, but the old cottages hid Duffy from view, and Liam too, mercifully. "Who's to say you aren't just making this up for a bit of trouble?"

"There isn't time for this!"

The guard folded his arms and sighed. "Now, you're a bit hysterical for this time of night, hm? Why don't you go back to sleep and I won't tell the Patrician you were outside after dark." Anger laced the edges of his patronizing tone.

Maeve huffed her frustration, searching for an answer amidst her fearful bafflement and wishing she didn't find it so difficult to put words together while under duress. "A man is dying and you call me hysterical," she sputtered. "If you—if I am lying and the Patrician finds out, I'll pay for it, not you. But if the Patrician finds out that the person responsible for mending your weapons has died because—because you were asleep at your post, you'll suffer for it!"

He shifted. After an agonizing moment of silence, he heaved another long-suffering sigh. "All right, all right. I'll go. Don't get so agitated, miss. I'm on my way."

"Hurry!" Maeve hissed at his retreating back. "Or you'll have a man's blood to account for!"

She waited until he disappeared around a bend in the street, then tore back down to Duffy and Liam. The shepherd's sleeve lay soaked in crimson on the ground. "Don't." Maeve stopped him from tearing his other sleeve off. "Let me. Or they will wonder how I stopped the bleeding with someone else's clothes."

She tore a wide strip from the hem of her dress. Then, with a little guidance from Liam, pressed the fabric against

Duffy's wound. She shuddered when he groaned, his eyes shut tight and his breathing rapid. "I don't want to hurt him," she whispered.

Liam shook his head. "He's already in pain, Maeve. Those are bite marks on his side."

She failed to suppress a shiver. "You have to go. I told the guard I was inspecting the orchard, but you have no good reason for being out here so late."

"I could say I was searching for the beast that attacked the sheep."

Duffy groaned, his head turning from side to side. Maeve reached tentatively with her free hand and patted his uninjured shoulder.

"Shh," she said. "Help is coming." She turned back to Liam. "Please," she urged, "it's too risky. I will be fine alone." This lie faltered the moment it left her lips. *I am terrified of him dying, for myself as much as for him.*

But to her surprise, Liam didn't argue. He rose swiftly. "I'll find a way to see you soon," he promised. "But I'm waiting for the guard to come. You shouldn't be alone out here. I'll keep out of sight. Don't worry."

He slipped away into the shadows, and Maeve did nothing but worry as profusely as the blood soaking her hands through the cloth. "Please don't die," she whispered. "Please stay awake."

The minutes stretched interminably. Maeve stripped another piece of fabric, making sure this one was wider, and replaced the soaked one. Uncomfortable questions raised their heads in her mind. *Is it the same beast who's been killing sheep? And why was the blacksmith here, of all places, in the middle of the night?* Familiar prayers begging for protection rolled off her tongue. She had no prayers for healing a man who lay dying.

Duffy's moans became wisps of words. He began to turn his head back and forth again, agitation increasing. "I'm here," Maeve said, worry clamping down on her in a fresh wave. "The Patrician is bringing help. You'll be all right."

Duffy's head stilled. His eyes opened and focused on her. In the moonlight, his eyes looked wild, though with pain or the throes of death, Maeve couldn't tell. His eyes widened. His distress must be growing.

"What is it?" Maeve leaned forward to listen, trying to force her stomach not to rebel at the hot, coppery scent of gore.

Duffy muttered a slew of unintelligible words until one formed, crystalline as hardened honey. "Danger." The word burst raw and wet from his mouth. "Stone. The apples. Stop—you must—"

He coughed harshly and fell silent, his breath stirring her hair. Maeve drew back with a racing heart.

Heavy footsteps on the bridge made her look up. The Patrician descended the hill, flanked by several guards. Maeve felt weak with relief.

"God have mercy," the Patrician breathed. He bent down to examine him for a moment, then stood. With a wave of his hand, the soldiers surrounded and lifted the man from the ground and bore him away. "How did you find him, Maeve?"

She recognized the guard from the side entrance among the others. He must have told the Patrician his own version of her story, and she was almost grateful for the chance to tell it again. *Even if it's laced with lies.*

"I thought I heard something and went to check on the orchard."

She shuddered. Cold seeped into her skin, and her hands were sticky with blood. She couldn't stop shaking. The Patrician nodded patiently and waited. The guards carried Duffy up the hill and toward Quin amidst grunts and the clatter of boots against stone. The sound faded to silence. "I knew it was a human cry, not an animal, and I—I found him." Her voice failed her.

"It's fortunate that you did. I must go at once to stitch and clean his wounds. Go and clean yourself and get some rest. I'm sorry you'll be the one to break the news to Finna and not I, but it cannot be helped."

"Can you save him?"

The Patrician didn't pause his stride. As he crossed the bridge he spoke, his voice rising above the persistent rush of water: "If God wills it, Maeve. If he wills it."

Cries howl throughout my restless dreams. Sometimes they are human; other times, animal. Both are so twisted with pain and rage that I shake like apple tree branches in a winter gale. I wake to a watery gray light, my thoughts trampling through my mind, as if they have never stopped and never will. What if I drew Duffy's attacker by entering the downs last night? I am not of Lochlyn or any other clan. At least, I don't think I am. I would chafe with impatience, waiting for word from Dumar, if there weren't other, closer concerns that worry my head. I wonder again if Ragad would set one of their horned mounts on us as punishment for being pushed away from Quin's commerce. But why would they? And why would they go after Duffy? As far as I know, he never gave them any cause for grief.

I push myself out of bed and shiver as my feet touch the cold floor. My mind is as full of thoughts as the downs are full of strange beasts, and I hardly understand the first better than the second. I shiver into my second dress and go to the kitchen. It's surprisingly cold; the fire has burned to ashes, and the bucket of cold water where I left my blood-stained dress to soak is filmed with ice. I go to find the tinder when a sound signals Finna's entrance.

Still undressed, her braid hanging over one shoulder, she's hunched and her nose is red. Of course; I've forgotten. She works herself into an illness every autumn and it's come upon her now. She looks at the flint in my hand and nods imperceptibly, tightening her shawl around her narrow shoulders. Then she's shuffling back into her room and the door shuts.

We both know the rhythm of the year, and this part is no exception. She quakes in bed with the fever that will inevitably grip her. I will take on all responsibilities. Sometimes I think she stores all her sickness for the year and only allows herself to succumb to it after the apple harvest is complete. It feels like another reminder of what is most important to her. I will always fall second to the orchard.

When at last I've lit a fire and begun the first brew, I hold my hands to the warmth. Finna lies ill. Duffy lies dying or dead. The Patrician is weak and oblivious to so many things. And Liam . . . but I can't think about that now.

If this is adulthood, I'm already weary of it. I think of the days when Katherine and I would play in the abandoned cottages and the worst thing I encountered was Finna's icy coldness or harsh punishments. But then, that is one thing that hasn't changed. People still age and leave me long before death takes them. No one is who I thought they were. Perhaps adulthood isn't so different from the life I've always known.

Maeve was not surprised to find Thomas and Declan had accompanied the Patrician when he came to see to the cure. Nor was she surprised to learn the guards would be standing watch at the orchard after the previous night's discovery.

"How is Duffy?" she asked after they'd said the prayer. "Is he . . ."

"Still alive. Sleeping." The Patrician frowned. "We don't know yet if he'll survive. But he lasted the night, thank God. I have administered a draught of something to help with the pain. Mrs. Campbell has made use of her garden for their healing herbs."

"What do you think did this?"

"We don't know for certain, of course. But with the attempt on the church, and the ravaging of the flocks, I'm afraid it all points to a specific group."

Maeve swallowed, her throat having sprouted a stone. *You never saw anyone at the church that night but me. The wild men—Lochlyn—don't control the wild animals like sheepdogs.* Still, the attack on Duffy didn't seem to fit with these things. And if wild animals did prowl the northern hills and feast on sheep, then why hadn't they found more evidence?

"Have the shepherds found anything more?" she ventured. "I heard you were putting protections around the pastures. Should we be more worried about the orchard, if they got past that?"

"I prefer not to speak of this in the village. The people have a tendency to panic. The protections I placed on the pastures are impenetrable. I don't understand how the attacks happened in the first place. But something is stirring on the downs. No doubt the rot started it all."

"Have you any idea what caused the rot in the first place, sir?" Maeve inquired.

"I still have none, and we may never truly understand. Perhaps the rot and the evil of the downs feed off of one another. The important thing is the cure." The Patrician waved a hand at the trees.

They had moved the shelter to the middle of the orchard, closer to the diseased and rotting trees. The trunks were nearly black with it, the silver crepuscules clustering thickly. The leaves had long fallen from those trees, and the smell grew stronger, a sweetness so rotten that Maeve felt grateful for the bitter smells of the herbs in the pot and the fire smoke. She stood with her back to the dead trees and wondered again just how a week-old brew and prayers—no matter how sacred—could bring them back to life.

But the brew continued to lighten in color, as the Patrician said it should. Today it was the thin gray of a winter's gruel.

"If this cure should not work, and these attacks continue, I will be forced to take more significant action."

Maeve's heart stuttered in her chest. "Sir?"

"The Lord Protector gave me permission to send the additional soldiers into the downs if need be. I have held back, though they have expressed their willingness. Let us pray that tomorrow we may begin administering the cure and that my men and I can return home, along with the additional soldiers."

"You've said you believe in the cure." Maeve swallowed. "Why are you saying this now? Has something changed?"

The Patrician looked at her, his face drawn in tension and concern. "I hope not," he said quietly. "But with Duffy struggling to live . . . it is more important than ever that we keep inside Quin's walls. You must report anything you see that could place someone in danger. Can I trust you to remain steadfast? People have done strange things under sudden duress. I would not want you to think that I care any less about you and the orchard, should something out of the ordinary take you by surprise."

Maeve nodded, not trusting her voice to speak clearly. His words held such an undercurrent that it took all her efforts to school her face into what she hoped was an acceptable expression. She often misunderstood people's words when they spoke in subtleties and hints rather than straightforward means. Her heart leaped like a frightened rabbit's, and she hoped rather than believed the Patrician was not hinting at what she feared most.

"You have not asked after the letter I sent to Dumar. I see your patience, Maeve, and it shall be rewarded soon." A fatherly smile lit his features, and doubt shadowed her suspicions from a moment ago. "I will see you here tomorrow. Just as they did last time, Thomas and Declan will provide for themselves, so you needn't trouble yourself with them. Now, go see to your foster mother. Perhaps the news of the cure will cheer her."

He put a hand on Maeve's shoulder briefly. She tried not to flinch. The two guards leaned against the wall; Declan was trimming his nails with a knife, and Thomas watched her with a glare of a wolf. She hurried after the Patrician, unwilling to remain behind with the two of them.

"I look forward to tomorrow," she said. "I will pray tonight that the cure will work."

"Good." The Patrician smiled again. "Keep safe, Maeve. Do not go into Quin without Declan or Thomas for escort. We will continue tomorrow."

She went with him to the bridge, where the water sang its song and the sounds of Quin greeted them as a muted hum. The blend of the village noise seemed quiet without the clanging of metal. *I hope Duffy would not tell anyone that Liam and I found him? But perhaps he does not remember anything.* The thought gave her a weak pang of guilt. She did not want the blacksmith to die, but neither did she want anyone to discover her real reason for leaving the cottage at night, or who was with her.

She shivered at the Patrician's words. *Can I trust you to remain steadfast? People have done strange things under sudden duress.* She had feared, after the dance, that the wild magic of the downs had somehow changed her or marked her in some fashion that would give her nighttime adventures away to anyone who looked at her. The more she learned from Liam, however, and her subsequent visit to the clan made her realize just how removed she was from magic of any kind. She had no more of anyone's magic than the Campbells' cat did. She may have felt feral, but she was only a girl who tended the orchard and had gotten tangled in too many things. Lochlyn's magic, whether it belonged to them or simply let them interact with it, was something she only experienced as an outsider. And that felt like more than enough.

The Patrician nodded to the guard at the entrance and disappeared from view. Her body sagged with relief, and her gaze dropped from Quin to the jumble of rocks and half-fallen structures below. The space where she and Liam had found Duffy, innocent now of all bloodshed and secrets. The stream cut past it before disappearing into the hollow. It looked as if nothing had happened at all.

In the cottage ruins, then, something flashed—a face in an opening that had once been a window.

A face Maeve knew well.

21. Secret

Katherine Monaghan, Quin's newest bride and wife to a wealthy merchant, was hiding in one of the old cottages.

The guard at Quin's entrance stared into the distance with a bored expression. Maeve glanced behind her for Thomas and Declan. They stood as she had left them, with Thomas facing her, though he conversed with his companion as if she were of no concern. But Maeve did not trust that to be true. Thomas watched, and she doubted he missed much.

She fidgeted at the bridge, trying to think of a way to get down without attracting anyone's attention. She began walking toward her own house in a meandering, slow walk, and darted a glance up at the orchard. Both men had moved. Behind her, the other guard was still lost to his own thoughts. Maeve measured her steps down the hill.

Once out of the guards' sight, she bolted.

The cottage remains stood on this side of the stream, closest to where Duffy had been attacked. The thatched roof had more holes than roof, and likely hundreds of mice; one side of the stone wall had caved in completely, and the door had long been removed and used for something else. Maeve looked up once more before going inside. The orchard wall hid her from anyone there unless they leaned over it, and she couldn't see Quin's entrance. She drew a deep breath and went inside.

The smell of damp straw and earth nearly choked her. She bit back a scream as dozens of tiny feet scampered away. Why on earth was Katherine in here? This must be some odd game. Katherine was making it up to her after sending her away, or trying to resume one of their childhood games . . . but that didn't seem like the woman Katherine had become.

Had Maeve imagined the sight after all?

"Katherine?" she whispered, and coughed from the mustiness pervading the space. "Katherine, it's me, Maeve."

She couldn't see the window from there, but something shifted in the dark. Footsteps, unmistakably human, drew closer.

"I hoped you'd find me."

It was Katherine's voice, small and worn and scared. Maeve held out her hand and any thoughts of imagining things fled at the sensation of her friend's cold grasp.

"Here. Sit down. There's room enough on the blanket."

Maeve obeyed. The ground was cold but the blanket provided some comfort and offered protection against the dirt. "I don't understand."

"You must promise not to tell the Patrician, or Finna, or anyone," Katherine said in a rush, her voice a shaking whisper. "Promise me, Maeve. Promise or you're no friend of mine."

Stunned, Maeve nodded, then remembered it was dark. "Of course," she said. "We always kept each other's secrets, remember? But I thought you didn't want my friendship now that you're married." A thread of bitterness crept into her voice, but Katherine gave a strange, strangled laugh.

"Married! Not for long, Maeve. Conlan is a stupid, stupid man, and now I will pay for it!" Katherine grunted and pounded her fist against the floor, jostling her unkempt braid.

"What happened? Please tell me, Katherine."

"Something has changed, Maeve. Something has happened to me. And I'm so scared."

Katherine's cold hand enveloped hers again. Instead of holding it, she pressed it against her dress, at her stomach.

"I'm with child."

Maeve inhaled. Beneath the fabric she felt the smallest swelling, round and firm. She withdrew her hand. "It's not—is it—"

"Of course it's his."

"Then why—"

Katherine made a sound somewhere between a sob and a groan. "He used to visit me on the hills when Father left me with the sheep. I never thought what we did was wrong, because I loved him. I know the priest's teachings as well as you do, Maeve, so don't lecture me. But what does that leathery old man know of love or marriage? He's nothing but a sputtering old fool.

"I thought Conlan would be happy when he found out. We'd spoken of children often since our betrothal. We both wanted them. But I began to show so quickly. One day we were married, and scarcely a week later he saw me dressing in the candlelight and—he asked me when it happened. I told him I'd missed my courses four months ago."

Maeve didn't understand why this should pose a problem, but she remembered Katherine's outburst and held her tongue.

"He said he won't be disgraced. He's gone to Dumar, and he's coming back soon."

Dumar—Cromwell House?

Sudden shock tumbled through Maeve. "What does he want, Katherine? Why should he be upset?"

"Don't you understand? Four months, Maeve. We've not been married one. Everyone will know."

Kate's voice was raw with an angry desperation Maeve had never heard. "Are you saying he'll send you away?"

"I thought he loved me." Anger and hurt bled into Kate's voice. "All his talk of the best house, and all the comforts he could buy, and living together as man and wife. He always liked to be in control of things, but he couldn't control this," she said, rubbing her belly.

Conlan had tolerated Maeve's presence but never more than that; she'd always put it down to his lovesick focus on his bride and paid it little heed. In light of what Katherine told her, the possessiveness of the young man's actions and temperament now seemed worse, as if his wife were another pretty object to be brought home among merchant wares. The image of the torn dress at the wedding made her shudder. Shock turned bitter with anger.

"He disgraces himself," Maeve said hotly. "If his love is so easily broken by something he did, it was never love at all. He is to blame. He *should* bear the blame!"

"I'll not go with the other disgraced wives." A tired anger colored Katherine's voice, the souring of something once sweet, too thin to be stronger than watered vinegar. She sighed. "I've nowhere else to go. I don't know what to do."

"For now, I will make you as comfortable as I can." Maeve stood, her head spinning. Katherine, with child and homeless, rejected. Finna was probably waiting on her and shouldn't be kept any longer. But she would find a way to bring Katherine more supplies while they thought of something.

Should anyone else get wind of Katherine's whereabouts, no doubt she and Maeve would be in trouble; they might even both be sent to Cromwell House. *I won't let either of us go. The Patrician can ask all the questions he wants. I'll tell him nothing. Besides, what does Katherine's presence have to do with wild beasts or wild men?*

Now that the first shock had abated, her caregiving skills took over. "You'll need food and another blanket. What else? You won't be warm tonight with only one and no fire."

"I've two blankets, a jar of water and some food, but they won't last long. Maeve?" Katherine tried to get to her feet but Maeve bent down, gesturing for her to stay. "That last time you came to the house, I only wanted to protect you. I worried Conlan would come back, and I thought he might vent his anger on you."

Maeve nodded. "You were scared. I understand now." She squeezed Katherine's hands, still cold. "But understand this, Katherine Monaghan: do not underestimate our friendship. I may not know much, but I am loyal and always will be."

Katherine squeezed her hands in return. "You always have been. Fear does terrible things to me, Maeve. I wish you hadn't been the one to bear my outburst."

"When is Conlan due back? It is a two days' journey there, isn't it?" *How long does it take for one to secure a place at Cromwell House? Hopefully as long as it takes to find records of an orphan's parents.*

"I don't know, but he left three days ago. I panicked and came here early this morning. One of the neighbors—nosy Mrs. O'Neil—wouldn't stop prying into my affairs. I am sick of her questioning. I miss comfort, but I don't miss my cage."

Maeve rose. "I'll come back as soon as I can. Finna's ill and I don't want to raise her suspicions. Oh, Katherine." She squeezed her friend's hand a final time.

"I'm stubborn as you are loyal, Maeve. Go home. I won't run away." Her voice hinted at her old sauciness, and her smile almost reached her eyes.

Only when Maeve stepped into the faded autumn sunlight did she remember another obstacle to visiting Katherine. The entrance guard was now reading a small book; she scoffed. At least there didn't seem to be much of a threat in that quarter. It was the other two she worried about. She steeled herself for confrontation, hoping to think of some excuse should they question her. To her surprise, when she reached the cottage door the only guard standing in the orchard was Declan, and something about him looked unusual. He was hunched and pale, as if ill, and didn't even seem to notice her.

There was no time to muse on the subject, however. The moment she pushed the door open and stepped into the cottage, the unexpected sight of Finna greeted her.

"Finna." Maeve swallowed, taking in her foster mother's appearance. Though still as pale and drawn as before, she was dressed and wore her hair up; a rare occurrence when she was ill. Two points of color burned on her thin cheeks, a sign the fever had arrived. Her pinched features briefly reminded Maeve of Declan. "Are you feeling better? What do you need?"

"What took you so long?" Finna's voice was dry, tired. "You should know better than to tarry, after Duffy..."

She didn't finish the sentence. Her voice caught, either on her sore throat or some unspoken emotion.

"I had to run an errand." Maeve hurried to the fire, hoping to avoid further questioning. Though the amount of lies she told grew by the day. Just now all she wanted was to deflect Finna's attention to her whereabouts. "I'll make some tea. Go back and lie down."

"Don't go into the village, Maeve. I expect you to obey me, ill or not. Understand?"

Maeve nodded and coaxed the fire up again. "Yes, Finna. I'll bring you the tea when it's done. Are you hungry? We might have an early meal." Silently willing her foster mother to go back to bed, she put tea leaves in a cup.

"Yes. That would be wise." Finna left the room like a shade melting into darkness.

God, is there room in your goodness for a girl who tells lies to help others? Help Katherine, then, and if not for my sake, then for hers.

Maeve's hands didn't stop trembling until after she finished serving Finna.

I expect to avoid the guards when I leave the next morning, carrying a pillow and some food wrapped in a blanket for Katherine. I am not expecting to see the Patrician standing outside the cottage door.

He smiles as if this is his ordinary arrival time and all is well in the world, but I feel nothing of the kind. I freeze, unable to say anything.

"No doubt you are surprised to see me," he says, as if it isn't obvious I'm shocked speechless. Perhaps he can't read my expression. I don't even feel my face. "I find myself without duties this morning and wanted to attend to the cure early. I hope I haven't interfered with caring for Finna."

Now he eyes the bundle in my arms.

"Yes. No." I force a smile across my face with the ease of practice and the difficulty of hiding so many things. "I'm only shaking these out for her. The fever makes her so uncomfortable."

"Do go on. I am early, after all, and wouldn't keep you from your other duties."

After a silent pause, his words make me realize I'm still standing with the bundle clutched to my chest. If I shake it out, I'll drop the food, and how would I explain that? "I already saw to it," I answer. "Just finished. I'll bring them inside and be right out." And hoping he'll excuse my rudeness, I dart inside and shut the door, leaving the Patrician of three villages on my doorstep in the chill. I shove the bundle into a scantily stocked cupboard, hoping Finna won't surprise me with another unforeseen trip to the kitchen; then I breathe deeply and step back outside, my smile so large that my face hurts.

"Thank you," I say for no other reason than I am well practiced in thanking my elders for anything they do.

"See. The cure is done." The Patrician held out the page for Maeve to inspect. He withdrew it from a place in his robes, and it was still warm when she took it, although the warmth flew away at her touch. She studied it, as she had many times: the obscure language, the faded ink, the elaborate swirls across the page. She was so distracted with thinking of the woman hiding between orchard and village that she could scarcely understand what she read.

"It is the right color." Maeve took a stab in the dark, and the Patrician nodded.

"It is the right color." He returned the page to a hidden pocket and gestured to the small pot simmering in its shelter. "Would you say the final prayer?"

Maeve repeated the words, forcing herself to say them slowly, reverently, while her own thoughts bubbled in her head. She hoped the Patrician was right and her lies hadn't tainted this cure. How she wanted the trees to be whole and hale again, for everything to return to the way it was, even though she knew it never would. She wasn't sure if her silent words were prayers or wishes, or if there was even a difference.

The Patrician waved Thomas over. He was alone, looking as awful as Declan did yesterday. The Patrician, who must have noticed, asked him about his companion's absence.

"Indisposed," was the tight-lipped reply.

"Ill?"

"Something about sleeping outside, sir."

"Soon you will be home, Thomas," the Patrician said with the patience of a loving father. The irony did not escape Maeve. "You of all my guards are here to witness this miracle."

He told Maeve to take the ladle and administer the cure, starting with the trees closest to the bronze apple still on the wall. Beside her Thomas carried the pot; Maeve did not look at him. She focused on pouring the milk-white liquid around the base of the first tree, watching closely, scarcely daring to breathe. The cure hissed on contact with the dampened earth.

Maeve gasped, almost choked. The smell of the herbal brew grew so strong that it seemed to cloud the air. Sickly sweet, the liquid seeped into the earth and returned the rotted soil to its original brown. The encrusted trunk became healthy bark again as if leeched of its poison.

"Now another ladleful for the next," instructed the Patrician. Maeve distributed the cure to one tree after another until all seven were treated. The same results followed. Those that had rotted bore fewer leaves than the rest, but the entire orchard stood whole and healthy, and by all appearances, free of rot.

"Thanks be to God." The Patrician laughed with relief, echoing Maeve's surprise.

"Is it really that easy?"

"Easy?" He looked around the orchard, a smile crinkling the corners of his eyes. "Maeve, you have tended the cure for a whole week. Every faithful prayer, every time you offered proof of your devotion—I would not call this easy. But I would call you constant and true."

The expansive feeling of relief stumbled and grew sharp in her lungs, like a beast that suddenly sprouted claws. She murmured her thanks. Turning her attention to the nearest tree, she ran a loving hand across the healed bole, breathing her own prayer of thanks. To whom, she hardly knew.

Perhaps it was to the trees themselves. Regardless of where she went at night and how many lies she'd told, she had rescued them and avoided Cromwell House. The monumental outcome felt too great to fully comprehend just now.

Slipping down to the old cottage felt so easy that Maeve almost found it amusing. *If I spend any more time outside at night I might become an animal.* Then she thought of the attacks on the herds, and of Duffy, and of the bloody fight she and Liam had encountered on their way to see the chief, and she wiped the absurd thought from her mind. There was nothing humorous about it. Between the orchard, Finna, and Kate, she'd been at home even more than usual for this time of year. She wished she'd thought to ask the Patrician about Duffy, and whether anyone had seen anything else dangerous or unusual. *He would have mentioned if anything noteworthy had happened, wouldn't he? What else* has *happened since I saw Liam? Is he still safe?*

There would be time for that later. The night was cold and damp, and the moon shone down and revealed every dent and crack in the stones of the cottage Maeve entered.

"Kate. I've brought food."

In the shaft of moonlight, Kate's eyes lit up and she rose from her mat. Maeve waited until her friend had eaten and drunk her fill before speaking.

"We have to find some way of helping you. Isn't there anyone you could go to? Any people your father interacted with as a shepherd who might be willing to aid you?"

Even as she said this, she knew it was a foolish question. Kate looked at her hands as Maeve went on. "What about your cousins in Ferre? Would they—"

"No. They wouldn't help me." Katherine's voice was hard, thin. "And Conlan's father holds power not just here, but in all three villages. He knows all the merchants by name. His parents were kind to me, but they are loyal to the Lord Protector through and through. There is nowhere I can go."

"Not even back to your parents?" Maeve hazarded.

"And bring my shame upon them?" Kate shook her head. "A daughter just married doesn't run from her husband. My mother has hidden a bruise or two from my father and would expect no less from me. Not even their own grandchild would sway them. Besides, Conlan could deny the child is his if he wanted. No one would believe my word over his."

They sat in silence awhile, leaning together for support. How long ago their childhood seemed. Maeve had always seen the Campbell home as the most loving place in Quin. The thought had instilled in her both comfort—knowing such a place could exist at all—and ravenous jealously. Learning the truth beneath the appearance made her feel as if she were falling rather than sitting on a dirt-packed ground.

It is a feeling I should be used to by now.

A terrible thought hooked its teeth into her mind. *Is love always so dangerous? Can a woman ever love in a way that doesn't put her in harm's way?* Kate may not have fled through the downs at night or danced with dark magic, but her failing had been discovered. Her punishment was just as bad as Maeve's would have been. It seemed life was a morbid kind of dance, a dance of carefully constructed steps and measured movements, and one move too soon or too late condemned the dancer. Was openly breaking free of these restricted motions ever worth the risk?

"Kate," she said after some time. "Can I ask you something? Do you wish you had never fallen in love?"

Kate drew a slow breath. "I don't know. Sometimes I hate Conlan with every fiber of my being and think of vowing to never love again. Sometimes I wonder if I really loved him at all. All I wanted was for someone to prove his love for me, to shower me with grand gestures. But my fine house is nothing but a cage. I thought my future was good. Now I don't have one."

"Yes you do," Maeve said, rubbing her friend's shoulder. The defeat she heard in Kate's voice alarmed her. "You will, Katherine. I'll help you. We will find a way for you to escape. Please, promise me you won't give up? As long as I'm on your side, you aren't alone. Conlan be hanged."

Katherine regarded her with a faint smile on her lips. "This is not the friend I left, Maeve. I want to know where this anger of yours came from. What happened to you since I married?"

So much. Too much. Enough to make me long for the days when we could tell each other everything in an afternoon and return to our mundane tasks for the rest of the day.

"Another time. You need to rest now." Over their years of friendship, Kate had grown to understand when Maeve was out of words. She tried to tell her that she had reached that place now, but a tremendous yawn nearly split her face in two.

"Go home," Katherine urged. It seemed she understood after all. She rubbed her belly absently, accentuating the rounded shape beneath her dress. "Thank you for all you've done, Maeve. I don't know what I'd do without you. I need you to rest as much as you can."

"You're sure? I'm worried about you." Even as Maeve spoke, the cottage swam before her eyes. *If I keep going out at night, I'll simply give myself away by sleeping for a week.*

"I'll be all right," Katherine said. "Things always seem terrible when I'm alone, but you've been here with me, and I want to sleep too. Go, before you doze off and risk getting caught for my sake."

"I'm already taking that risk," Maeve said, giving a half smile as she stumbled to her feet.

"I wish I were as brave as you."

The voice that followed Maeve to the door sounded tired and childlike. Kate had always been the one to try new things, to plunge fearlessly into the unknown. Maeve had clung to her and hoped her best friend knew enough to see them through whatever small adventure they chased. Now this was no adventure. Kate's life hung in the balance. And Maeve, for all her newfound, secret rebellion, had no idea what to do next any more than when Kate had cajoled her into stealing a horseshoe from the blacksmith. Growing up hadn't lent her the fearlessness she used to long for. It only revealed more terrors.

"Brave?" Maeve choked on a halfhearted laugh. "I'm scared, Kate, for you and for myself. I'm scared of things I can't even name to myself in the dark. But at least I can take care of you."

She was so tired that she barely registered anything beyond her own labored steps. Only when she reached the cottage door did she think to look for the guards. But fatigue muddled her thoughts and dulled her senses. Which explained why, in the dark kitchen, the shadows loomed taller than usual.

Maeve blinked. A shock like cold water brought her fully, painfully awake as one of the shadows spoke.

"I knew it. You've been sneaking off behind my back."

A thin form, a braid over one shoulder, the cold voice. Finna rose from her seat and Maeve's eyes had grown accustomed to the dark enough to see the lines of angry exultation on her foster mother's face.

"Now, girl, tell me where you've been."

22. Tell

Maeve's mind raced. She could not lie her way out of this one. She could not even speak.

"Is it a boy?" Finna demanded.

"No." *Not this time, at least.* She bit her tongue to keep from following the urge to split herself open and let Finna see everything.

"Have you given your virtue to some scoundrel?"

"N-no!"

"I don't believe you." Finna took a step closer and raised a hand.

Maeve shrank back. "I'm speaking the truth! I haven't given my virtue to anyone. Please, believe me!"

"Did he force himself on you?"

"No." She shook her head. "Look at my clothes if you want to, even the ones I wear. Search my sheets, my shawl, the whole cottage—you'll find no evidence!"

To her surprise, Finna paused and lowered her hand, but the angry gleam in her eyes remained. "Then what is it?"

"Someone is in trouble. I only wanted to help her." Maeve took a gulp of air and went on, still stumbling over her words. "She had nowhere else to go. It isn't her fault. Please, please don't tell anyone."

I'll do all the housework for a year without complaint almost escaped her lips, but something checked her. She would do far worse than that if it meant protecting her friend. But she would no longer sacrifice herself to Finna's ire in the process. She was younger than her foster mother and still had much to learn, but she would no longer grovel to make Finna do what she wanted.

It was time to act like the equal she was.

Maeve drew a deeper, slower breath. "Being angry at me won't change what I've done," she said. Her voice still trembled, but she found the words, and she forced herself to slow down. "And you should consider this other person. Everything you feared would happen to me has happened to her. But not because of the wild men. It's because her husband is the *pinnacle of respectability* that she is in trouble."

Confusion and something else passed over Finna's face. "What has happened to Katherine?"

Finna took the news of Kate's pregnancy and Conlan's errand with a face as impassive as ever. She sat down wearily and didn't speak for a few minutes, leaving Maeve to hang in the balance.

"If word of her escape gets out," Finna said, "the guards will comb Quin without respect for anyone's privacy. Where do you think they will look first?"

Maeve suspected that the Campbells' farm wasn't what Finna's meant. "What are we going to do for her? If you tell them I aided her, blame will fall on you just as much as it will on me."

"I'm not going to tell anyone, foolish girl. You will show me where she is, now."

"Now?" Maeve glanced out the window, but an overcast sky veiled the moon. "What about the guards?"

"I might ask you the same thing," came the acerbic reply. "Why do you think the Patrician's boys have been sickly of late?"

"I've no idea."

Finna took her boots from near the door and sat back down to tie them on. "I've heard they still aren't allowed alcohol rations. They won't be too keen on providing the Patrician with a list of what they've consumed, then, should he ask them to explain their sudden attacks of the gut."

"How would they . . ."

"You're quite daft, Maeve. Mrs. Campbell isn't the only one who knows a thing or two about herbs. Added to whiskey, some are near tasteless."

Maeve's mouth dropped in horror. "You've been *poisoning* them?"

Finna secured the second boot with a final yank of the strings and rose slowly to her feet, still hunched. She inhaled deeply. "Oh, their illness. I wouldn't have needed to take such measures if the Patrician hadn't sent those lusty youths here. As if we didn't keep to Quin's walls and rules. We don't need more protection from the downs! That man loves this orchard more than people, and has he ever done anything for it? No."

Maeve kept from mentioning the Patrician's aid in the cure and Finna's similar love for the orchard. It hardly seemed worth arguing about, now.

Once they reached the abandoned cottage, Maeve stopped at the doorway. "Kate!" she called. "It's me. I've brought someone to help."

At first there came no reply. Finna pushed at her back and Maeve went in, peering into the inky dark. Then she heard muffled sounds of crying. Maeve picked her way back with Finna on her heels, and as her eyes adjusted, saw her friend lying curled up. Her heart twinged with fear again.

"What is it?" Maeve sank down and put a hand on Kate's shoulder, shaking her gently.

"Maeve." Her voice was small, tight with pain. "Something's wrong."

Finna knelt beside them, bringing a smell of herbs and sweat. "Is it your womb?" she asked, her voice unusually gentle.

Katherine nodded, clutching her abdomen.

"For how long?"

"It began just after Maeve left," she whispered. "What's happening?"

"I don't know. Perhaps nothing, hm? Sit up, Katherine. This floor is too cold, even with my blankets on it."

They both helped her into a sitting position and Kate gave a short cry. "It's warm," she said. "I'm bleeding. Maeve, I'm bleeding so much."

Finna frowned and bundled up one of the blankets. "Sit on this."

"Am I going to lose it? I don't want to lose it."

Maeve clutched her shawl with one hand and rubbed Kate's shoulder with the other, feeling utterly helpless. Finna eased Kate onto the blanket, stood up, and steered Maeve into a corner.

"There's nothing else we can do for her now," Finna said in a low voice, "but keep her warm and supplied with rags. Tomorrow we'll make certain she's well fed. But if Conlan returns then, time may be on our side."

"What do you mean?"

"Once her pregnancy ends, she can go back to Conlan. She can say she was ill. Perhaps even tell people it was an early loss. No one will suspect, and she will keep her honor intact."

A whimper sounded from Kate. Maeve stared at the outline of Finna's face, horrified again. She wanted to go to her friend, to take the pain on herself and spare Kate the burden, but Finna's hand locked on her arm like an iron chain.

"Finna, is there nothing we can give her for the pain at least? You said you know herbs. Can't we get some others? Maybe there is something to stop the bleeding and—"

"Listen, Maeve. Her being here is a danger to us as much as her. Do you think we can get herbs from Mrs. Campbell's garden without her or the guards noticing?"

"But she doesn't want to lose it." Maeve pulled her arm free. "And how can you talk about us being in danger? What if she loses too much blood?"

"There is nothing we can do at present. Tomorrow, I will invent an errand to the Campbells' and see what I can get. But we may not be able to stop her womb from emptying if nature's course is determined."

"I know you're talking about me." Kate's weary voice broke through their whispered discussion. "If you think you can hide my death from me, you are both very foolish."

"You aren't going to die," said Maeve, striding back to her and crouching down. "She isn't, right, Finna? Does it hurt that much, Kate?"

Kate nodded, a patch of moonlight revealing her pale face. Maeve had never seen her in such pain. Kate had been known to use choice words to alleviate discomfort when her parents weren't present, but it wasn't Finna's presence that silenced her now.

"I'll be back as soon as I can," Maeve said gently. She gave Kate's shoulder a final squeeze and stood up. "Finna, there is someone who can help her. And I'm going there now. Don't ask if you don't want to know. They are good people and I can trust them. They have helped me before. I will not leave my friend to suffer when I know a way to help her."

Finna's face had turned as pale as Kate's. She shook her head as if to refuse the reality Maeve offered. "No, Maeve," she whispered. "You must not go. You've already . . . no. I forbid it."

"You can forbid me, but I will do it anyway. I never meant to disobey you, Finna, whether you believe that or not. But this is more important than obedience."

She left the cottage trembling with the weight of her own words. Before she even reached the stone wall, the downs seemed to well up and greet her—vast, wild spaces that felt more dangerous and frightening the more she got to know them. *I wish you were here, Liam. But I can't wait for you this time.*

She was going to find Lochlyn on her own.

The black dog loomed over her, red eyes like points of fire in the night, emitting a low, throaty growl that made her bones go soft with fright.

Maeve had found the clan successfully, but Aodh seemed to judge otherwise. The creature's breath blew warm and wet on her face—a damp, canine smell.

"Aodh," came Breena's warning voice, "you'll smother her with your underworld stink, you know that?"

The creature leaned down. Heart pounding, Maeve screwed her eyes shut, anticipating the sharp-toothed mouth. A loud snort enveloped her in the Cú Sidhe's breath. The sound of paws moving away made her open her eyes, and the black dog was leaving. It was like watching a hill walk away.

"I wasn't sure if he was going to bite your head off or slather you with drool." Breena grinned down at her from a little rise. Her teeth glinted in the moonlight, almost reminding Maeve of the hound itself. The grin faded. "I doubt he would've bitten you. He only kills what he eats," she said, and though her words were less than reassuring to Maeve, the cocky tone was gone.

"Is Orlenn awake?"

The guard nodded. "I guess you want to see her." She jumped down from her hiding place and slipped into the opening Maeve always missed. "Come on."

The camp was as quiet as the last time Maeve had visited, but a different energy hummed about the place. She'd been surprised that Breena didn't ask why she'd come, but something was brewing with Lochlyn. Perhaps it was on the forefront of everyone's mind.

The chief's hut was welcomingly warm and bright with hearth fire. Maeve felt some of the tension leave her cold, weary body as she took in the scene. Colm stood at the little table with Orlenn, bent over a map. His eyes crinkled into a smile when he looked up and saw her, and Breena slipped outside.

Orlenn greeted her first, though she didn't look up from her map. "Maeve. The villager who promised never to return. What was so important that you both came out again, on a night I haven't called Liam?"

"I'm alone, Orlenn," Maeve answered.

At this the chief looked up. "So you are. Not very wise. Perhaps very desperate. I've already told you: I have no control over the wild beasts that share this place with us. You'd best stick to your blessed walls if you want protection. Lochlyn isn't answerable for every foolish villager who goes wandering the downs."

"I'm not here for that. I'm here for someone who needs help. My friend is with child, but she's bleeding. She doesn't want to lose it. I can only offer you something within my power in exchange, but I'm able to trade. As an equal. Can you help her?"

"Is there no one in your village who cares?" Orlenn continued marking something on the page. "Quin promises to take care of its own, if I recall. Surely someone there is better suited to the task."

"She's in other danger, too. Her husband wants to send her to a workhouse in another village."

"And why would her husband do such a thing?"

"Because of honor—or some idea of it, at least, and money, and—well, why are you asking me?" Unwelcome anger simmered up her throat, catching the words as they rose. "It's the rule of Lord Protector. We receive our rules from him, and because of him, Quin's rules are terrible and stupid!"

Orlenn studied her a long minute. Maeve expected a rebuke, another cutting question, or a lofty, puzzling remark, but none came. Why was saying this aloud so difficult? She had admitted as much to herself before. Why did she squirm beneath this formidable woman's gaze, when the chief had no real authority in her life? She would not be distracted.

Maeve swallowed, clasped her hands behind her back. "Chief Orlenn, I've come to ask for more than help. I need to know if my friend could take shelter with you until I can find a safe place for her to live."

Now the chief met her gaze. "You ask a lot of us," she said, "especially since we are leaving these hills before two more nights have passed."

That explained the energy Maeve noticed when she arrived. But she cast her thoughts about, grasping for a chance for her friend. "Can you take her with you? She wouldn't stay with you, of course. Aren't there other villages where you're going? She could make a new life for herself there. She wouldn't be a burden on your hospitality for long."

"You say she is bleeding. How can you be sure she wouldn't slow us down?"

"I'm not. But if you help her, you'll be helping someone escape Quin's rules."

"And why does that matter? Whether or not we follow your rules, we would still be wild men. Quin's rules are nothing to us." She went back to studying the map.

Anger flared in Maeve's chest. She leaned against the table, willing the chief to look at her. "You told me that we are all connected, even those who do not acknowledge it. I acknowledge it now. Don't help my friend to spite Quin, if that means nothing to you. Do it because she is a person."

A faint smile traced Orlenn's face. "And you? What will you ask for yourself?"

The question confused her. "Myself?"

"You advocate for this girl. You fight for your orchard, and you risk disembowelment by wild creatures to discover who is attacking your flocks. You are dancing along the edge of a choice, Maeve, and if you do not choose for yourself someone will push you. When will you see that you also exist as a person?"

"I didn't come here to be lectured." Her own answer startled her, but she couldn't take them back. Orlenn's words unsettled something within her, stirred up a different kind of anger, one that knocked her off-balance. Her claim as the equal of the woman before her seemed a mockery now, vanishing like mist. She suddenly felt weary of always having to defend herself to the chief and of conversations that spun her in every direction like a child's top.

Kate needs me. I want to go home. And I am so, so tired.

The yawn she'd been fighting took over. When she opened her eyes, Orlenn was pulling a jar from a shelf. Colm stood, hands behind his back and head cast down. He glanced at Maeve with raised eyebrows, but she couldn't tell if the expression was one of rebuke or something else.

"This will help with the bleeding." The chief handed her a satchel of herbs whose scent Maeve didn't recognize. "If she is losing the child, I'm afraid there is nothing I can do to stop it. I would offer a spell, but that would no doubt interfere with the Patrician's magic."

Maeve nodded, grateful for the herbs and that the chief didn't speak any further on the subject. Even if a spell could do the impossible, it would alert the Patrician to Kate's location and put her in imminent danger. "Thank you, Orlenn," she said, and she meant it. "I will do whatever I can for you, as thanks. I already know any attempt to buy your approval would be worthless."

"True." The chief returned her wry smile. "As it happens, you can do something for me. Liam has expressed interest in joining our clan. Morning is not far away. Please convey to him that he must decide now. If he does join us, he will come with you and your friend when you bring her to us tonight."

Maeve struggled to make sense of the chief's words. "I didn't know," was all she could say.

"With all the unrest, I have decided to move my people away from Quin for the time being. Your 'Lord Protector' has a long and greedy arm. He and his underlings won't be content to ignore us much longer."

Of course she would keep her people safe; that wasn't what surprised Maeve. "Does that mean Liam will never come back to Quin?"

"You'll have to ask him yourself. Now go. You don't have much time before dawn."

The moon was a curl of wax in a sky bleeding pink at the edges when Maeve reached home. She caught a glimpse of the guard dozing at Quin's small entrance. Thomas and Declan were nowhere about, having left after the cure.

The stone cottage, when she approached it, was terribly silent, which set her heart hammering again. She could see inside clearly enough. Finna stood blocking any sight of Kate, but Maeve caught the sound of quiet weeping. The place stank of blood and mold.

Finna turned and stepped aside. She carried a balled-up, red-stained blanket, and at Maeve's questioning look, she shook her head.

A shudder ran through Kate's body. She sobbed, a crumpled-up sound like the first release of grief. Finna left quietly.

"Please take some of this," Maeve said, offering the leaves a third time. Inwardly, she raged against her own helplessness as her friend grieved things she could neither understand nor console. "It doesn't smell good, but it will help the bleeding."

Kate shook her head in the early morning light, her face pale and drawn. She continued to refuse the herbs while Maeve fretted and fussed. When Finna returned empty-handed, Maeve looked to her with some relief. Her foster mother took the satchel and sniffed the contents, then gestured for Maeve to follow her.

Maeve did so, annoyed at being pulled away from Kate but too tired to protest.

"Well? I recognize the herb well enough. Don't tell me everything that happened. But I know you have a plan for her. And I know it involves those—" She put a hand to her mouth and shuddered. "So tell me what that is."

Maeve spared a glare for her foster mother. "You said Kate has no place to go. So the chief of the Lochlyn clan has agreed to take her with them tonight. Are you going to forbid that, too?"

"No." The answer surprised Maeve. Not so much the word itself, but the way it was spoken, as if Finna had been handed her own escape and refused it.

"I see well enough you're too fool-headed to argue with. You've always been a challenge. But it seems this time it's warranted." Finna sagged against the wall. The night must have caught up with her. Shadows pooled in the hollows of her cheekbones and pressed bruises beneath her eyes. In all her years of autumn illness, she had never exerted herself this much, and certainly never for Maeve. "You've been worse than fool-headed. You've endangered the both of us. But we'll talk of that later, once we take care of Katherine."

Leaving Maeve angry and bewildered, Finna strode over and crouched next to Kate.

"Now, listen to me, girl." Finna's voice softened, so different from the voice Maeve was used to. "What's done is done, and you cannot turn it back. You've got to go on, Katherine. Letting yourself waste away is a fool's choice. Take this."

Kate ignored the satchel and cast a baleful, red-eyed glare at Finna. "Where did you put her?"

"In the orchard. No, no one saw me, and you cannot see it. You can't spend another night in this godforsaken hovel, either."

"I'm not leaving."

"God's teeth," Finna muttered, "you're worse than Maeve. I had a time getting the guard to leave his post at the entrance, and the other two won't bother us, but we have to get you inside now. I won't have you bleeding all over my kitchen floor. So stop arguing and take this now unless you want me to force it down your throat."

Kate relented at last. Barely had she swallowed the satchel's contents when they helped her to her feet and brought her inside to Finna's bed. "No," Finna said when Maeve offered hers. "Who knows how little sleep you've gotten lately. I'll take the sofa."

The early sunlight hurt Maeve's eyes. She was so weary that her jealousy over her foster mother's attentions to her friend barely registered. But as she stood at her doorway, some of that jealousy spilled over.

"Finna, the wild men are led by a woman. This whole time, you've been afraid of a woman who is your equal in age and superior in authority. You only have me to order around. She has an entire clan." Maeve watched for any kind of reaction, but the shadow of the doorframe obscured Finna's face.

"Few things in this life are as they seem," she said in a faraway voice. "Very few things."

"Is that why you're afraid? Because you don't understand?"

"No. I'm afraid because understanding a thing makes your own powerlessness more visible than when you were ignorant."

Finna retreated to the parlor, leaving Maeve to stare after her, wishing words with Finna could make sense.

23. Protection

It was afternoon before Maeve awoke. She remembered Kate, and going to Orlenn. *The Patrician—he'll come to see the cure and the orchard and find her—*

She tumbled out of bed and was half-dressed before she remembered the cure had healed the orchard, and the Patrician wasn't coming today. No one guarded the trees; no one was expected today, and no one would find out about Kate because they were going to Lochlyn tonight. And she had to tell Liam.

Kate slept in Finna's bed, her face pale but peaceful. Maeve breathed a sigh of relief and stole quietly into the kitchen, where Finna stirred porridge over the fire.

"I've got to run an errand," she said, seizing her shawl from the hook and running out the door before Finna could stop her. The woman might be feeling well enough to be up and about after such a night, and Maeve didn't want to risk being kept at home. *I've had enough of that.*

Making her way through the streets, she wondered if the orchard being cured was on anyone's mind today or brightened anyone's spirits. She missed her trees. She would have to see them soon, to thank them for growing healthy again and for not leaving her as so many people would.

Boyle stood at his post by the shepherd's gate. He chewed on his pencil and studied his little book, his posture relaxed.

"Hello, Boyle," she greeted him. "Have there been any attacks since the Patrician visited the pastures?"

"Well. Maeve. How are you? No, there haven't been, matter of fact. Not a whiff of mischief, and now I hear the trees are cured. Quin is as it should be." He beamed. "What're you up to on this fine day?"

His words gave her a small measure of peace. "I've got to see Liam," she said. There was no point in lying about her intentions now. Even the possibility of being watched by guards mattered little. "Where is he?"

"Due north, just between those rocky outcroppings," Boyle said, pointing. "Be careful, now!"

With a quick word of thanks, she climbed up and over the fence in one motion, wobbling only a little, and landed on Quin's pasture lands.

The wind soon swallowed Boyle's protests as she ran up the hill. Slowing to catch her breath, she took in the rumpled horizon as it reached to meet the sky. For a moment she could almost understand Liam's detachment from Quin, from everything, out here where the sky descended to touch the earth.

The outcroppings Boyle had pointed out offered a brief reprieve from the wind's shrill battery, though she could hear it whistling overhead. As she came out from the shelter, she heard the bleating of sheep. Another minute and she saw Liam sitting on the grass, a black-and-white form nestled at his side.

He was stroking Whistle and watching over his scattered flock, looking for all the world as Maeve had imagined him out here in the hills. Something unknotted within her and she exhaled in relief.

Then he turned and revealed a face streaked with tears and the crimson stains on the little black-and-white body lying too still to be asleep.

"Liam!" She flung herself down beside him and took the still hand at his side, her pounding heart pushing a sob into her throat.

"It was broad daylight," he said, still looking out at the hills and speaking as if he stood on one of them, far away and small. "He was just behind that rise. I'd left him for . . . I don't even remember. One bark, that was all. I should've stopped it. I should've been there for him." His voice tightened and his hand twisted in the muddied fur, tugging as if trying to draw some animation back into the lifeless body.

"Oh, Liam." Maeve made herself look at the once-joyful Whistle, his body rendered still and broken by violence, and reached out a tentative hand to stroke his curly flank. He already felt cold and stiff. She lay her head on Liam's shoulder, wishing she knew how to comfort him. She knew by the sinking feeling in her body that something more than Liam's companion had died.

"He was all I had left. Something killed him. No amount of the Patrician's so-called magic could stop it. So I have to."

"How?"

A light in Liam's eyes had hardened, a gleam of something so bright and dark at once that Maeve felt a pang of worry. "Are you sure it was the same creature?" she asked.

He nodded. "What else has come here? I found footprints. Magic or not, I'll kill it."

"Or you could go with Lochlyn."

Some of the distant anger faded from his eyes. "What?"

"Orlenn says you are to go with them tonight. The clan leaves tomorrow, and you have a place in it."

He looked at her, his eyes narrowed. "You went there alone?"

"My best friend is in danger. She's going, too."

"And—?" A flash of hope lit his eyes. He didn't finish the sentence. A bloom of dread, the culmination of many thoughts and fears, swelled in Maeve's chest. She tightened her hand around Liam's and chose her words.

"Quin is my home, Liam. I don't think I can leave it."

"Don't? Or won't?"

How do I say this? How can I tell him that everyone I try to hold close changes, or leaves, or proves themselves a liar? How can I tell him that I know I can't keep things the same, that I would rather let him be safe and without me than go with him and risk something changing him? I wanted to keep what we have forever. Now I know better. Nothing lasts forever, and I was a stupid girl to think that this could. I can no longer live in the present. I must think of my future. I think I must break his heart.

But I don't think I can.

"Maeve." Liam gripped her hand. "You worried once I wouldn't take you seriously. But you don't take yourself seriously. Not where it counts. Why won't you leave this place? Is it for the trees? Trees that tell everyone a nice story about the Patrician and his grandfather? What good do they do you? What has Quin ever done for you that makes you have to stay?"

"You wouldn't understand." But her resolve crumbled as she spoke. For a moment, impossible fantasies crossed her mind: Leaving all that was familiar, all that was safe, and risking the unknown to be with Liam. She studied him, his own gaze intent and almost desperate.

I was afraid he wanted something I couldn't give him. But he's given me more than I imagined anyone could ever share with me.

What if I go with him? What if my strange thoughts are more than hollow fancies? What if there is something more for me?

"If I tell you I will think about it, will you promise me not to hunt for this monster?"

He released Whistle's fur and took her hand, his own trembling. Maeve grasped it in both of hers and willed her own strength to steady him.

"I promise."

It was hard to leave him.

Boyle had left his post by the time Maeve reached the shepherd's gate. Villagers went about their business, no one sparing her a glance. Even the knot of guards stood relaxed and talking to one another. She slipped past them, and only when she'd gone down the street a ways did she note the footsteps behind her.

"Just keep walking."

Thomas's voice sent a jolt down her spine and her thoughts scattering, buzzing like a swarm of bees. Her feet moved senselessly forward. And then she stood in a narrow alleyway, and there was no way out.

"You must think you're very clever." Thomas stood over her, so close she could see the gold flecks in his green eyes. "I know it was you. Poisoning us. Little witch."

"I didn't poison you." She regretted the words as soon as they escaped.

"Oh no?" He paused. An eyebrow lifted, almost quizzically, and for one frantic heartbeat he stepped away and left Maeve the space to hope he would leave. "Oh. The old biddy. Didn't like us 'boys' in her trees, did she."

Half-formed words lodged themselves in her throat. When Thomas spoke again, his breath was a hot, alcohol-infused stink on her face.

"Maybe it was you. Maybe it wasn't. But you're here. Right place, right time. And it's time I made good on my promise to you."

He seized her arms, driving her back against the rough stone wall. Maeve's strength leeched out of her like water from a dishcloth. The knot in her throat tightened and bobbed, releasing a choked whimper.

"Quiet, now. No need to struggle." He lifted one hand and traced a finger down her cheek, her neck, while his other hand held fast to her arm. "One scream, one quick movement, and it'll be much worse for you. Just stay still and silent. From what I've seen, you're good at both."

His hand fumbled down her skirts. Maeve lurched once, desperately, her hands pinned and useless at her side, and bashed her head against the wall. Black spots bloomed across her vision.

"What seems to be the trouble?" a voice called down the alleyway.

Thomas's voice was turned away from her. "Just reminding this young girl of her place, sir."

Rough hands released her. Sudden cold took their place, the feeling of falling, a waterfall's roar in her ears.

Someone was offering his arm. Someone who wasn't young, but who wore a rich cloak and graying hair to his shoulders, someone whose eyes were kind.

She was walking with the Patrician down the street and Thomas was gone. She shuddered. A kindly voice was talking about something in a casual, ordinary tone; a thin line tethering her mind to her body. Maeve nodded like a puppet. When they reached the exit from Quin, the kindly voice formed into sounds and words she recognized.

"I have that letter from Dumar, Maeve. I thought you'd like to hear it from me before I left."

As we cross the footbridge, I can't tell what shakes more: my heart or my limbs. I must not let him go inside. Of this much, I'm certain.

The Patrician seems content to stand in the orchard. Without releasing my hand from his arm, he pulls a piece of parchment from a pocket, opens it, and reads.

Fragments of the letter reach me. My father was a tradesman, my mother kept house. If they had names, I do not hear them. They died sixteen years ago of the fever and sent me to Cromwell House. A woman then brought their infant child to Quin, when it was discovered that the orchard keepers' daughter was unmarried and likely to remain thus.

The crinkling of parchment paper recalls me from silly dreams of the short time I lived with my parents. I am no part of Lochlyn or any other clan; I am from the Lord Protector's villages as much as any person born in Quin, and I always will be.

"I see that you are very tired, no doubt from caring for Finna. Yet I hope this news has brought you a measure of comfort."

I nod numbly. "It has." It is not totally a lie.

The Patrician looks over the trees, and my gaze follows. Every tree looks as healthy as it did yesterday. The cure, whatever it was, seems to have held fast and done a complete job.

"There is something else I wanted to tell you in person. The Lord Protector has required my permanent return. I cannot outrun my fate any longer."

"Sir?" I say automatically.

He pats the hand clutching his arm. His own hand feels paper-thin and dry, the skin of a very old man. "Thank you for your devotion to the orchard, Maeve. I am glad to be leaving it in your care. Quin's legacy lives on, thanks to you."

A finality in his words breaks over me. "What do you mean?"

"This body grows too weary for the journey, I'm afraid." He smiles as if greeting an old friend in the distance. "I have been able to hide the truth for some time, but no longer. The illness has been with me for too long. I doubt I would survive another journey to Quin."

His meaning dawns on me. Too many thoughts and feelings choke me; I realize I have uttered the sound aloud.

"But do you not see God's provision? It's as if you were brought to Quin for this very reason, Maeve: to protect the orchard. I must leave, but you are here, just where you are needed. You have always been at the right place at the right time."

Silence covers me like a wool hat shoved over my head. I may fall asleep standing up; I reach for that, welcome it, the feeling of leaving this troublesome body behind.

A breeze brushes my skin and leaves rattle loudly in my ears. I experience a moment of distant anger at the orchard for taking me from my respite rather than providing it for a change. The Patrician comes into focus, and I see the look of fatherly concern on his face, and for a moment I want to believe everything good he has ever told me. That it is not such a terrible thing to belong in Quin. Belonging in Quin is simple. Familiar. I long for that more than ever.

"Maeve?" he says, and I realize I haven't heard everything he's been saying to me. A gentle hand supports my elbow. "How rude of me to keep you. Go rest. You can read the letter whenever you wish. Farewell, my child."

I nod. I wish that he would die quickly; I wish he would not die at all. I wish he could die and return as the Patrician I thought existed but never did.

He is gone from the orchard, and I am still here, and I do not know how long it takes me to go back inside the cottage.

24. Goodbye

Neither Finna nor Kate noticed Maeve's quiet state, and for that she was grateful. *If I try to talk about it, I will sit down and cry instead. Perhaps I won't get up. I have no time to cry.*

Kate was still pale, but her bleeding had slowed considerably. Finna fed her broth and bread with hearty slabs of butter, then told her to go lie down until it was time to leave. The kitchen felt oddly hollow. Finna let the fire bank down after dinner and lit one precious candle. The light threw dancing shapes across the walls and made Finna's face look more aged than ever.

"Maeve. Sit a moment." She patted the table and went to pour some tea. Maeve waited in her seat as familiar kitchen sounds broke the silence: the clank of the pot, the chink of spoons on cups, the splash of water. Finna brought two cups to the table and sat down.

"What if we left Quin?"

Maeve paused mid-sip, staring. "Leave Quin?" she repeated. *I must not have heard correctly.* Her foster mother was as tied to the orchard as she was, by birth even more so. "Why?"

Finna drew a deep breath and looked down at her cup. "Your friend may escape tonight, but how long before people start to wonder? How long before Conlan looks our way? There is no place in all three villages where he could not pursue us and charge us with the crime of aiding a disobedient wife, and then"—she swept a hand across the table—"it's Cromwell House for us after all."

"I've already been there," Maeve murmured, but Finna didn't hear. "But where else could we go? I don't even know the names of the other villages or how far they are. How would we survive the journey?"

"There are inns along the way. Do you think the Patrician would have left so late today otherwise? The man loves his comfort." She frowned and took a drink from her cup. "I have some money set aside. We leave at the first sign of spring and pay the innkeepers enough so they don't ask questions. By the time the Patrician arrives in Quin, we will be long gone and miss him altogether. We could do it."

Maeve almost said the Patrician wouldn't likely be in Quin next spring, but one small word stopped her. *We.* Had Finna ever referred to them both taking on an endeavor together as equals? With the orchard it was always, "You will do this" or "We will do that," but her tone left a clear message: *You are doing this because you are here and we both have no other choice.* This plan of escape felt very different in light of Finna's confiding in her something so dangerous and outside the usual.

She was no longer the girl who scrabbled at any soil for the tiniest seed of affection, and she was too aware of Finna and her actions to be totally won over by this invitation into the woman's confidence. One conversation wouldn't erase the past. Even planning for a new and different future where their shared hope of freedom might allow them room to grow, was not enough to change Maeve and Finna into people with a true mother and daughter bond. A little stain of jealousy remained in Maeve's heart when she thought of how quickly Finna abandoned her upright principles for the sake of her friend. But, when she looked closer, the stain was no more than a watermark. It wouldn't last.

And she had to look to the future.

"The Patrician is dying," Maeve told Finna. "He said he won't be back in the spring."

If she expected a surprised reaction, she was mistaken. "His post won't remain empty for long," Finna said. "Quin's rules will follow us as long as we remain in the Lord Protector's domain. This is why we must go far, far away."

"North?"

Finna regarded her before answering. The frown lines were no less sharp on her face, but her eyes lacked the usual suspicion. "We might go west. From there, more settlements line the way south."

Something quivered in Maeve's chest, a sleeping bird stirring. *Orlenn is taking her people south, and Kate and Liam—*

Liam. She missed him so much it hurt. When she'd seen him in the pastures, he'd been distant with grief, a grief she could do little to assuage. *Like Kate's loss.* But she couldn't get him out of her thoughts, couldn't stop remembering the way he'd looked at her when they danced in firelight and starlight and when they lay in the orchard looking up at a blue, blue sky. The touch of his lips on hers, the warmth of his hands.

A shiver cut off her thoughts. She pulled her shawl tighter against the onslaught of sensations both vague and sharp: A stone wall at her back. Hot breath in her face. Searching hands.

The hot cup in her palm tethered her to the present, where one friend waited for Maeve to take her to safety, and where another awaited her answer to his question. A question that Maeve had seriously considered only hours ago, as though it might involve a simple, happy choice.

It was too good to last long. I was right. Nothing good comes from that kind of love.

"Maeve, you don't have to marry. No matter where we choose to live."

She looked up, surprised. "Is that accepted in other villages, do you think?"

"I don't know. But if two women arrived in a village, what could be stranger than that? I know people talk about me here, and marriage is as certain as the seasons. They call me an old biddy, but what of it?"

"You told me I had no choice," Maeve said. "You told me I wouldn't be accepted if I didn't marry or follow Quin's rules." She felt no need for an outburst this time. Indignation like hot ice burned down her arms, as calm and steady as a frost creeping across the hills. Even when Finna's expression faltered, the only thing Maeve noticed was how inevitable it all felt. She had never stood up to Finna, and in the last two weeks she had done it twice. Already the act held all the familiarity of a worn garment, though it lacked warmth.

"I wanted you to be safe. You're always off somewhere in your head, far away from sense and reason; how could I hope to let you take over the orchard like that, when the world is as it is? I only wanted to protect you."

"You did a terrible job." Bitterness bled into Maeve's voice, and she didn't try to stop it. *I speak the truth.* "You've never noticed how hard I tried or that I existed, apart from carrying out your tasks. I wanted your affection and kindness, Finna, more than I ever wanted your apple cake."

Finna stretched her hands over the table, as if trying to fend off harm, and lowered her head.

"Why did you never marry?" Maeve pressed, the bitterness gone from her voice.

Finna hesitated. "I could never give him what he wanted." Each word sounded pained, and Maeve asked no more.

Silence hung between them. It remained unbroken, jagged with years of dead things rearing sharp-toothed heads called to life by speech. From another room, something rapped at the window.

"It's him." Maeve rose, a fresh dread suffusing her limbs. "The other one I told you about, who is going to Lochlyn too."

Liam seemed different even in the faint moonlight, looking up at her with a bag slung over one shoulder. Maeve's insides clenched with fear. "You'd better come in," she whispered, stepping back from her window.

Liam clambered over the sill with a slow ease that almost belied his grief. When he righted himself and shook out his hair, half his face was shadowed, and Maeve was almost certain that he'd missed her flinch when he stepped toward her. His eyes glinted in the half-light. "Well, Maeve," he said.

"I can't go with you." With great effort, she pushed the words out and let them fall into nothing. She couldn't take her eyes off him, either, willing him to speak.

"I knew it." He gave a bitter laugh, half sad resignation, half self-defense. "You've got roots here like your trees, haven't you?"

She nodded. It would have to do. *How else could I explain it to him?* "You belong with Lochlyn," she attempted. "I don't. I never will. But I won't be here forever. Finna says we might go south in the spring. I might find you—I would look for you—"

"Don't." He sounded only sad. "I understand. You don't have to come looking for me just to make me feel better." He strode to the door in two steps. "Bring your friend. I'll wait in the kitchen."

Maeve left her room, tears blurring her vision, as Finna's low voice greeted Liam.

"So you're the boy on the wall," said Kate.

It felt entirely too strange to be real. Liam, Kate, and Finna all stood in the kitchen with Maeve, and the air felt heavy with unasked questions. Her tears hadn't fallen and she'd remained in control of herself. Only Kate voiced one of her thoughts aloud. Despite Kate's weakened state, a faint grin lit her face as she looked once from Maeve to Liam.

Kate's teasing seemed to pass over him. He kept glancing around the kitchen with a hunger that had nothing to do with food. The firelight brought every detail of his face into relief. Sadness had scuffed up his foolhardiness and made him look worn down, beyond the faint bruises beneath his eyes. Maeve longed to embrace him, to tell him everything would be fine.

Finna, however, was looking him over with her usual hawk-eyed stare.

"It's time to go," Maeve said, breaking the awkward silence. She was uncomfortable, but discomfort would be the least of their concerns if they didn't leave soon. "Kate, do you have everything?"

"Yes." The mood was serious again.

Liam, whose attention had returned to Maeve, caught her eye and held it briefly. "We'd better go."

Kate thanked Finna, her voice catching when she spoke of the bundle buried in the orchard. "Look in on her often, won't you?" Kate said to Maeve. Maeve nodded and squeezed her hand.

"I'll wait up for you," Finna told Maeve. "You'll need something warm after that long walk in the chill." She eyed Liam once more, who regarded her with a careless half-measure of scorn. "Safe travels to you," she said to him, then strode from the room, leaving Maeve surprised yet again.

The night was cold and heavy with finely misting rain; there would be frost on the earth by morning. As Maeve led Kate through the window and down to the cleft in the first wrinkle of hills, Kate paused to look over her shoulder.

"Don't worry. It'll be like running into the blacksmith's shop. But this time, you'll be with me," Maeve reassured her, but Kate chuckled darkly.

"I'm not worried. Goodbye, village," she said, her smirk holding some of the old sauciness. "May all your young men rot."

They set out at a quick enough pace. The path felt well-worn to Maeve now, and she felt little anxiety. No one spoke. Several times, she caught Liam's eye and he seemed on the verge of speaking. But he never did. They both put their attention to helping Kate navigate the rocky path. Kate, who protested at first, soon walked slower and slower, until Maeve began to feel alarmed. She jumped at every twig snap or rustle in the brush. But they saw no sign of any beast, though she never stopped looking and guessed Liam did the same.

A thin, wavering note of music reached them, dark and haunting as the night sky. The vast blackness shivered and twisted into a mass of sleeping roots like an inescapable embrace. Then Maeve blinked and the sky was itself again, curling over the earth instead of beneath it, but the familiar sensation of being pulled from one world and into another where she did not belong, left her like a slow ache.

Once they reached the camp, Maeve exhaled in relief. Colm and Breena were waiting for them just outside the chief's hut. There was no sign of a large, red-eyed dog anywhere—another cause for relief.

Kate stumbled and nearly sat down on the ground, but Colm and Maeve steadied her.

"There, lass. Can't have you collapsing here. Come inside and lie down."

"I don't want to rest," Kate declared, though her face was pale in the low firelight. Her mouth twisted in stubborn refusal. Maeve, who wished she could curl up in bed herself, propelled her friend along.

"I hope you and the chief know what you've agreed too," she said to Colm, attempting a light-hearted tone. "I've known her my whole life and she knows how to cause trouble."

This brought a smirk from Kate, but no answering jab. The smirk faded when she saw Orlenn in the hut, commanding as ever, putting several rolls of parchment into a bag. Maeve wondered if the chief ever slept. She addressed them without looking up.

"You'll lie down over there and sleep until we leave. I won't have you slowing us down." Orlenn glanced up and studied Kate briefly, who did as she was told without another word. There was something about Orlenn that no one questioned.

And this was goodbye. Haltingly, Maeve followed Kate and knelt at the cot, grateful for the comfort and rest offered her here.

"Promise me you'll try to be happy, Kate. I'll be miserable if you don't."

"Are you trying to make an ill woman feel guilty?" Kate grinned sleepily. "I'll try. But only if you can do the same. Can you do that, Maeve? Try to be happy? Whatever shape that takes." Her voice drifted into silence as her eyes closed, and she gave Maeve's hand one feeble squeeze.

A gentle hand patted Maeve's shoulder. "Let her rest. She is weak but she is safe with us. She will be all right, now." Orlenn waited for her to stand before gesturing to the door. "Remember, someone else wants to say goodbye."

Liam was waiting just outside, hands shoved in his pockets, nudging the ground with his boot. He looked up when she came out. A hundred emotions passed over his expressive, handsome face. Maeve went to him feeling shy and sad.

"I didn't mean it," he said, looking down at his boots. "Earlier, about you not coming to look for me. I hope you do."

He sounded so raw, his words like a new wound shown only to a comrade in arms. *He doesn't hide from anyone. From me. He's just good, just himself.* But she remembered the way he looked at her in the orchard and during the dance: like Conlan used to look at Kate. *I hate that every man I know has ruined this—us. It's better to separate now before something worse does it for us. He will be shaped by Lochlyn in ways I don't understand. What we had is gone.*

"I know you didn't," she said soothingly. "You aren't yourself."

He reached for her and she was in his arms, resting her head on his chest. He smelled of the plants they'd walked through and of sheep; mentally, Maeve clung to those details.

"I won't ask you to come with me again. But I want to."

"Thank you. For seeing me, Liam. For being my friend."

His arms tightened around her briefly. "Just your friend?"

Maeve leaned back so that he released her, and she looked at him. "You know it was more than that. For a little while."

"Will you kiss me again?"

She kissed him, and he seemed to cling to her like a memory. His hands shifted, gripped her waist. Maeve jolted away.

"I'm sorry," she said breathlessly. "I'm sorry." She gave him one more kiss, quick enough to escape her own memories and long enough, she hoped, to leave them both with something good. They held hands without saying anything.

"You know, I'm not afraid of magic anymore," Liam said.

Maeve looked up to see a sad smile on his face.

"I still don't understand it," he went on, "but . . . it isn't trying to take anything from me."

"I'm glad," Maeve said. *I have to go. Please, please let this not hurt so much as it does now.* "You'll find your way, Liam. I know you will."

Nearby someone cleared his throat. She released Liam's hands.

"Wait," he said. "Orlenn says we will come back here in late spring. So if you've not left by then, you won't have to look so far."

"I won't be here in the spring," she said gently. "I have to leave Quin with Finna. You understand. I've been between the village and downs too much. I don't belong in either anymore. It isn't safe."

He nodded. "Well. Just in case you're still here, you can listen for the music. There's nothing wrong with that." A faint smile tugged at his lips.

"No, there isn't." Maeve's face was wet; she realized she was crying silently, for all she would leave behind. She wanted to kiss him again and be held by him again. It was best to leave while that still felt bittersweet, before it all turned bitter.

Someone cleared his throat again, and Colm materialized from the shadows. "You'd best get some rest, lad," he said, patting him awkwardly on the shoulder. "If you can. Sorry to interrupt."

Breena appeared, her arms folded. "Watch out for big black dogs on your way back," she said. "We won't be here to protect foolish wanderers anymore." She grinned. "And all the best to you, Maeve, even though you are a villager."

She had nothing else to say—and everything—but she was taking Colm's proffered arm and looking behind her as she went, until the camp was swallowed up in darkness and Liam was just an image seared into her mind and a tingling memory on her lips.

I will never see him again.

The world was too big, and survival too all-consuming. The clan was a world beyond her. Kate would not stay with them; who knew where she would start her new life? *Better to adjust to a future without them than to hope for something that will hurt more by its absence.*

"There, lass. Let the tears fall. It's medicine, that."

Colm patted her head with an exaggerated grimace, eliciting a wet laugh from Maeve. "We all must move on, whether by our own two feet or by the changing of our minds," he said. "It's the heart that finds change the hardest."

This only dislodged a harder bout of weeping, and Colm went on, "Oh, but look what you've done: no villager has ever braved the downs, and that's something for pride, isn't it? No matter those stuffy folks back home'll think otherwise. You'll live your life, sure as you've chosen where to live it, and your heart is soft enough to grow and strong enough to withstand the growing. What more could you ask for?"

"But what—what if—" Maeve began, hiccuping. *What if I'm not strong enough?* But the words wouldn't obey. The weight of all her goodbyes was too heavy. Colm seemed to understand, though. He gathered her into a brief, genuine embrace that startled her with its tenderness, then held her at arm's length.

"Ah, Maeve." His eyes crinkled into a sad smile. "I trust you, lass. Villager though you may be, you're akin to us Lochlyn folks. By heart alone, I mean, nothing else, that's for certain. You'll see. One day, you'll know it's true. That, I feel in my toes." He tapped his foot twice and gave her a knowing smile tinged with sadness.

"Colm, you don't have any magic, do you?"

Far from being perturbed by the inquiry, Colm stuffed his hands in his pockets and rocked back on his heels, looking over his village with affection. The flickering orange light of the bonfire etched deeply the lines on his face. "None at all, lass," he said cheerfully.

"And that doesn't bother you?"

"Ah. Now it used to, at first. It's hard being different, even among those you love."

"What changed that?"

Colm shrugged. "Well now, you're an apple girl. I guess you might say I found my core. There's more to a person's worth than what they can do. Now go on, lass. This day'll not wait for any of us." Without another word or glance, the old man turned and disappeared down the hill. This time, Maeve did not watch.

25. Letter

The misty rain did indeed stop long enough for frost to lace the edges of the stream by that morning, when Maeve went for the ritual ladleful of water. Everything felt as if it had shifted. The light slanted differently, as if unsure of the season or time of day. The world sat differently around her, as accomplishment and emptiness competed within her.

Her closest childhood friend was gone. The Patrician was gone. She'd seen them both leave under very different circumstances. And out on the broad, climbing pasture hills, there was no dark-haired boy to share adventure or kisses with.

Maeve hefted the dripping bucket and climbed up to the path, fixing her eyes on the orchard. She wondered what the point of this ritual was now that the trees had survived rot and recovered. But as she entered the archway and made her way around, the familiar fondness stole across her and she couldn't help but greet each tree with a smile.

"I'm sorry."

Finna had spoken those words last night when Maeve climbed wearily through her bedroom window and went to say goodnight. Finna had stayed up as promised and asked no questions, only offered a pot of tea warmed on the fire's banked embers. Maeve hadn't asked what she meant. She'd only nodded, accepted the tea, and gone to bed, where she slept deep and dark for a few brief hours, woken by uncertainty and finality both.

While Maeve visited her trees, Finna was visiting Duffy. The word was that he was improving. Maeve was relieved. She no longer feared he would give Liam away; the blacksmith spoke few words, and she doubted he had reason to give away the names of those who found him and saved his life. She remembered the blacksmith's rebuffed attempt to speak to Finna the night of the village meeting. She remembered Finna's answer to the question, *why did you never marry?* and wondered what they might have been to each other, under different circumstances.

Different circumstances. Had her parents survived the fever, Maeve would be living in Dumar, would never have seen the blessed orchard or anyone in this village, would never have even visited Quin. She brushed a hand down the rough bole of one of the trees and thought of the letter. *You may read it anytime,* the Patrician had said. She'd barely heard him that day. Everyone in her life was gone, save Finna. A desire to read this letter for herself quickened her step. She hung the bucket on its nail and set off for the Patrician's rooms, where he had stored the letter.

The side entrance was unguarded. The streets seemed quiet and strangely empty after the recent influx of guards. Something loosened in Maeve's gut, but she didn't stop to examine it. Boyle stood guard at the church entrance, and he greeted her with his customary smile.

"Morning, Maeve." The lightness in his voice mirrored her own sense of relief. "Finna send you on an errand?"

"No. The Patrician left a letter for me in his room. May I see it, please?"

He stepped back and held out a hand in a dramatic gesture. "Of course. Watch out for our priest, though. I don't know if he's still in or not." He dropped a knowing wink as Maeve passed.

The priest was nowhere to be seen. The Patrician's rooms felt empty and cold now, their grandeur faded in the weak autumn light. Dusters covered the furniture and the fire grate sat full of gray ash and soot. She wondered who would fill this space when he died, and who else knew that several months from now someone else would be riding into Quin as its leader.

Where would he keep the letter? She wished she'd heard more yesterday. A sound made her heart race, but it was only the opened door swinging on its hinges. Maeve hurried to shut it, wishing there was a lock.

The desk held nothing but writing supplies. One cupboard held spaces for the bronze apples, which must be on their way to Dumar now. The final cupboard revealed a neat pile of folded parchment. Their broken, crimson red seals clacked together like soft coins in a purse as she pulled them out and began going through them one by one. One was sealed with brown wax.

To the Patrician, regarding the matter of the girl's parentage, it read. Maeve opened and scanned it rapidly, feeling an increasing sense of disappointment as she did.

It told her nothing new. Everything she remembered from yesterday sat in scrawling ink on this page, leaving her no more illuminated than when she came in. It was signed by a soldier whose name she didn't know.

There was a postscript, however.

See the enclosed letter from the Lord Protector, sir. He requests that you read it at once.

Maeve shuffled the papers until she found it, a smaller letter dated the same and sealed with red wax. It must've been from the Lord Protector, for who else would address the Patrician by his name –a name heard so infrequently she'd forgotten it–instead of his position?

To Carlyle Bromley—it is a great pity about Miss Maeve MacGowan. You had mentioned the possibility of her holding powers which would have enabled you to pass your illness onto her, but unfortunately, this has not proven to be the case. Almost more alarming, by your frequent and thorough reports, you say she is not as docile as you had once thought, and that is the trouble of underestimating these women. They grow entitled in this post.

Your power rests in the orchard in ways the villagers will never understand. Their continued ignorance keeps them under your sway and ensures your control. Protect that at all costs, and our legacy, the crown's legacy, is secure. It is a shame you could not utilize the girl more during the cure.

It is, to a lesser extent, a shame about the attacks, but they, too, have served their purpose. Should the heathens ever crawl out of the downs, we will annihilate them swiftly.

But you must focus on the orchard and the two women. Do what you must to secure our legacy. Then return to Dumar immediately, where, for your service to the crown, you may live out your days comfortably and undisturbed. You will not fail to remember that I can carry out your rule from here when the need arises. No one will trouble you and your illness shall remain a secret.

Signed, the Lord Protector

Maeve gasped for air as she pounded the cobbled streets home, careless of everything but the words in the Lord Protector's letter.

Foolish, stupid Maeve!

The Patrician may have left, but his power over Quin remained. His magic remained. And she and Finna—every villager—were still in danger.

The very trees I saved have fed our fear and hatred of the so-called wild men. I have fed his power this whole time.

She wasn't sure how the Patrician used his magic to influence everyone through the trees. But it was more than the great recital. The trees were always the key to his power, and she had been unable to see just how important they were.

I have spent my whole life loving the orchard, trying to prove myself worthy, this whole time dying to hear him call me good. I have only given all my power to a man who controls everything for his own benefit.

A sob escaped her as she reached the village exit. Her dear trees beckoned in the breeze like innocents inviting her into a sacred space. *I have crept around him, trying to do everything behind his back, thinking it was enough to subvert him. Thinking that I had to save myself from Dumar, when Dumar is all around us. Dumar is the Lord Protector is the Patrician is the crown is Quin. And I have kept it alive.*

The rot was not Quin's downfall. The rot was Quin's cure.

Oh Finna, please understand. Oh dear trees, forgive me.

The tinder set the first tree alight with ease. Maeve watched the leaves catch fire and blaze against the sky. She set each tree afire, one after the other, and watched as the dry bark blackened and crackled and charred. Smoke filled the air. It billowed up and tumbled into the wind, which tossed and carried it far away, scattering pieces of the trees across the downs they were meant to keep at bay. Blue heat licked at Maeve's tears. The only thing that pierced the pain and wrongness of it all was knowing that she was destroying the Patrician's hold on every life in Quin.

When the flames had devoured every remaining leaf, and the trunks were blackened and stunted, Maeve doused them with water from the stream. The blackened, limbless stumps smoked, and the trees with them. The Patrician's hold was broken. She turned her back on the orchard.

We must not wait for spring to leave Quin. I must warn Lochlyn, tell Finna.

Finna would be back soon. Would Quin understand one day? The guards might present a problem, but if Finna had found a way to poison two of them, she could undoubtedly do it again. Maeve began listing things she would pack when she opened the door and stepped into the kitchen.

"Ah, child. What have you done?"

Cold dread doused her from head to foot. The Patrician stood in the room.

26. Twist

"Maeve, you have not been honest with me."

The Patrician gestured to a chair, just as if she had come to him in his comfortable room for nothing more interesting than stirring a pot. Maeve could not move. She knew that through the kitchen window, the Patrician witnessed the smoking remains of Quin's sacred orchard.

He continued in the same calm, patient voice. "Something deeply troubles you."

"You said you were leaving." Her voice was tight and dusty and distant. It surprised her, as if someone else spoke on her behalf. "You lied."

"I sensed something was wrong. I'm glad to have returned. Why not confide in me? Do you no longer trust me?"

Such blatantly feigned care triggered a hot stab of anger, snapping her out of her stupor. "Your magic. You control everyone with the orchard. There is nothing to trust."

"Control? Child, what do you mean?"

"Stop pretending," Maeve snarled. "I can't play this game anymore. You used me. You use all of us."

The Patrician sighed heavily, a long-suffering sigh. Maeve wanted to scream but her throat had closed up again. "How do you think this magic of mine controls people, then? The magic I use for healing and lighting the way in the dark? You know the truth well, because I have told you before. The only way magic is connected to the orchard is in our history, in the cure, in the way it protects us from the wild downs. And now that is gone. Oh, the villagers are going to be very displeased about this. Who will protect you when they see what you've done?"

Finna's fiery warning rang in her ears: *I hope your shared blood is enough to cover your defiance.* Oddly, it was Finna she now thought of, searching desperately for something to fall back on. Keeping quiet and playing along wouldn't provide a way out this time. But with the Patrician here, every guard answered to him, their numbers forming a net to snatch its prey at a moment's notice. She had nowhere to go.

The beginnings of panic overtook her ebbing anger and muddled her thoughts, even as she fought for clarity.

"You know, I have been patient. I gave you so many chances to tell me you had become entangled with the wild men. Even when you crossed the wall at night, I did not accuse you. Finna would punish you worse than anything I could devise, and I wished to spare you from that, and from public humiliation. You are so like me, you see. Both of us striving desperately to be worthy of the task assigned to us, both of us unable to quell the secret rebellion twisting in our cores. But you, against all my suppositions, actively fomented that inner rebellion and let it settle in your soul like a tick gorging on sheep's blood. And what has it done to you, Maeve? The Lord Protector is concerned for the guardianship of the orchard. His fears have proven more than justified now."

He nodded his head, and shadows in the hall moved. Someone groaned and vague figures took shape. A cry escaped Maeve as Thomas and Declan dragged Finna into her kitchen. Maeve lunged for her, but the Patrician stopped her with the same infuriatingly calm voice.

"I would be very careful, if I were you. My men are not themselves."

Thomas's grin caught her eye briefly, blade-sharp and gleaming. She tore her gaze away. "Finna?" Maeve choked on a sob, on her own powerlessness. A dark stain spread across Finna's dress over her ribs. What was wrong? Why did she look so tired and pained? The woman who had always stood proud and tall before others sagged between the two guards, her eyes begging something of Maeve that she couldn't understand.

"What have you done?" Maeve cried. "How could you let them do this? Let her go!"

Finna mumbled something, but the Patrician spoke over her. "Unfortunately, I cannot stop the damage. The branch is rotted, Maeve. It's time for something new."

Thomas and Declan released Finna, who dropped to the ground with a moan. Maeve ran to her. The tall, once rigid frame felt thin and bird-frail as she struggled to lift Finna onto her lap and press a handful of her dress to the terrible stain. Immediately her fingers came away sticky and red through the layers of fabric.

"She needs help! Finna, Finna." The woman's eyes had closed. Her face was gray with pain, her skin cold against Maeve's trembling hand, but her ragged breaths formed into something coherent.

"Don't go with him."

Finna's words were a murmur and a sigh that never repeated. Her body lay still on the cold kitchen floor, and all Maeve knew was the final weight on her lap and the sobs that shook her body.

"There is still a chance for you, Maeve, in the midst of this tragedy." A hand fell heavy on Maeve's shoulder. "Come with me quickly, and leave your shame behind."

Red flamed in Maeve's vision. Rage prickled down her limbs like blistering fire. With a scream she twisted upright and flew at the Patrician. Something heavy knocked the wind from her lungs. Red turned to black spots dancing in her vision as hands tightened their grip on her arms. She choked, coughed, and fought for breath. The cold flagstones bit into her knees. With great, gasping efforts, she drew clean gulps of air again and her vision cleared.

The Patrician knelt eye to eye with her. When he inhaled to speak, Maeve sucked on her cheeks and spat in his face.

Another blow stung her cheek as Thomas struck her. The Patrician made a quelling sound and rose to his feet. Maeve felt the guards shift, hold back, and struggled to stand. "I am a tolerant man; that was my downfall. I should have cut everything off at the quick. Now your secrets have forced this upon us. Bring her to my quarters," he told the guards, "then return and dispose of the body."

"Should we leave it outside the wall? Make it look like—"

"No. We will have enough to work with here."

The guards dragged Maeve to her feet and from the cottage. Finna lay sprawled across the stones, and even Maeve's ragged cries could not move her.

"Let her walk unassisted."

Obscenely cheerful sunlight illuminated Quin's crowded houses and uneven streets, as if this were any other day. Maeve could see the gates and their stone apples. The sounds of the usual village business with the singed smell of burnt trees. One or two people darted a look at them as they passed, but did nothing more than nod to the man who led the group.

When Thomas's hand dug harder into Maeve's arm, she did not resist. *Why would I?*

"Thomas." The Patrician's voice held a warning and the guard obeyed, reluctantly. They had almost reached the square. The Patrician waited a beat and kept pace beside her, the false protector he had always been, forcing Thomas to join Declan at the rear. Maeve kept her numb march in the strange procession. *A stupid sheep among wolves.*

But unrest gathered in the streets.

A small crowd of people stood at the church entrance, speaking to the priest. The man gestured wildly, his eyes wide and the chain askance about his neck. Murmurs arose and several people turned as they approached. Fear twisted within Maeve when she recognized Conlan among those speaking directly to the priest.

"Thank God," the priest said in his sanctimonious voice when he caught sight of the Patrician. The murmurs died down. "We had all thought you gone, Patrician, but what providence brings you back! These good folks are troubled, for we see vast quantities of smoke. I would have investigated at once, but not a moment later this young man brings word that one of our young women appears to be missing . . ." His eyes narrowed as he took in Maeve's appearance. "Patrician, I trust you bring news to quell our troubled minds." He sounded almost gleeful, though whether this was for the news or the troubled minds was less certain. A gleam leaped into his eye that he barely subdued.

Another face and then another turned to Maeve, and their familiarity jolted her out of her numbness: the whole Campbell family stood near Conlan. Tears stained Mrs. Campbell's face. Her husband glowered, and their two young daughters watched Maeve with equal parts horror and fascination. *I must be covered in soot.*

"Good people of Quin," the Patrician began, and everyone quieted.

His voice was like the return of good sense and balance, and the nervous energy seemed to still with just a few words. Yet Maeve saw something in his eye. He was too practiced in subtlety for anything so blatant as the priest's greed and hunger for misfortune, for a reason to warn of judgment and disaster. The Patrician could turn a crowd with a single gentle word and make them believe that he had done nothing. It was startling how he could do so little and achieve so much violence, and everyone would praise his good sense. For the first time since Finna had been dragged in by the guards, tiny seeds of dread curdled in Maeve's stomach.

"I wish to assure you that the fire poses no immediate threat," the Patrician went on. "It has been quelled. But let the young man speak before I say more on the subject. He is greatly agitated." He gestured to Conlan.

"My wife is missing." His voice shook with what most would take for grief. "I return from trade business in Dumar to find my bride is gone. Her family hasn't seen her. Someone must know where she is."

Maeve sensed that people were looking at the Patrician, but not with expectation. With wariness. Fear. Horror.

They were looking at her.

Voices broke out at once. "Where is she?"

"What is happening to our village?"

"First the attacks, and now this!"

"We've got to find her!"

Conlan was still fixed on Maeve. Two or three more people left their businesses to join the crowd.

Oh, Orlenn. I hope you have left by now. Run and do not delay.

Two women who'd said nothing at first looked at each other knowingly, as if they'd foreseen this. "Wild," said one of them, and Maeve recognized her voice from the wedding. Now their speculations seemed to bear evidence of truth.

"Where is my wife?" Conlan cried. "Sir, give us permission to find her."

The Patrician raised his hand and the cries died down, though agitation thrummed through the crowd.

"Good people, I will not lie to you, though the truth is sad and grievous. Indeed, you already know it. The attacks, the rot in the orchard so recently cured, and this missing young woman—they are all connected. And you, good people, know by whose hand these tragedies have befallen us."

"The wild men!"

Maeve could not see who said it first. The words rose like a greedy tide around her, repeated over and over.

"No!" she shouted. "It isn't true! Listen to me!"

To her shock, the crowd fell silent again—the Patrician had quieted them, and was watching her. No good could come of this. Likely no one would believe her, but she had to speak the truth.

I've shut my mouth for too long.

"Conlan was going to send Kate away to Cromwell House. And for what? Their own child, that he gave her! The only thing you're grieving, Conlan, is the loss of respect you think you deserve."

Her blood pulsed heavily through her and throbbed painfully beneath her eye. She was trembling, but still felt a stab of pleasure when Conlan's face turned red, his eyes wide with impotent anger. He forced his way through the crowd and stopped to look her in the eye.

"Where is she?" he demanded. "What have you done with her?"

Maeve shut her mouth. Behind her, one of the guards chuckled. The priest's eyes darted from the crowd, to her, to the Patrician, burning with a frightening hunger. The desire for violence swelled among the crowd like rotten fruit about to burst.

"We will find your wife," the Patrician assured Conlan, speaking loud enough so the whole crowd could hear. "I am so sorry it has come to this, my friends. For the other news I have to share with you is almost as grievous. Let me address the fire before we act. The orchard is burned to the ground."

Gasps rose from the crowd. Murmurs of shock, grief, anger.

He is enjoying this.

"This is all connected, as we have said. Maeve MacGowan has, for some time, been consorting with the wild men. They have troubled her mind. She is why our sacred orchard is gone, and your young wife delivered to their schemes. Your fears are true: the wild men have taken Katherine. They have plagued us far too long. We have been patient, and this is how they reward us. We will get her back and avenge her purity upon those who stole it."

Maeve was too stunned for shame, too wild with fear. Later, she would marvel that he could speak more than a sentence without the crowd bursting through the gates and into the downs. His words stirred the air, fed their hunger for vengeance, their desperation to restore their world to the story he had fed them until it was the only story they could see. The Patrician held them at bay, drawing them taut as a bowstring, and he would be the one to release them like a weapon.

Her throat hurt; she realized she was shouting. Not for herself, but for Lochlyn, for Kate, for Finna lying cold on the floor. But no one heard.

Several villagers stabbed the air with rakes, rods, makeshift weapons, and guards gathered with their swords. Maeve lurched and found herself dragged back. She fought, though it was pointless. She fought because when she died, she wanted to do it resisting.

"The trees needn't have burned, Maeve," the Patrician said in her ear. "Their power is symbolic; they are nothing more than that. And now you will be a symbol these people will never forget. You see, you are still of use to me."

He drew away and addressed the crowd in a ringing voice: "My children, before we go into battle, you deserve to know one final thing. Maeve MacGowan is a danger to herself and to everyone else. These attacks are not the work of the wild men. Not even of their wild beasts. This innocent-looking girl is behind them, a pawn of the wild men's magic. That is why she must go with us. God will use her for justice that she might be redeemed."

She was looking into the Patrician's eyes, where she saw herself reflected. Her face was smudged with soot and her hair disheveled. A bruise bloomed on one cheek. Wide-eyed, small, cornered, her own fear staring back at her. She looked like insanity.

"I won't obey you," she cried.

His smile terrified her. His dark blue eyes flashed with an inhuman light. "You may say that. But you have given me a gift, one you do not understand. You will be of use to me yet."

"Everyone's blood is on your hands!"

"These hands?" he asked, holding them out. "When have these hands ever shed blood? You are the one who will spill blood today, Maeve. Not me."

With a ringing cry, he released the crowd. He urged them not to fear whatever they saw on the heathen downs. He urged them to trust.

And somehow, as Maeve was dragged along, her body thrumming with rising panic, she knew they would believe him to the end.

27. Monster

How strange to walk these paths in the light. How strange to walk, not with the fear of being caught but with fear for those she would encounter, and fear of the person walking at her side with all the fervor of one certain his course is true and right.

Thomas's spear jabbed her in the back, biting more than once. The crowd went before them and the Patrician held her back. They weren't close enough yet for her to call out. She would wait until the last minute. Then at least she could die knowing she had spent her last breath warning Lochlyn.

What if they've already left? What if they know we are coming? Perhaps they'll kill us before we can even lift a hand . . .

How strange to wish for the death of all those around her. She felt she had already died.

The villagers walked with purpose, confident in their steps. They were furtive, quiet, if not completely so. Something led them on. She realized with horror how true the Patrician's words were about the symbolic power of the trees. They did not need magic to inspire them to violence, not when Quin's history was steeped in it.

Far too soon they stopped and gathered at a place Maeve recognized. Smoke rose in wisps beyond the next rise, sending dread pooling in her throat. She stood at the back, her arms in Thomas's hold now, and the Patrician was about to speak to the villagers.

Something hot and sticky covered her mouth before she could open it. There was no calling out, no warning them. She could not speak. *Orlenn! Liam, Kate! Death stands at your door.*

"Do not be afraid of what you will see." The Patrician's quiet voice carried, setting the villagers' eyes alight. "See what happens to those who defy God and defile themselves with those who reject him. See what happens to those who rebel."

Maeve shook her head, shaking uncontrollably, her body heavy, her mind screaming. *I won't obey you! I will rebel until the end!* She threw her head back and met something painfully hard. Thomas swore, but no answering blow hit her. Instead, the heavy weight in her chest, her lifelong companion, spread deeper and deeper like treacle sinking into soft bread. The Patrician was watching her now, an eerie, desperate smile set on his face. She felt her body slipping away from her, though terror pumped through her veins. Her hands constricted in a rictus. Sudden pain, everywhere yet undefinable, pulled another ragged cry from her lungs. She could hardly stand upright despite the grip on her arm.

The Patrician leaned close so only she could hear. "I'm not going to kill anyone, Maeve." His smile widened. She was gone from the reflection in his eyes; it showed a face she did not recognize. "You are."

The heaviness swelled and spread and poured into her limbs. It oozed from her pores and dragged her to the ground, making her so clumsy she could no longer stand. She fell to her knees, twisting and writhing as pain tore through her body. Her skin itched and exploded; fur sprouted from every inch of her. Her back hunched. Her crumpled hands, bracing her against the earth, shortened, sharpened, grew black nails. And over it all, something gripped her, propelling her to motion, every step an agony. Her silent cries of protest became howls of pain.

She had a flash of understanding: the creature in the Patrician's eyes was something on all fours. Then there was nothing but movement flooding her limbs and the irresistible urge to kill.

28. Kill

The world is blood and shouts and tearing, smears of terrified human faces. I am swift. I am leaping and snarling and teeth meeting flesh and bone. I tear and pull and taste copper. Blood spills and fills my mouth, hot and liquid and galvanizing.

The pushes against my body cannot stop me. So much shoving, so I tear them all away. So many teeth. A growl, familiar and savage, reaches through the human cries and sharp teeth sink into my shoulder. My body moves without thought, twisting and snapping and finding purchase in my attacker. I feel something ripping from my body, but I push and bite and growl without stopping. I must not stop. I cannot stop. I will not stop.

Ice enters the steel of my mind, and I fight that too—or is that the intrusion?

I am wounding. Killing. Someone is making me do it.

This distraction will cost me. I shake my head and seek a new hold, my teeth slicing into flesh. I sink deeper, worrying the prey, and a cry of pain is my reward. My enemy stills and hangs heavy from my mouth. I drop the weight and seek more.

The smell of death is pungent in my nostrils as bodies still jostle and press, fall, rise, and fall again. The distance I feel grants me a satisfaction. I see no distinction; I only kill. I taste nothing but blood. I feel nothing but hard, brute intent.

"Maeve!"

A voice—the ice weakens the steel of my resolve again. Who calls me? Why does it matter? War breaks out in my head, tearing and painful. I am fighting. I fight—what?

The distance is gone. Panic grips my throat; I see bodies lying stained in crimson, ribbons of clothing and flesh. I hear my name again. I must answer. I must.

A face appears, distinct as the pain in my shoulder. I see terror and grief. Bile rises in my throat.

And then I see nothing. The cries fall away around me. The jostling bodies are nothing but wisps of air. I meet the ground and nothing else matters. Everything fades.

I wake alone.

That is the first thing I notice: the silence, the absence of bodies moving and still. The second thing I notice is my body, inhuman and battered.

Without the distance and urge to destroy, an abyss of horror opens up within me. Blood soaks my paws; it sticks to the fur on my muzzle. The stench of it fills my nostrils still. I whimper and try to wipe it off, but I cannot.

Then a breeze brushes cool fingers against the fur on my back, the gentlest whisper. I look up and see the apple tree. It stands alone, amidst a patchwork of burnt stumps that I had not seen before, and there is a wall stretching all around us. But it is the tree that catches my eye. The bole and branches look hale and strong, and gleaming among smooth green leaves are red, gleaming clusters of ripe fruit.

I leap for the tree, desperate to taste it. All my longing to eat the fruit right from the branch returns with the force of a storm, as if it's been waiting for this moment. I rear up on my hind legs and paw at the fruit. I know if I can eat one, I must return to myself.

It takes many attempts. It feels awkward to stand this way and my front legs shake with the effort of reaching.

278

After many missed attempts, I succeed at last, grasping a smooth apple between my paws. But it bursts at my touch, running down my forelegs in a sticky, pulpy mess, the smell too sickly sweet to be appealing.

I back away in horror, then try again. The second apple melts just like the first. Circling the tree, I leap again and again, and each time the apples burst and melt, sticking to my fur like gore. A whimper escapes me. Perhaps my touch ruins it. Perhaps I ruined it when I set the trees on fire. How could they recover from such devastation?

Faint music reaches me from far away. It is not the lively, strange, goose-bump-raising tune I am expecting; it is the somber music of a wedding or church meeting, and the sound sinks all the way down to my toes, heavy and suffocating. The apples swell and bulge on the branches. The tree sways and groans with the rapidly expanding weight, as its rotten fruit grows to the size of large potatoes, then small pumpkins, and the music may as well be a funeral dirge.

But for whose death?

I howl in frustrated grief. Something sharpens within me, like a sixth sense, and that's when I see it. Them. At every apple. How could I have missed it? For at each stem there pulses a faint light, a knot of blue in the brown. And I know it doesn't belong.

It was not my touch ruining these apples. These apples were not even real. They were failing because someone had put them there and they did not belong in the first place. This tree was never meant to bear their weight.

Stretching up, I seize a branch between my paws and shake, slip, and try again. I shake and shake until the tree releases its rotten burden and the apples splatter around me, slicking my fur. It doesn't matter. I could wash that off; these apples won't stain me because they are not a part of me. Their rottenness never belonged to me at all.

The bark prickles against my palms. My own hands clutch the branch, the weight in my chest lightening as little knots of blue die and wither on broken stems.

I jump again and again, pulling the heavy branches and freeing them of the rottenness that clings. I might look ridiculous, dancing like that around the tree, half-human, half-creature. That does not matter either. This is my tree, and I know what belongs. I laugh once at the thought and pull and dance and bob, glorying in the motion of my strange body and the feel of the bark in my hands. The music is fading. It is very distant now, and it is out of tune and awkward.

When at last I am shin-deep in slimy morass, the tree stands upright and free. I stand on my own two legs, a naked girl. I leap once, purely for the joy of it, tendrils of red hair swirled around my shoulders, and land on clean grass. I feel more feral and free than I ever did as a creature on all fours, because I am myself. The music is a faded jumble, like old, balled-up strings, growing fainter and fainter until it rolls away and disappears altogether.

Creamy pink-and-white apple blossoms erupt all over the tree. They sprout tiny green nubs which swell and darken into red fruits, hanging by their delicate brown stems. I pluck one from the tree and hold it to my nose. It smells clean, ripe—perfect. The air is full of the scent of healthy fruit. I bite into the juicy flesh and a sharp, sweet taste floods my mouth. It is crisp and spicy in a way that makes everything I've ever eaten taste like mush.

And with that bite comes the understanding of two things:

The reflection in the Patrician's eyes is not mine, but his.

And he is afraid of me.

I wake to overwhelming pain throbbing in my shoulder. For a time I stay there, floating in that miasma of a body that is not my own, yet screams for all my attention. Slowly, other things become clear: The smell and taste of blood still thick in my mouth. The jostling in my body. And the sight, swaying back and forth beside me, of a large black dog, its head thrown back at an angle too sharp for it to be alive.

Last, my hearing returns. Someone is shouting in one long, groaning cry, and I see an apple, large and dead-looking and upside down.

Above the blood I smell sweat and sour fear, zealous triumph. I'm surrounded by bodies whose shouts I can't understand. But I do understand that the apple I saw was one of the stone apples. The groaning shout is the gate swinging open, the mouth of Quin yawning as the village swallows me whole. I understand, when I see the Patrician standing before a pile of bodies layered like discarded garments, that the village will witness the destruction enacted on the downs and brought within the walls as evidence of righteous victory.

And the pieces fall into place. I understand something Duffy told me the night he was attacked: the power is not in the orchard, but the apples. I understand who attacked him and what he was searching for that night.

I understand that the taste in my mouth is the death of many.

29. Heart

Maeve could not look away from the sight. Comprehension blinked in and out of her mind as the pile of bodies—Cú Sidhe and human—swam in and out of focus. Something in her demanded that she not look away, so she looked at the crowd, where she could focus on individual faces.

The priest stood with his teeth bared, his eyes frenzied. Mr. Campbell looked harried, hollow-eyed, as if he had lost something again and couldn't quite believe it. Boyle was scrubbing a hand across his cheek. His motions grew more frantic and he tried to flee the crowd, but two guards stood in his path.

Doubt and fear and disgust showed on others' faces as they looked from the pile of bodies to their leader, and despite their uncertainty, they remained fixed on him. The Patrician stirred them like the contents of a pot. Just as he had stirred the cure so carefully, just as he had released them onto the downs when he was ready, he would say the right words once again and provide a remedy that would restore order and keep his world intact. He would return their world to order for the price of lives deemed disposable. The crowd ebbed and flowed around him like troubled waters, uncertain, waiting for commands.

Troubled waters.

Those words stirred a memory: swimming in a cold pool, her feet missing, then finding, the rounded stone floor. The world tilted and something crashed against her, sending pain shooting through her body. Rough hands deposited her on the cobblestones in a heap of blood-matted fur. When she saw the large, limp body of the black dog dragged away and thrown onto the pile, she came painfully, fully alert.

Aodh.

A frenzied desperation replaced lucid thought. She searched the pile of bodies, looking for a long golden braid or a tangle of dark hair, a weathered human limb or a cloak the color of moss. Bile rose up and thickened her throat. She turned and heaved onto the cobblestones, retching and choking.

At any minute someone would come and kill her. She received a shock when her strange body stopped disgorging itself and felt only the stabbing pain in her shoulder.

I've got to know.

How many had she killed? Who lay buried, crushed, torn by teeth she had wielded? It was impossible to distinguish who was animal and who was human. She tried to scrub the sick off her muzzle and felt bare skin trembling against her sharp-toothed mouth. Her own fingers, gray with fur, had replaced the paws. Already the fur on her body was shortening, and she felt a weight of long, red hair on her head. In a moment she would stand naked on her own two feet.

"Up you go."

Rough hands seized her and dragged her toward the crowd, the Patrician, and the stench of death. Maeve struggled against Thomas as her strength faded and the pain in her shoulder grew sharper. This close to everything, she could see the dead Cú Sidhe in detail. Their red eyes dull and unseeing, their shining fur bloodied and torn. Some had their throats torn open. Some of them had no heads. The pile was massive, arresting, terrible. Shreds of human bodies protruded here and there, but she could scarce comprehend what she saw until Aodh caught her eye. The once magnificent beast stared at her with sightless eyes, his beautiful form pitiful in its desecration. Maeve sobbed for them all. *I am sorry. Did you die protecting Lochlyn, or are they buried here, too? Who escaped? Anyone? I am sorry. I am sorry. I am sorry.*

Thomas's hands burned hot on her cold skin. She must be fully human and naked, but what did that matter? Someone flung a rough cloak around her and shoved her. Pulled her onto the bloody mound of bodies and forced her to climb. Her bare feet slipped on fur and gore and loose, broken limbs, and torches blazed around her as cries joined in a single purpose.

She must die.

Somehow that phrase sparked a fire within her. If dying was the Patrician's will, she would fight it. Her death was another means of securing his story as the only one, and it wouldn't end there. He might die in six years or six days, but his story would remain, taken up by those sent to fill his role and those who saw him as their savior from the wild and frightening, untamed downs.

Who do you think you are, Maeve MacGowan, to give up now? Death is an escape. It is time to fight. The advantage is that no one thinks I will.

She waited as people set fire to the corpses she stood on. Someone shouted and escaped the crowd unhindered, but her eyes were on the flames. She waited as the tongues of orange and yellow licked around the edges of black and gray and the smoke filled the air with the terrible smell of burning hair and flesh. She waited until the Patrician stood in front of her, watching with a calm face and eyes alight with flames both natural and magical.

Then she smiled at him.

The air was thick with heat and stench, but she was thinking of water. She was thinking of the blacksmith and his tools for stoneworking. She was thinking of how the

Patrician had been honest about one thing, and when her smile did not fade she felt a flicker of satisfaction to see his confidence falter, just for half a moment. It wasn't the apple orchard that held the Patrician's power. He had told her of his struggle as a boy to control his power. He had told her of his illness, growing beyond his control.

Another face appeared at the edge of the crowd, a face she had hoped to see. But there was no way to send a message. There was only time to act. She smiled widely at the Patrician again. And then she moved.

Without knowing fully whom she left behind, Maeve leaped down over the bodies, the fire, the startled figures, and landed with a bone-jarring thud on the cobblestones. Clutching the cloak about her, she rose, shaking, and ran toward the gate, her shoulder throbbing as if every step drove a dagger into it. Shouts and footsteps sounded behind her. She whimpered and hobbled, black spots blooming in her vision. The shut gate and its stone apples rose up before her. Two guards outpaced her and took their positions on either side of it, hands on their sword hilts and eyes trained on her.

This will be over very fast if I can't get that open.

"Duffy!" she shouted, but her voice came out like a squeak. Something heavy slammed into the gates. A heavy fist swung once, twice, and the two guards fell to the ground. The blacksmith, looking almost as pale as the bandages around his chest, leaned against the gates and gripped the handles.

"Be quick," he panted, nodding at her. "Push that stone down and send it back where it came from. Get it back to the pool. I'll get the other one." Then he pulled open the gates.

Maeve heaved against one of the stone apples, trying to budge it from its pedestal. It was infuriatingly heavy. Duffy turned and roared; fights broke out behind her. With a shout, she shoved the stone down, barely missing her feet, and pushed it through the open gates, down the road, toward the little path where she'd once looked for herbs. It didn't make sense that she moved unhindered by anything but her own body, but there was no time to look back. Every part of her trembled and burned as she rolled the stone over tiny hillocks of grass. Then she swerved to the right, looking for the small space where once a bronze apple had rolled and found a place to hide, a place that had not given it up easily.

It might not fit.

She would carry her stone burden, if needed, and throw the stone back into the pool from where it had been taken. A shout made her look back in time to see a fur-cloaked shape hurtling toward her. She caught a glimpse of Duffy surrounded by guards choking the open gates like foam in the mouth of a rabid beast. She caught the second stone apple and pushed them further, further.

White-hot pain seared into her calf. She cried out, stumbled, and fell, losing sight of her twin burdens.

"You belong to me!" The Patrician lay on the grass, his hand still outstretched and holding the slim, bloodied knife. His disheveled hair fell about his face, but Maeve could see the frantic light in his red-rimmed, weary eyes. He dragged himself toward her. "You will pay for your disobedience for the rest of your life, and I assure you, it will be a long one."

"You've got blood on your sleeve," Maeve said. Her voice was tired and thin but calm, her own. Vaguely, she thought it would be a good idea to move away from that blade before it struck again. "You must be truly desperate, if you're willing to get your hands dirty."

A distant *splash* arrested them both. The Patrician's face contorted once, as if he saw a terrible vision. His cry, unearthly. Maeve flung herself away, toward the apples, and saw the second one perched alone at the edge of the rise. Her fingers brushed it when a hand grabbed her ankle and pulled her back.

"No one will ever care for you now." His face was a distorted mask, more terrifying than his smile had been. He was so fixed on Maeve's face that he didn't blink when she reached up with her outstretched hand and felt again the smooth surface. "You are injured, alone, and disgraced, Maeve MacGowan. Do you even know whom you've killed? You will live chained to these burdens for the rest of your life. How will you bear it? You may outlive me, but you will die in your shame. Nothing and no one will ever take it away."

Every fiber of her body threatened to snap. Her skin was cold and damp, too damp. The Patrician rose to his feet with his back to Quin and stepped on her ankle, digging it into the soft, cold earth. She hissed as pain shot through her leg, then lay perfectly still and shut her eyes.

She wrenched herself out from under his boot. Something in her leg twanged and broke, as she twisted, reached, and shoved, spots blossoming across her vision. She could just make out the stone vanishing from view as it rolled over the edge. Maeve scrambled upright and dodged the *whoosh* of the knife.

The second stone apple fell.

Splash.

With a soft *thunk*, the blade fell to the grass. With a cry, the Patrician followed. His body twisted and shook, withering into a mass of gray fur and a foaming, sharp-toothed snout, all encased in a faint blue glow. In other circumstances, Maeve would have been terrified. He had succeeded in adding to her burden of shame with his soft words and willing support of Quin's laws. But he had failed to transfer this one burden to her, and it was time to return the other one she had taken on herself, wearing it like a heavy cloak for so long. Maeve stood over him and willed him to look at her. A cold, wide blue stare met hers.

"I don't need anyone to take my shame. I leave it with the source. You wanted to put the curse of your own magic on me? You failed. And I leave it all with you."

"You cannot," he snarled, his voice unnatural, his humanity fleeing. "You are weak. You are only a girl."

Maeve knelt and collapsed as sharp pangs tore through her body. He was frightening, even in the end. Even amidst the fur and elongated teeth and the strange form the Patrician's power remained almost tangible. But just as he had become twisted and controlled by his own greedy powers, he would never know what it meant to be fully human, fully wild. Something panged within her, something terribly like pity.

"Why, Carlyle Bromley? Couldn't you have given up your powers before they destroyed you?"

"I am my power."

"And I am the kind of feral you fear the most," she whispered. "I am a girl you could not control forever. And my voice will outlast yours."

The creature, the salvation and ravager of Quin, shuddered. His eyes glazed over. He lay still. The blue glow faded and was gone.

He didn't even hear me.

As several people rushed from the gate, she crawled away from the body, wanting a little distance, just a little. Her bare legs stuck out from the cloak. One of them didn't look right. Her hands were slick with blood, and she wasn't sure how much of it was hers. Spots blackened her vision again. Before they overtook her, she clung to one last lucid thought.

But I heard myself, my own words. I suppose that's what matters. I suppose that's a start.

30. Epilogue

"That's the last one," Maeve said. She wiped her hands on her apron and surveyed their work. Rows of new cabbage and potatoes spread in uneven lines. She had wanted to plant a row of flowers as well, but had decided in favor of practicality this time. Nothing would replace the apple trees. She felt there was no need to try, that it was better this way, but Maeve promised herself that at the next opportunity she would add something beautiful to this beloved space. She felt not happy exactly, but that one small part of her had settled with the planting of seeds and the rich, comforting presence of tilled earth.

In one corner near the stone wall, a young mother worked at planting seeds while her tiny daughter toddled nearby. Some villagers had accepted Maeve's plan to make a garden out of the old orchard and had come to cultivate their own plots or help with another's. But many still regarded anything related to Lochlyn with fear and distrust, and would not enter the stone arch. How quickly reverence had turned to fear.

Duffy set down his shovel with a grunt and wiped his brow. It was pleasantly warm for an early spring evening, now that the early rains had slowed. A good day for digging.

"Have you heard yet?" he asked, gesturing over the hills. Maeve didn't answer and the blacksmith didn't press the matter.

Maeve leaned against the wall and shut her eyes, letting the first timid breezes of spring play with her hair. The smell of freshly turned earth filled her nose. The burned smell was little more than a shadow beneath it all. In the weeks that had followed since the Patrician's death, people began to make their own meaning of what had happened that day on the downs.

Some believed that Lochlyn had cursed their village leader. Some, like Duffy and Boyle, understood that the Patrician's magic became tied to the stone apples when his father had Duffy's father cut them from the pool floor. Such a loss left the pool protective of itself ever since, waiting to reclaim its stolen pieces and the life tied to them. Despite Duffy's witness, some villagers didn't know what to believe. A few avoided Maeve on the street and refused to acknowledge her. She could guess what they believed.

"Got to get back to the forge," said Duffy, recalling Maeve to the present. "Need anything?"

"I don't think so." Maeve offered him a half smile. Between him and Boyle, she'd not been without friends. She'd even come home a few times over the winter to find a basket at her doorstep, full of herbs, root vegetables, and candles. Mr. Campbell regarded her with glaring distrust and Mrs. Campbell avoided her, but Maeve knew the baskets were from her.

"If you ever want company, visiting the graves," said Duffy, and Maeve understood the rest.

"Thank you," she said. He'd helped her bury Finna in one private corner of the orchard with the solemnity of a lover, next to a tiny grave. He'd helped her bury what was left of the Cú Sidhe in the shadow of the downs. Most villagers wanted to burn them, but she'd fought for burial and prevailed. They'd borrowed a cart and horse, and in the end it was her and Duffy, Kate's sister Brigid, her little face stony with rebellion, and Boyle, who went through the gates to put the great beasts to rest out on the hills. Brigid hadn't flinched when they found the corpses, two from Quin and one from Lochlyn, mauled and broken among the dead. Maeve recognized one as the father of the boy whose arm the Patrician had tended; she had vomited. Boyle had gone home and tried to hang himself. *I should have tried harder to stop him*, his note said. Or so Duffy, who'd found him and cut him down, told Maeve.

"How is Boyle today?" she asked. "I haven't seen him yet. He said he was excited to plant flowers."

Duffy nodded down the lane toward the village. "Ask him yourself." A figure in a worn, brown uniform walked across the bridge.

There weren't as many uniforms in Quin now. Everyone who'd arrived with the Patrician had left with Thomas and Declan. Both men had threatened to send word to the Lord Protector of the violent death wreaked upon the village leader. Maeve had no doubt they'd hold true to their word.

Boyle and Duffy have gone home, promising to say hello tomorrow, a promise I know they will fulfill. I cannot help feeling an ache watching the young mother and child leave the garden hand in hand, the little girl skipping for joy and the mother's laugh echoing across the hills.

It is one thing to look at the Patrician and to tell him that I reject a lifetime of shame. It is another to choose to reject that shame in the days that follow, when I struggle to understand the full extent of what I've done, when I have no way of knowing just how much harm I have caused. My deeds gape before me like the bottom of a pool, obscured in darkness.

And yet I know that to believe I alone am responsible for all the destruction is foolish and quite convenient to the Patrician's goals. I know little of what it meant to truly work in tandem with others, living as I have in my small, isolated world; but at least I can reject the notion that everything falls upon my shoulders alone, and begin with the smallest thing that is mine to right.

"Nobody else human died," Boyle has told me, over and over again. "It was a blur once he did that terrible thing to you, and we were all frightened out of our wits." He means that no one died while the Patrician and I wreaked bloody havoc on the Cú Sidhe, but that does not mean that the wounds I inflicted didn't leave death in their wake. I have no way of knowing if he saw correctly, that the shock and chaos did not hide the truth from him. At least I do know that someone saw Kate and a girl matching Breena's description far from the fray, a fierce, gray-haired man holding the second girl's arms to keep her from throwing herself into the fight. At least then, they were safe.

I wonder where Kate is, and if she's happy. I must believe she is. I can barely bring myself to think of the others, though screams of their dying, both human and beast, haunt my dreams. Sometimes I wake in the night and cannot go back to sleep for terror of that day on the downs. For the terror of what I did. For the dead weight that threatens to return and crush me as if it never left and has now found new ways to cling to me.

I've done horrible things, and I don't even know all of them. I don't know where I belong anymore. I don't know how Lochlyn would receive me, or if they even would. They might reject me for all I've done.

As if waiting for the right moment, strains of lively music drift over the hills. It's not the first time I have heard this tune. I have heard it every night for the past three nights, and before that, I heard it in the orchard, on the same flute that plays now.

Orlenn once told me that if I did not wake up to my choices, someone would choose for me. The Patrician chose to make me his weapon. My choices now are mine and mine alone.

I may not know where I belong, but I know I must find that out for myself. And how can I do that if I continue to stay behind the wall?

The sky deepens to purple as the music continues. Stars blink on, like sleepy eyes opening. A familiar twitch tugs at the music, like someone pulling at a knot in a thread, and my own breath catches. There is one person calling to me, and I am listening.

I am shaking and uncertain, but I am moving, and without a backward glance I leap over the orchard wall and run toward the gathering shadows among the low and secretive hills.

ACKNOWLEDGEMENTS

This book was four years in the making. While I wrote Maeve's story from a personal place, it wouldn't be in your hands today without the many people who helped it come to life. Here are the people I'd like to thank.

To my earliest readers, many of whom have read many drafts: Damaris, Bethany, Dawn, Jessica, and Laura, thanks for believing in this story in its messiest stages. To my wonderful editor, Jessica Allowoski, thank you for handling my story with such care and understanding. To all my fabulous ARC readers and everyone who helped spread the word, you are the best cheer team I could ask for.

As always, thanks to Mike for your support, and for asking questions I didn't want to consider. Thank you to my children, who deserve to live in a world where they don't have to suppress any part of themselves in order to experience safety and belonging.

And finally, I want to thank you for reading this book. I hope you know that at your very core, you are worthy of love.

ABOUT THE AUTHOR

Stephanie Ascough is a neurodiverse author of fantasy and fairy tales who writes books for quiet people with loud thoughts. She is obsessed with folklore and fairy tales, finding out what her kids love, dates with her man, dark chocolate, hiking, reading romance and books that feel like a hug for her younger selves, all things Celtic, ghost stories, and her demanding cat/fae overlord. Stephanie and her family live near Chattanooga, TN. You can sign up for her newsletter, The Purple Vale, at purplevale.substack.com, and find her on Instagram @author.stephanieascough.

ALSO BY THE AUTHOR

If you enjoyed *The Secret Heart of Maeve MacGowan*,
please leave a review!

A Land of Light and Shadow
Upper middle-grade fantasy novel for grown-ups & kids

Flower and Cloak
Five fairy tales for the curious, romantic, and deep-feeling
souls

The Wistful Wild
Fairy tale poems of longing and ferocity

Double Alchemy
A NA romantasy inspired by Beauty and the Beast

www.ingramcontent.com/pod-product-compliance
Lightning Source LLC
Chambersburg PA
CBHW031337020726
47499CB00005B/1308